CHRONICLES OF THE KING

BOOK 1

THE LORD IS MY STRENGTH

A NOVEL

Lynn N. Austin

Beacon Hill Press of Kansas City
Kansas City, Missouri

THE LORD
IS MY STRENGTH

*The Lord is my strength
and my song;
he has become my salvation.*

EXODUS 15:2

ISBN 083-411-5387

Printed in the
United States of America

Cover Design: Crandall Vail
Cover Illustration: Keith Alexander

The following paraphrase of the Bible is also quoted in this work, as well as a number of the author's own paraphrases. See page 300 for a list of the page numbers on which quotations from these additional sources are found.

10   9   8   7   6   5   4   3   2   1

Dedicated to my husband,
Ken,
who never doubted

ABOUT THE AUTHOR

Lynn N. Austin is a full-time freelance writer and speaker. With her husband, Ken—a Christian musician who has performed with "Truth," Sandi Patti, Steve Green, Bill Gaither, and others—Lynn has lived and worked in Bogota, Colombia; Ontario and Manitoba, Canada; and several states throughout the United States. The Austins currently reside in Orland Park, Illinois, with their three children. Lynn is a contributing editor for *The Christian Reader* and editor of *Profile,* the journal of the Chicago Women's Conference.

Lynn received her bachelor of arts degree from Southern Connecticut State University and has completed graduate work in biblical backgrounds and archaeology through Hebrew University and Southwestern Baptist Theological Seminary. She and her son spent a summer in Israel participating in an archaeological dig at the biblical city of Timnah.

Lynn's articles have appeared in *Moody* magazine, *Parents of Teenagers,* *The Christian Reader,* *The Lookout,* *Teen Power,* *Discipleship Journal,* and *Teachers in Focus,* for which she has written on assignment. Lynn was named the 1993 "New Writer of the Year" at Moody Bible Institute's Write-to-Publish Conference.

A NOTE TO THE READER

Shortly after King Solomon's death in 931 B.C., the Promised Land split into two separate kingdoms. Israel, the larger nation to the north, set up its capital in Samaria and was no longer governed by a descendant of King David. In the southern nation of Judah, where the story of this book takes place, David's royal line continued to rule from Jerusalem.

The narrative centers around events in the lives of two kings of Judah: Ahaz, who ruled from 732 to 716 B.C., and his son Hezekiah, who ruled from 716 to 687 B.C.

Interested readers are encouraged to research the full accounts of these events in the Bible as they enjoy this first book in the "Chronicles of the King" trilogy.

Scripture references for *The Lord Is My Strength*
> 2 Kings 16
> 2 Kings 18:1-3
> 2 Chron. 28:1-8, 16-27
> 2 Chron. 29:1-14

See also:
> 2 Chron. 26:3-5, 16-23
> Jer. 26:18-19
> The prophecies of Isaiah and of Micah

Prologue

The Singer elbowed his way through the narrow, crowded streets of Jerusalem, searching for the right place, the right moment to sing his song. He felt the crush of people suffocating him, and he tucked his lyre close to his chest to shield it from the push and shove of men and women mobbing the streets. Nothing must prevent him from singing this song. The urgency of his mission burned inside him like a fire.

If an observer had looked closely, he would have seen that this trim, compact man with the reddish beard and piercing blue eyes was not an ordinary traveling minstrel, but a man of refinement and dignity, possessing the unmistakable aura of royalty. But the Festival of Spring was in its third day, and few people in the overcrowded city took notice of the Singer as they gathered to celebrate the rebirth of spring and the promise of bounty from the awakening earth.

The Singer paused beside a crowded booth where a spiritist performed rituals with animal entrails, hoping to entice people into paying to see more. When her demonstration ended, the crowd quickly formed a line, eager to hear their future or communicate with departed loved ones. The Singer drifted away along with those who were not willing or able to pay.

Nearby, flutes and lyres played the strains of a familiar song, and the Singer followed the sound. A band of musicians had assembled on a busy street corner with their instruments to perform for the gathering mob. It would have been a good place for the Singer to perform his song, but he was too late. He would have to find another one. He headed in the direction of the marketplace.

"Out of the way!" came a shout from behind. "Caravan coming through! Move out of the way!"

The Singer flattened himself against the wall of a building as the narrow street cleared for the caravan like the parting waters of the Red Sea. Ishmaelite traders, grimy with dust and sweat, prodded their camels through the narrow, twisting streets with harsh cries and short sticks. The goods they brought from distant lands were undoubtedly costly, but they ventured the rugged journey up to Jerusalem, knowing they would find willing buyers at any price in this city of prosperity and peace. When the last camel had passed, the crowd surged back into the street, and the Singer resumed his search.

In an open square near the water gate, a troupe of acrobats and jugglers performed as swarms of excited children clambered around them, wide-eyed and laughing. The Singer watched for a moment, then walked on, guarding his lyre carefully. As he passed the Street of the Taverns, a group of drunken peasants staggered and reeled past him, arguing loudly. The wine flowed freely at festival time, and before nightfall many would lie drunk in back alleyways and stinking gutters.

At last the Singer reached the marketplace, where a host of sounds filled his ears and a nauseating blend of smells assaulted him: rotting fish and pungent spices, charcoal and roasting meat, wet wool and unwashed humanity. Merchants in brightly colored stalls bargained loudly with their shouting customers. But the busiest booths sold carved figures of Baal and Asherah, for many shepherds and farmers believed they must enlist the help of these powerful gods of fertility in order to guarantee plentiful harvests and herds in the months to come.

A huge crowd had gathered in the center of the market square, forcing those in the outer fringes to crane their necks for a better view. The Singer advanced slowly, patiently elbowing his way through, and he soon saw the center of attraction. Ritual prostitutes of Asherah stood on display, enticing the crowd to join them in their rites of worship.

The Singer knew he need look no further. He had found the perfect place to sing his song. As the bargaining ended and the prostitutes began to leave with their customers, he leaped gracefully onto an empty oxcart, strumming the chords of a popular tune on his lyre. He had timed it perfectly, and the crowd's attention quickly shifted to him. He played a familiar tune, but the words were the Singer's own:

My loved one had a vineyard on a fertile hillside. He dug it up and cleared it of stones and planted it with the choicest vines. He built a watchtower in it and cut out a winepress as well. Then he looked for a crop of good grapes, but it yielded only bad fruit.

He had the people's undivided attention. Suspense hung heavily in the air as he paused.

The vineyard of the Lord Almighty is the House of Israel and the men of Judah are the garden of His delight. And he looked for justice, but saw bloodshed; for righteousness, but heard cries of distress.

Passion and anger ignited the Singer's words as the Spirit of Yahweh filled him. "See how the faithful city has become a harlot!" he shouted. "Woe to you . . . the city where David settled! Add year to year and let your cycle of festivals go on. Yet I will . . . encamp against you all around; I will encircle you with towers and set up my siege works against you. . . .

"Woe to those who rise early in the morning to run after their drinks, who stay up late at night till they are inflamed with wine. They have harps and lyres at their banquets, tambourines and flutes and wine, but they have no regard for the deeds of the Lord, no respect for the work of his hands. Therefore my people will go into exile for lack of understanding."

The Singer's passion startled the crowd. They stood

before him silent and stunned. But as he paused for breath, they began to recover, and once again he saw apathy and scorn reflected on their faces. They had realized that the Singer was a fraud, a prophet of Yahweh masquerading as a troubadour to gain their attention. Many turned away in disgust to search for entertainment elsewhere. Others decided to make the prophet their entertainment and shouted insults at him. But the Singer drew a deep breath and continued to prophesy, undaunted.

"But you—come here, you sons of a sorceress, you offspring of adulterers and prostitutes! Whom are you mocking? At whom do you sneer and stick out your tongue? Are you not a brood of rebels, the offspring of liars? You burn with lust among the oaks and under every spreading tree; you sacrifice your children in the ravines and under the overhanging crags. The idols among the smooth stones of the ravines are your portion . . . when you cry out for help, let your collection of idols save you!"

A middle-aged man, whom the Singer recognized as a priest from Solomon's Temple, shouted from the crowd, "We still worship Yahweh! We go to His sacred assemblies at the Temple!"

"No!" the prophet cried. "The Lord says: 'These people come near to me with their mouth and honor me with their lips, but their hearts are far from me. Their worship of me is made up only of rules taught by men.'"

"False prophet!" someone shouted, and the mocking crowd took up the chant to drown out his words. "False prophet! False prophet!" From the middle of the crowd, someone lobbed a ripe pomegranate, and it exploded against the prophet's shoulder, splattering his clothes and sandals with vivid patches of red pulp and slimy seeds. But he continued to shout, though few in the crowd could hear him above the laughter and jeers.

"'All day long I have held out my hands to an obstinate people . . . a people who continually provoke me to my very face . . . I will pay it back into their laps—both your sins and the sins of your fathers,' says the Lord."

At last the crowd lost interest in heckling and slowly dispersed, shrugging off the prophet's words as simply another diversion among the festival's many forms of entertainment. But the Singer remained on the oxcart, not caring if he had an audience or not. He gazed straight ahead, as if watching a drama being enacted before him, and sadly described a scene only he could see to the few people who had remained to listen.

"They have rejected the law of the Lord Almighty and spurned the word of the Holy One of Israel. Therefore the Lord's anger burns against his people; his hand is raised and he strikes them down. The mountains shake, and the dead bodies are like refuse in the streets."

In the Singer's mind, the sounds of the marketplace faded in the background, and he heard instead the rumbling of distant chariots, the thundering of pounding hooves, the clash and ring of sword against shield, and the terrified cries for mercy that came too late.

"He lifts up a banner for the distant nations, he whistles for those at the ends of the earth. Here they come, swiftly and speedily! . . . Their arrows are sharp, all their bows are strung; their horses' hooves seem like flint, their chariot wheels like a whirlwind."

The Singer closed his eyes. He could not bear to witness what would soon happen to his nation and to his people. His shoulders drooped as the fire within him faded and died, and he spoke the final words of his prophecy in a whisper:

"And if one looks at the land, he will see darkness and distress."

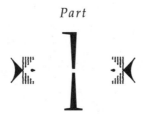

1

Ahaz was twenty years old when he became king, and he reigned in Jerusalem sixteen years. Unlike David his father, he did not do what was right in the eyes of the Lord.

—2 Chron. 28:1

1

The rumble of voices and tramping feet awakened him. Hezekiah lay in the cold, dark room, and for the first time in his short life he was terrified. Unfamiliar sounds of turmoil filled the hallway outside his room: men's voices shouting orders, doors opening and closing, children crying. Overnight his safe, quiet world in the king's palace had vanished, and he listened with mounting panic as the commotion grew louder, closer.

He sat up in bed, his heart pounding, and saw that his older brother Eliab was awake too. Hezekiah quickly scrambled off his bed to be near him, to seek comfort from him.

"Eliab," he whispered, "who's out there?"

"It sounds like soldiers."

"Why are they here?"

"I don't know." The boys huddled together, staring at the door, waiting.

In the distance, the mournful cry of a shofar trumpeted an alarm over the sleeping city of Jerusalem as the sound of footsteps thundered up the hallway, approaching their room.

"I'm scared," Hezekiah whispered, swallowing back tears. "I want Mama."

Suddenly the door opened, and soldiers, armed with swords and spears, poured into the room like a flood, pulling Hezekiah and Eliab off the bed. Hezekiah was powerless to stop them as they stripped off his short tunic and forced a long, white linen one over his head. Fear stiffened him, and the soldiers, their hands cold and rough, fumbled awkwardly to dress him. The palace servants usually dressed him gently, making up little games, slipping him treats, smiling as they tousled his curly brown hair. But none of the soldiers spoke, and in the darkened room their cold silence terrified him. They dressed Eliab too, then tied their sandals on and herded the two boys out of the room.

More soldiers and a dozen priests in flowing robes crowded the hallway. In the flickering torchlight, Hezekiah saw his younger brother and half-brothers dressed in identical white tunics, standing together and whimpering softly. His Uncle Maaseiah, armed with a sword, bow, and a quiver of arrows, appraised the frightened children huddled in front of him.

"These are all of the king's sons," he said. "Let's get on with it. My troops have a long march ahead."

"We've prepared everything, my lord," the chief priest assured him.

"Wait! Where are you taking them?" Hezekiah's mother hurried down the hall from the king's harem, hastily wrapping her outer garment around her as she ran. Her dark hair flowed, uncombed, down her back. Hezekiah yearned for the warm comfort of her arms and tried to squeeze past the soldiers to go to her, but strong hands held him back.

"What are you doing?" she cried. "Where are you taking my children?"

Maaseiah's frown deepened. "My army must march north to repel the invasion and—"

"What invasion?" She hugged her robes tightly around herself and shivered.

"The northern kingdom of Israel has formed an alliance with Aram. They've attacked our northern border areas."

"What does that have to do with my children? They're only babies."

Maaseiah seemed impatient. "King Ahaz has called for a special sacrifice to the gods, to pray for protection and victory before the army marches. He wants all his sons to take part."

He signaled to his soldiers, and they moved across the hallway to block her path, separating her from her children.

"No! Wait!" she cried. "What kind of sacrifice? Which gods?"

Maaseiah did not answer her. "Let's get on with it," he muttered and motioned for his men to follow.

Hezekiah heard his mother scream, and the sound filled him with terror. Her face had turned as white as the linen robe he wore. She fought desperately against the soldiers, who held her as her screams echoed down the hall. They were hurting her. He wanted to go to her, but a soldier's hand squeezed his shoulder, guiding him, propelling him against his will, down the palace stairs and through the maze of corridors to the courtyard.

Outside, the sky had begun to lighten as the sun emerged from behind the eastern Judean hills. A brisk wind cooled the air and whipped the hem of Hezekiah's tunic against his legs. The thin fabric offered no warmth against the morning chill, and he shivered with cold and fear.

A huge assembly waited for them in the palace courtyard, spilling over into the broad main street outside the palace gate. Hezekiah had never seen so many soldiers before, lined up in even rows, their swords gleaming, standing at attention before his father, the king.

King Ahaz wore every symbol of his authority on his stout body—the royal robes, the insignia of the house of David, the crown of Judah—as if to impress the crowd with his power and perhaps help them forget his relative youth and inexperience. He had inherited the fair, ruddy coloring of his famous forefather King David, but, unlike David, Ahaz was no soldier. His corpulent body, the result of his indulgent lifestyle, made him unfit to lead troops into battle. He could scarcely walk up a flight of stairs without pausing for breath.

The soldiers formed a procession and began to march, led by King Ahaz and his brother Maaseiah, who would command the troops in the king's place. Behind them walked the priests, the city elders, the nobles and princes of Judah. But instead of climbing the steep mount behind the palace to the Temple of Yahweh, the traditional place of sacrifice, they proceeded down the hill, through the narrow, twisting city streets. Except for the sound of hundreds of tramping feet, they marched in ominous silence.

They passed the spacious, dressed-stone mansions of the nobility, then marched through the central market area, now quiet and deserted, the booths tightly shuttered, the colorful awnings rolled up for the night. Curious women and small children looked down on the solemn procession from rooftops and peered from behind latticed shutters.

As the street narrowed, the soldiers squeezed closer, and their swords pressed coldly against Hezekiah's side. Where were they taking him? What was going to happen to him? Twice he stumbled as he missed a stair in the street, but the soldiers gripped his arms and pulled him to his feet.

They finally reached the massive iron gates on the southern wall of Jerusalem and passed down the ramp, out of the crowded city. Now the silent dawn began to echo with the throbbing beat of drums pounding in the distance. Directly ahead, blocking all means of escape, rose a craggy wall of cliffs, dark and foreboding, guarding the entrance to the Valley of Hinnom. The procession turned into the narrow valley, and a column of black smoke billowed high into the air ahead of them, carried aloft by the wind.

The priests began to chant, "Molech . . . Molech . . . Molech," and the men in the procession joined in, to the throbbing beat of the drums, "MOLECH . . . MOLECH . . . MOLECH!"

Suddenly the wall of soldiers parted, and Hezekiah caught his first glimpse of Molech. He knew he wasn't dreaming. He knew the monster was real, for he never could have imagined anything so terrible. In the midst of undulating waves of heat and smoke, Molech stared down at him from a throne of brass. The fire in the pit beneath the hollow statue blazed with a furious roar. Spears of flame, like hundreds of malicious tongues, licked hungrily around the edges of Molech's open mouth. His fierce animal eyes glared, his greedy arms reached out for his victims, forming a steep incline that ended in his open, waiting mouth.

Hezekiah's instincts screamed at him to run, but his legs buckled beneath him as if made of water. He couldn't move. "MOLECH . . . MOLECH . . . MOLECH . . . ," the crowd chanted to the pounding rhythm of drums. Hezekiah's heart throbbed in his ears as the soldiers carried him up the steep steps of the platform that stood in front of the monster's outstretched arms.

A half dozen priests waited on the platform as the soldiers herded the white-robed children into a cowering group before the monster's throne. Hezekiah found his brother Eliab and huddled beside him as the billowing heat of the monster's anger burned their faces.

The high priest faced Molech with raised arms, pleading with him in a frenzied cry, but the chanting crowd and Molech's deafening roar drowned out his words. Then, when the priest finished his prayer, he lowered his arms and turned to face the whimpering children. The cold, intent look on his face terrified Hezekiah. He cried out and tried to back away, but Molech's priests hemmed him in. He had no means of escape.

"Which one is the firstborn?" the high priest demanded.

Uncle Maaseiah's golden signet ring flashed in the light of the flames as he laid his hand on Eliab's head. "This one."

The high priest grabbed Eliab and scooped him up in his powerful arms. Slowly, clearly, and with every movement forever etched in his mind, Hezekiah watched in horror as the priest tossed Eliab into the monster's waiting arms. Eliab rolled helplessly, sickeningly, toward the open mouth. He clawed at the brazen arms to stop his fall, but the gleaming hot metal was polished smooth. He couldn't hold on. Eliab's pitiful screams wailed above the roar of the flames and the pounding drums, even after he had fallen over the flaming rim of Molech's mouth and the monster had devoured him. His cries, coming from the depths of the flames, lasted only an instant. They seemed like a lifetime.

Then a terrible stench, unlike any he had smelled before, filled Hezekiah's nostrils and throat until he gagged. His stomach turned inside out, and he vomited, as if trying to vomit the memory as well.

But the nightmare didn't end with Eliab's death. The priest grabbed another child, then another and another, and tossed each of them into the monster's greedy arms. They rolled helplessly, one after the other, into Molech's open mouth, to be devoured by the flames. Hezekiah cowered in a heap and covered his face to escape the sight of their torture, to blot out their screams of pain and terror, and the stench and bile that filled his lungs and throat. But the horror of this day was engraved on his soul. Hezekiah began to scream, and he screamed and screamed as if he would never be able to stop again.

＊＊＊

Zechariah stared at the empty wineskin through reddened eyes, his gaunt body huddling over it protectively. He had consumed its entire contents in an effort to forget, but he had not forgotten. The vivid images of Molech's sacrifice played over and over in his mind.

"Why didn't I stop them?" he murmured to himself. "I—I just stood there—watching. Why didn't I make them stop?"

Zechariah had awakened to the sound of shofars that morning and followed the procession to the Valley of Hinnom. But as he had watched the king and city elders sacrifice their firstborn sons to Molech, horror had paralyzed his limbs and sealed his lips.

When it finally ended, he had wandered back to the city in a daze and stumbled into this inn, seeking refuge in the familiar, numbing power of wine. But not even the wine could erase the memory of those children, *his own grandchild*, little Eliab, thrown into the idol's fiery mouth. And he had done nothing to save him. He covered his face with trembling hands, but the image refused to disappear.

"O God, let Your judgment fall on me," he moaned. "Punish me, not innocent babies—not my own flesh and blood."

Zechariah was tall and lean, once broad-shouldered and strong, but now his shoulders stooped as if bearing a heavy load. His lined face appeared intelligent, distinguished with a prominent nose and bushy brows that jutted out over his green eyes. But he looked pallid, drained of life, and his white beard and hair made him appear much older than his 55 years.

Night fell, customers came and went, but Zechariah remained oblivious to the noise and gaiety around him, nor did anyone seem to notice him, alone with his wine and his torment. Gradually the inn emptied as the other revelers went home. The innkeeper swept the dusty stone floor and snuffed out the oil lamps for the night. Only Zechariah remained.

"Zechariah . . . Zechariah, my friend . . ." Through the numbing haze of wine he heard someone calling his name and looked up into the round, jovial face of his friend Hilkiah. "Come on, Zechariah—the innkeeper wants to close. He asked me to walk you home." Hilkiah extended his hand to Zechariah.

Too drunk to argue, Zechariah clutched the empty wineskin and rose from his bench like an obedient child. He let Hilkiah guide him through the door and into the deserted street.

"It's late, my friend—you should be home in bed by now," Hilkiah said gently as they walked. His voice sounded soothing, though Zechariah could make little sense of his words.

High above, a sliver of moon and a few faint stars provided the only light. The streets were cool and shadowy, dark and still, as Hilkiah led him through the central market district and up the steep, deserted streets in the darkness. The square stone houses, like Zechariah's jumbled thoughts, lay clustered and stacked on top of each other, with one man's door looking down on his neighbor's roof. The houses, built from the native, rosy-beige limestone, seemed gilded in the pale moonlight.

As they labored up the hill, Zechariah leaned heavily on his friend's arm. Hilkiah was a short, plump man, whose balding head barely reached Zechariah's sagging shoulders. He knew where to take him. He had helped him home many times before.

"Why are you doing this to yourself, my friend?" Hilkiah asked gently. "You're a servant of Yahweh— blessed be His name. You shouldn't be wasting your life like this."

Zechariah stopped short as a memory flitted through his mind: the Temple of Yahweh . . . the splendor and honor . . . the holy sacrifices. Then, like a cloud passing before the moon, it vanished. He let out a soft moan.

"What's become of me?" he slurred. "What's happened to my life? I had so much . . . I was a holy man . . . but now . . . now . . ."

He thought about what his life had once been and what his life was now, and the chasm between the two seemed so vast and fathomless that he wondered how he had ever crossed the gulf. Nor could he imagine crossing back and becoming, once again, a holy man. He bowed his head in despair and pulled on his beard.

"O God—I don't deserve to live anymore!" he moaned. "I deserve to die!" His deep voice echoed through the quiet streets, and Hilkiah shivered. Zechariah stood waiting, yearning for God to answer, longing for Him to strike him dead in payment for his sins with a lightning bolt, with leprosy. But nothing happened.

"Yahweh speaks to Isaiah now," he said sorrowfully. "Not to me. He's finished with me." He broke into anguished moans, crying, "Why doesn't He punish me? Not my children!"

A dog began to bark, and someone lit a lamp in a nearby window. Hilkiah pulled the old man's hands away from his face and tugged on his arm. "Come on, Zechariah. You'll wake up the whole city. You need to go home." They started walking again.

"I live in the Temple of Solomon," Zechariah slurred.

"Yes, I know, my friend. Come on."

"I'm a Levite," he said with pitiful pride. "I can name all my ancestors back to Levi, son of Jacob." He looked at Hilkiah expectantly.

"Not tonight, Zechariah. It's late. Maybe another time."

"I was leader of my tribe, chief among all the other Levites. I once taught Yahweh's holy law." He suddenly felt a need to talk about his former life, as if by talking he could discover how he had crossed the chasm to this nightmare world where innocent children perished in a torrent of flames.

"God gave me wisdom and understanding from the time I was very young. So King Uzziah sent for *me* when he wanted to learn God's law. I taught him to fear Yahweh and . . ."

He stumbled over a loose brick in the street and lost the flow of his thoughts. The night fell eerily silent except for Zechariah's wheezing breaths as he labored up the hill.

The higher they climbed, the larger and more lavish the houses became—one of the largest was Hilkiah's. His family had supplied fine linen for the Temple garments and rich embroidered cloth for royalty for many generations. But the two men continued past Hilkiah's house, climbing until they reached the gates to the courtyard of King Ahaz's palace. Only the Temple of Yahweh on the hill above stood higher than the palace.

Zechariah stopped and pointed a shaking finger. "I used to live in the king's palace. I commanded the nation, second in power only to the king. Uzziah told me—he promised me—if I ever had a daughter, she would marry into the royal house of King David. Imagine that! Before Abijah was even born she—"

He stopped abruptly. Abijah. Eliab's mother. He had let Eliab die. It was his fault.

"O God!—O God!" he groaned and fell to his knees, gazing up into the starry sky. "I'm so sorry! Oh, Eliab, my child . . . I'm sorry . . . I'm so sorry . . ."

Hilkiah quickly pulled Zechariah to his feet and dragged him up the hill away from the palace. "Come on, my friend. This way. Come on."

"I turned my back on God," Zechariah cried with horror. "Slowly . . . slowly . . . year after year. Eating at the king's table, drinking his wine, listening to the flattery . . . slowly . . . until one day," he shook his head, ". . . one day God was a stranger to me."

That was how he had crossed the gulf. Zechariah remembered now. Not in one great leap, but so slowly, so imperceptibly, that he had not noticed the downward slope, had not realized how far he had separated himself from God until it was too late.

He remembered those years, how he had lived to please himself instead of God, giving little more than lip service to His laws or His covenant. And now when he cried out to Yahweh, his numberless sins swallowed up his prayer before it reached heaven. They filled the yawning gap between him and God.

"Shh . . . shh . . . ," the little merchant soothed. "Never mind, now. Come on, my friend." They reached the top of the Temple mount and opened the gates to the outer court.

"You're almost home, Zechariah. There's the Temple."

"Leave me here, Hilkiah. I know the way."

Hilkiah studied his friend then looked up into the starry sky. "God of Abraham, how can I leave him here?" he shrugged. "He'll never make it by himself."

"Yahweh's Temple—the holy Temple—," Zechariah repeated, as if trying to recall something important. He stopped walking. "King Uzziah wanted to go into the Temple, into the holy place. Kings of other nations didn't need priests to offer sacrifices, so why did he need them? I should have known what to tell him. I taught God's holy law, but I didn't have an answer for the king. Uzziah went into the holy place, where he was forbidden to go. He started to offer his own sacrifice. But Yahweh saw him. And Yahweh cursed him with leprosy. It was my fault Uzziah died a leper. I should have told him . . . I should have stopped him . . ." He began to weep.

"That was many, many years ago," Hilkiah comforted. He gently pushed Zechariah until he started walking again. "Yes, I think every man in Judah has heard of the terrible fate of King Uzziah—may he rest in peace."

Hilkiah steered his stumbling friend in a wide arc

around the outer perimeter of the Temple courtyard, deliberately avoiding the holy sanctuary, as if not wishing to offend Yahweh either. He opened the door to a side entrance that led to the Temple storehouses, meeting rooms, and the Levites' private living quarters, and roused a dozing Temple gatekeeper. Together they helped Zechariah down the stone steps into his room on the lower level, removed his outer robe and sandals, and seated him on the bed. Then the gatekeeper left them.

"King Uzziah's gone now," Zechariah mumbled. "His son Jotham's gone too, and Ahaz is king. He's married to my daughter. Did you know that?"

"Yes," Hilkiah nodded patiently. "You have told me that before." He patted Zechariah's shoulder. "Well, good night, my friend. I must go home now." He turned to leave, but suddenly Zechariah clutched his arm in a desperate grip.

"Your children, Hilkiah! Where are your children?"

"My son Eliakim is at home," he said patiently. "He's probably sound asleep already."

Zechariah stared at him, his eyes wild, frantic. "You must diligently teach God's laws to him—and to his children after him! The Torah commands it! Don't make the same mistake I did. I failed to teach King Uzziah, and now—now King Ahaz is worse than all of the others. He has heathen altars on every street corner. He even sacrificed his son—to—"

But the memory was too painful for Zechariah to bear, even through a haze of drunkenness. "O God!" His anguished sobs echoed in the darkened chamber.

"God of Abraham, what can I do?" Hilkiah whispered. "I can't leave him all alone like this." He stood beside Zechariah, wringing his hands helplessly.

"I have the answer for King Uzziah," Zechariah suddenly cried. "I know why he is forbidden to enter the holy place." He fell on his knees in front of an empty chair, pleading with a king who was long since dead. "Don't do it, Your Majesty! You must not enter Yahweh's sanctuary! You must not! Hear what Yahweh has commanded in His Torah. This is what is written: 'Be careful not to be ensnared by inquiring about their gods, saying, "How do these nations serve their gods? We will do the same." You must not worship the Lord your God in their way, because in worshiping their gods, they do all kinds of detestable things the Lord hates. They even burn their sons and daughters in the fire as sacrifices to their gods.'"

Zechariah looked up, and the sorrow on his face brought tears to the little merchant's eyes. "I was in the procession to the Valley of Hinnom today," Zechariah told him. "And while I watched them sacrifice my grandchild, my Eliab, to a heathen god, I remembered what else is written in the Torah: 'For I, the Lord your God, am a jealous God, punishing the children for the sin of the fathers to the third and fourth generation.'

"Eliab died because of me—because I sinned." He fell on his face to the floor. "O God—not Eliab. Punish me. Let me die—let me die."

"Ah, my friend," Hilkiah wept, "how can I ever comfort you?" He knelt on the floor beside Zechariah, staying with him until the old man's tears were spent and he finally lay quiet and still. Then Hilkiah raised his eyes to heaven. "God of Abraham—how can he ever find peace under such a burden of guilt?"

—◈—

"Please, Lady Abijah—you need to eat something," the servant begged. "There's some fruit here, and some bread."

Abijah glanced at the tray of food and shook her head. "No . . . I can't eat." She bit her lip and tasted salty tears, as bitter as the anguish of her soul. How could she eat when her life had shattered into thousands of tiny fragments like a bowl hurled to the floor? She would never be whole again.

In the darkness of her room, Abijah sat by the window and gazed into the night sky. The stars shone faintly, fading and dying like the splendor of her husband's kingdom. The great eye of the moon was nearly closed, as if to shut out the horror that had taken place on earth. Abijah knew this night would never end, even when the sun rose in the morning.

She had guessed where Maaseiah was taking her sons and what would happen to them, but she had been powerless to stop him. The soldiers had held her back long after the procession had disappeared from the palace courtyard. She had heard Molech's pounding drums above her own desperate screams, but she could not break free to save her children. When it was over, Eliab—her firstborn—was dead. And her son Hezekiah had continued to scream, too young to comprehend the reason for the horror he had witnessed. Nor could Abijah comprehend it herself. All she could do when Hezekiah was returned to the palace was hold him in her arms and weep.

After long hours, Hezekiah had fallen asleep, but the servants could not persuade Abijah to lay him down. She longed for someone to hold her and comfort her too—to feel the safety and security of loving arms surrounding her. But only the cold stone walls of the palace harem encompassed her. Decorated with tapestries and carpets, warmed by fires in the brazier and hearth, the room had the appearance of warmth and comfort, but Abijah knew it was only an illusion. Beneath their elegant surfaces, the walls, like her life, were hard and gray and as cold as stone. With no one to help her pick up the pieces of her life, Abijah sat alone on the window seat, rocking Hezekiah gently, stroking his dark, curly hair.

"Starving yourself won't bring Eliab back, my lady." Hearing Eliab's name reopened the wound, and Abijah's tears began to flow once again.

"Oh, Eliab," she wept. "My beautiful Eliab."

Everything about him had been special, everything fresh and new: the first time she felt life moving inside her; his birth, both terrible and wonderful; holding a new little person, who really was not new at all but had been a part of her for nine months. Miraculously, they had been joined as one—then suddenly they were two. Her son Eliab: as the future king, his young life had been full of hope and promise. Now he was gone.

"I never even kissed him good-bye," she wept. She hugged Hezekiah close to her, then bent to kiss his forehead. He stirred in his sleep as a sob shuddered through him, but he did not wake up.

"My lady, you must put him in his bed now," the servant pleaded. "You need to change your robe, comb your hair. What if the king comes to your chambers?"

Abijah looked down at the front of her robe, which she had torn to shreds in her grief. She had not combed her hair, had not bathed or put on perfumes.

"No," she said quietly. "Let me mourn for my son."

"But you know you're not allowed to mourn. It's not as if Eliab got sick and died. His death was honorable, my lady—a glorious sacrifice to be celebrated, not mourned." For Abijah there would be no mourners to wail with her, no funeral procession or prayers for the dead, no grave to mark the place where her child lay.

"What kind of a mother could celebrate her child's death?" Abijah asked angrily. "What kind of a father would kill his own child to save himself? Only a monster could do such a thing! And only a monster would force his other children to watch!"

"My lady, be careful what you say! Your husband is the king!"

"Oh, I know that well enough!" Her voice was brittle. "'You will be married to the royal house of King David'— that's all I heard from the time I was a little girl. It was an honor, I was told. I would carry kings in my womb. I was blessed among women. No other woman in the kingdom was as lucky as I was." She paused and fingered her torn garment. "But look at the price I've paid for that honor: my son is dead. And I'm married to a man I will hate until the day I die!"

"My lady! Don't say such a thing!" The servant glanced around nervously as if someone might overhear.

"I don't care," Abijah said flatly. "I hate him. I hate him! Nothing can change that."

"Please, my lady. You don't mean it. It's only your grief speaking. You have a wonderful life here in the palace—"

"That's what I used to think . . ." Abijah's voice drifted off into silence. She had never questioned her destiny, never had any hopes or dreams of her own. Why should she dream when her life had been so clearly laid out before her, when there was never a possibility it could have been different?

As a child she had been promised to the house of David, and her life had proceeded in its orderly course toward that goal like the stars moving across the sky through their appointed festivals and seasons. Her wedding to Ahaz led to the purpose for which she was born. Eliab's birth fulfilled it.

How eager Abijah had been to leave home! She had wanted to escape from her father's melancholy, from watching him drink himself into a stupor every night while her mother struggled to hide his secret and hold their family together. During the day, Zechariah was able to carry out his tasks—serving in the Temple, teaching students his vast knowledge of the Torah, solving complex problems of the Law in great debates. He had hidden his sickness so well that few people ever guessed that he had stopped living when King Uzziah died. Moving to the palace seemed like a blessed escape from the pain of home.

"But this palace is no escape," Abijah murmured. "The beauty and glory of King Uzziah's reign are gone forever. The music and laughter are finished. And I'm a sparrow held captive in a tarnished cage."

She wished her life had taken a different course, and she thought immediately of Uriah. Her life would have been different if she had married him. The high priest of Yahweh's Temple would never have sacrificed his firstborn son to Molech.

As her father's brightest pupil and the future high priest, Uriah had been a fixture in her household as she was growing up. And when she remembered him now, she realized he had always cared deeply for her, had always gazed at her with eyes full of tenderness and love. She had taken that love for granted, imagining that Ahaz would feel the same way about her. But Ahaz never looked at her with anything but lust. Not long after she had spoken her wedding vows, she had given up hope for any tenderness or companionship. She was Ahaz's property, to be used for his own gratification and to produce an heir—nothing more.

"My children are the only things that are truly mine," Abijah said, turning from the window to face the servant once again. "Everything else was determined for me from birth. But they came from my body—my pain and blood and tears. When they took my Eliab, they took part of me.

"And I couldn't stop them," she wept. "I was helpless. My husband can kill my babies, and there's nothing I can do about it. I comfort Hezekiah—I tell him, 'It's all right. Mama will protect you.' But it's a lie. I can't! All my life I've let other people tell me what to do and think and feel. But now that I've felt pain and hatred and despair, I won't let anyone think for me or decide for me again!"

"Please, my lady. Don't do something you'll be sorry for."

"I'm going to make Ahaz hate me as much as I hate

him. Maybe then he'll banish me, and my children as well." She could see that her words had shocked her servant, but she didn't care. She crushed Hezekiah to herself.

"If I lose him—if Ahaz takes him away from me—I'll have no reason to live."

2

Hezekiah lay awake in the darkness, remembering, listening for the soldiers, terrified that they would come for him as they had come for Eliab. He had heard no word of his uncle's armies since the morning they had marched into battle, the morning Eliab had died, almost two weeks ago. What would happen when they returned? Would Uncle Maaseiah send them here to the palace for him? Would he be thrown to the monster the way his brother had been?

He remembered the cold, stony gaze on Uncle Maaseiah's face and the way his ring had flashed like lightning as he laid his hand on Eliab's head to mark him as the firstborn. He remembered, and a shudder passed through his body that jolted him upright.

Hezekiah felt helpless, vulnerable as he lay in his bed beside Eliab's empty one. The servants who slept nearby wouldn't save him. They hadn't saved Eliab. Only Mama had tried to stop the soldiers. Mama would help him hide. She would protect him.

Hezekiah slipped out of bed and, as he had every night since the soldiers had come, crept down the darkened corridors to his mother's room in the harem. Her door was unlatched, and he crept over to the bed where she lay asleep.

"Mama—" He tried to whisper but his voice sounded loud in the darkness. "Mama, I'm scared." She awoke and gathered him into the safety of her arms.

"Come here, my little one—hush now, don't cry." She pulled him into the bed beside her and dried his tears.

Mama was warm and soft and very beautiful. Her shiny, dark hair, unpinned for the night, flowed down her back in thick waves. Her bed smelled of fragrant aloes and myrrh. He was safe here. She would keep the soldiers away. She would stop the nightmares from coming. In the comfort of her arms, with the sweet perfume of her scented bed on his cheek, he closed his eyes and soon fell asleep.

The sound of voices and the harsh glare of torches startled him awake. Hezekiah cried out, terrified that the soldiers had returned, but there were no soldiers this time. Instead, he saw the large silhouette of his father filling the door frame.

"Abijah, send the boy to his room," Ahaz said harshly. His lungs wheezed from his climb up the stairs to the harem, and his pale forehead glistened with sweat. In the flickering lamplight, Ahaz's face looked menacing, and Hezekiah scrambled into the safety of his mother's arms. She sat up in bed. Her heart pounded against him as he clung to her, but she made no move to obey.

Ahaz loosened the belt of his tunic as he took a step closer. "Didn't you hear me? I said send him away."

Abijah tightened her grip on Hezekiah until he could scarcely breathe. Then, almost in a whisper, his mother spoke. "Murderer—"

Ahaz swiftly crossed the room until he stood just inches from them. "What did you say?"

"Get away from us, you murderer."

Without warning, Ahaz struck Abijah across the face with such force that Hezekiah tumbled from her arms and landed on the floor. "Mama!" he cried and tried to go to her, but his father grabbed him by one arm and flung him away. Hezekiah fell against a bronze lampstand, and it toppled to the floor with a crash.

"Get out! Go back to your room!" Ahaz's flushed face

twisted in anger. Hezekiah was terrified of him, but he feared for his mother's safety, too, as his father towered over her in rage.

"Get away from me!" she screamed. "You murdered Eliab! You murdered your own son!"

Her words sent a chill through Hezekiah that felt like shards of ice. His father? His father had killed Eliab?

Ahaz grabbed her by the shoulders and twisted her around, forcing her to face him. "Yes, Abijah! And now you will bear me another son to take his place."

Hezekiah began to tremble as the awful truth sank in. Uncle Maaseiah wasn't responsible. It wasn't the soldiers he needed to fear. It was his own father.

He turned and ran, not stopping until he reached his room. He slammed the door and leaned against it, as if to barricade himself inside. The floor, the room, the whole world tilted and spun and reeled until Hezekiah felt sick.

His father—his father had killed Eliab. Who could possibly protect him from his father, the king?

He was wide awake now, every muscle and nerve ending tingling with fear, his heart racing. Where could he hide? Even his mother's room was no longer safe. He was afraid to stay here, but terrified to leave. He stood frozen in place. The moonless night was dark, the corridors outside his room quiet and still.

Gradually his eyes grew accustomed to the dark, and his heartbeat, his breathing slowed to normal as he realized no one had followed him. When the familiar contours of his room began to take shape, the shadows seemed less menacing. He could distinguish the bronze lampstands against the wall, the ivory table beneath the window, the charcoal brazier glowing faintly, his rumpled, empty bed— and Eliab's.

Tears filled his eyes and ran down his face as he remembered his brother clothed in a tunic of white linen, sleepy and bewildered, forced to walk in the procession to the Valley of Hinnom. His father, dressed in his royal robes, had led that procession. What he did not understand was why. Why had his father killed Eliab?

Hezekiah stood against the door for a very long time, aware of every sound that penetrated the silence of the darkened palace: a cricket chirping in the courtyard below his window, an owl hooting softly in the valley near the spring, a wooden shutter scraping, creaking as the night wind blew past his window. Before long Hezekiah's legs grew weary, his eyes heavy with sleep. The night sounds grew into a steady, comforting rhythm.

Then, sudden voices shattered the silence. Flickering torchlight danced through the crack under his door. Footsteps pounded down the hallway toward his room, then past it. He opened his door to peek out. The hallway was deserted, but he heard insistent pounding and urgent voices coming from around the corner by his mother's room. Hezekiah listened, ready to run, his heart thumping in his chest.

A moment later the torches began to move down the hall toward him. Then his father appeared, rounding the corner with a palace chamberlain jogging breathlessly beside him.

"Your Majesty, please forgive me for disturbing you," the chamberlain said, "but with bad news pouring in from every direction, the situation was critical!"

Ahaz's valet hurried to keep up, tugging hastily at Ahaz's clothes, trying to pull them into place over his flabby body.

"Why does disaster always strike in the middle of the night?" Ahaz cursed. He smoothed his thin, pale hair into place and wiped beads of sweat from his forehead.

"I don't know, Your Majesty—"

"Well, what am I supposed to do now? I don't know what to do!"

Through the narrow crack, Hezekiah stared at his father hurrying past, and his stomach turned over in a mixture of fear and hatred.

"I've summoned your advisers to the council chamber. You'll have a few minutes to read the reports for yourself before they arrive, and . . ."

The voices grew faint as the men disappeared down the stairs. Hezekiah stood shivering in the darkness, the stone floor like ice beneath his bare feet. He had seen fear on his father's face and had heard it in the chamberlain's anxious voice. Something terrible must have happened.

Hezekiah slipped into his robe and quietly stepped out into the hallway. For a moment he considered running back to the safety of his mother's room, but then a greater need, the need to understand why, to pursue the source of his fear and hatred, overshadowed his wish for safety.

Hezekiah crept down the darkened stairway and through the deserted hallways without being seen, following his father to the council chamber. He slid past the heavy curtain that guarded the servants' entrance to the chamber and hid inside the small anteroom where the servants usually waited to be summoned. The tiny room was empty.

Hezekiah crouched down and peered around the carved pillars and into the council room. His father's throne stood empty on a raised dais at one end of the room, with Uncle Maaseiah's smaller throne beside it. Between them, a carved ivory table held a flask of wine and a goblet. Thick wool carpets and cushions were arranged in front of the dais for Ahaz's advisers, and the valet scurried between them, lighting the lamps and charcoal braziers. The pale, meager light barely penetrated the thick gloom of the chamber. When the valet finished, he left the council chamber, hurrying past Hezekiah without seeing him.

King Ahaz stood beside a lampstand, unrolling and reading several scrolls as the chamberlain handed them to him. His face looked paler than usual, his eyes wide with fear, his lips tightly drawn into a thin line. When he finished reading the last one, he threw it to the floor with an anguished cry and tore his robes. Hezekiah crouched lower in the shadows, waiting, listening.

"No—no," Ahaz moaned. "How can I run this nation without Maaseiah? I never should have let him go into battle." He covered his face with both hands and pressed his fingers into his eyes, wiping them. Then he gazed up at the thick cedar beams of the ceiling and drew a deep breath, as if trying to draw strength from their massiveness.

"What am I going to do?" he muttered, shaking his head. "I don't know what to do."

The chamberlain took Ahaz's arm and led him toward the throne, his voice smooth and soothing. "Why don't you sit down, Your Majesty? You're upset. You've suffered a great shock. But everything will work out. Give yourself time. Your councilmen are coming. They'll know what to do."

Ahaz stumbled up the steps to the dais and dropped into his chair, then gazed, bewildered, at his advisers as they straggled in. They appeared groggy and confused, many rubbing the sleep from their eyes. They glanced nervously at Ahaz in his torn robes as they took their places.

"Is it news of your army, Your Majesty?" someone asked gingerly.

Hezekiah stiffened. He remembered the soldiers who had yanked him from his bed, the soldiers who had filled the hallway and carried his mother away, the endless rows and rows of soldiers lined up in the palace courtyard who forced him to walk down the hill through the city, the soldiers who surrounded the monster's platform so he and Eliab could not escape—his father's army.

"Yes. It concerns my army," his father said hollowly. He blinked the sweat from his eyes. Everyone stared at Ahaz, waiting, but he seemed confused and distracted, unsure how to begin. He cleared his throat, then glanced at the empty seat on his right and quickly reached for the flask of wine. It rattled against the goblet as he poured, betraying his shaking hands. He took two quick gulps and wiped his lips with the back of his hand.

"They're all dead," he blurted out at last. The advisers gazed at him through sleepy, uncomprehending eyes. "The army I sent north to stop the invasion has been defeated. One hundred twenty thousand soldiers have been slaughtered. My three commanders . . . Azrikam . . . Elkanah . . . my brother Maaseiah . . ." His voice choked, and he could only gesture weakly toward their empty places, unable to speak. The advisers looked away or down at their laps as if embarrassed by the king's emotional state. The room grew so still as they waited that Hezekiah could hear the oil lamps hissing faintly as they burned, casting wavering shadows on the walls.

"All three men are dead," Ahaz said at last and reached for the wine glass again, quickly gulping two more mouthfuls. After a struggle he regained his composure, deliberately looking away from Maaseiah's empty chair and focusing on the blank wall above everyone's head.

"The alliance between King Rezin of Aram and King Pekah of Israel proved stronger than we thought. I've lost most of my army, and the enemy continues to march south across the northern borders. They've invaded all my villages and towns along their path and have taken captive more than 200,000 people."

Several of the advisers moaned in despair while Ahaz gulped another drink of wine, set down the glass, then gripped the arms of his chair as if to steady himself. "The enemy is heading here. They've plotted to make the son of Tabeel king in my place. They're going to attack Jerusalem."

A ripple of fear coursed through the room as the advisers realized their own lives were endangered, and everyone started talking at once in low, nervous whispers. As the shock wave reached Hezekiah, he began to shiver.

Ahaz grabbed his wine glass with both hands and quickly drained it, then pounded on the table with his fist. "Shut up and listen to me! There's more." Instantly the room grew silent. "I've had news from the south as well. The King of Edom has taken advantage of this crisis and has invaded my only seaport. Elath fell easily into his hands. It's lost." Once again the meeting dissolved into chaos. "Please . . . please . . ." Ahaz groaned, pounding the table again. "There's still more." The stunned advisers tensed, bracing themselves.

"Our old enemies, the Philistines, have come against us as well. They've raided towns in the foothills and the Negev and have already captured Beth Shemesh, Aijalon, Timnah—three or four other towns—I can't even remember."

"What are we going to do?" one of the advisers cried out while the men murmured fearfully. Ahaz waved his hand limply as if shooing away a fly.

"For the time being, I'll have to forget about the Edomites and the Philistines. Our most serious threat is from the north. Aram and Israel will reach Jerusalem within a few days. They are organized and powerful. And I have no army left! So you tell me. What am I going to do?" Ahaz's panic showed in spite of his efforts to control it. He gazed anxiously at his advisers, waiting for their help, but the men sat in bewildered silence, as if trying to comprehend the magnitude of the spreading invasion.

"Doesn't anyone have a word of advice?" he challenged. "You're my advisers! What am I going to do?"

The men stared at him blankly, then a grim, scowling nobleman seated near the front rose slowly to his feet. He was a thin, pompous little man dressed fastidiously, even at this early hour, with a gold ring on each of his fingers. When he spoke he gestured broadly with his hands, and as his rings caught the light, Hezekiah saw a pattern like fire-flies on the ceiling above his head. Ahaz leaned toward him, listening hopefully.

"Your Majesty, if Jerusalem is facing a lengthy siege, we must consider our water resources. The rainy season is months away, and the city cisterns are probably getting low. Is there any way we can build defenses around the Gihon spring? Otherwise, once we seal the city gates our water supply will be cut off."

"You stupid fool!" Ahaz roared. "I know where the spring is! I know Jerusalem doesn't have any water! But what can we possibly do about it now?" He stared angrily at the man, challenging him to answer, until he shrugged helplessly and sat down.

"So. He has no answers." Ahaz grunted and shook his head in disgust. "Does anyone else have some worthless advice to offer?"

From the back of the room, almost against the rear wall, a lone figure rose slowly to his feet. "Your Majesty, I do."

"Who are you? Come forward where I can see you."

"I'm Uriah, Your Majesty—high priest of the Temple of Yahweh." He spoke in a deep, resonant voice and, un-like Ahaz's other advisers, appeared calm and in control. He was a tall, powerfully built man with massive shoulders and arms like tree trunks. His steely gray eyes under bushy brows had an intensity that was intimidating. He strode forward with such a commanding presence that Hezekiah curled up in the shadows where he crouched, suddenly afraid.

Hezekiah could not help comparing his father to the imposing priest, and the king came up short on every point. Uriah was strong and muscular, with broad shoulders and chest; Ahaz was flabby and round-shouldered, with no muscles beneath the fat. Uriah's swarthy skin and thick, black hair and beard gave him a leonine appearance.

Ahaz's pale, doughy skin was blotchy, sickly, and the soft, reddish hair on his face formed only a scraggly beard. The priest seemed to have no wasted motion, his every gesture decisive and powerful, while Ahaz fluttered and fidgeted nervously, his hands quivering like a man with the palsy.

The king seemed awed by Uriah's strength and confidence as well. He perched on the edge of his seat breathlessly. "You may speak, Uriah."

"Your Majesty, our nation needs a strong ally to come to our defense in this crisis. I suggest that we quickly approach one of our neighboring nations to—"

"An excellent suggestion!" Ahaz interrupted. His eyes held a glimmer of hope for the first time. He glared at his other advisers accusingly. "Now the question is, which nation would be most likely to help us?"

"I've given it a great deal of thought, Your Majesty—," Uriah began, but Ahaz cut in.

"Which nation does our enemy fear the most? I want to choose an ally that will fill the Arameans' hearts with dread."

"Your Majesty, it might be better if we—"

". . . an ally that will make them retreat out of Judah as soon as they hear the news of our alliance. Which nation would do that?" Ahaz demanded.

Uriah thought for a moment. "Your Majesty, the nation that is their greatest threat is Assyria. The Assyrians are currently waging war with the nations north of Aram, and their empire is already vast and far-reaching. I'm sure the King of Aram fears becoming the next target of aggression. But I think I should warn you that—"

"Perfect!" Ahaz shouted. "Would the Assyrians be willing to ally themselves with us?" he asked Uriah anxiously.

"An alliance with us would certainly give them a foothold in this region, which is what they're looking for," he answered cautiously. "But I think we should consider a less dangerous ally first. The Assyrians are a vicious, violent, heathen nation, and I'm not sure we should—"

"The more violent the better," Ahaz replied. "Let King Rezin suffer the way I have." He closed his eyes and beat his breast with his fist. "My brother's death must be avenged!"

Ahaz's words jolted Hezekiah: *"My brother's death must be avenged."* But how? How could he, Hezekiah, avenge Eliab's death? Who would dare challenge his father, the king?

"Uriah's right," Ahaz continued. "We must convince another nation to come to our defense. We're in no position to defend ourselves without an army. The stronger that ally is, the better." He took a deep breath. "We will send a gift of tribute to Assyria and propose an alliance. The gift must be very lavish, to impress them that we are a worthy ally. And we'll need to act quickly, before the siege of Jerusalem begins. We'll send the best of everything in the nation: gold, silver, precious stones."

"But, Your Majesty," someone protested, "where will all these gifts come from? There's no time to levy taxes, and we've already emptied the royal treasures to equip Maaseiah's army."

Ahaz tugged at the neck of his robe as if it choked him. "I need air—I can't breathe in here," he mumbled. The chamberlain quickly threw open the shuttered windows, and cool, damp air flooded the room. Ahaz filled his lungs, then stared out of the open window longingly, as if wishing he and his problems could disappear through it.

Hezekiah followed his father's gaze and saw, in the faint dawn light, the outline of Solomon's Temple on the hill above the palace. Ahaz must have seen it too, for a moment later he fairly shouted, "We will remove the gold and other valuables from the Temple of Solomon."

The high priest, who had returned to his place in the rear of the chamber, scrambled to his feet.

"Your Majesty, the Temple storehouses are nearly empty. The only valuables left are the sacred vessels used for worship." Uriah spoke calmly, but his deeply knit brows revealed his distress at Ahaz's plan. "It's true that the holy of holies contains a wealth of gold, but it is part of the structure. There's no way to remove it without permanently damaging Yahweh's dwelling place."

Ahaz did not appear to be listening. "A wealth of gold," he repeated to himself, nodding. "Uriah, I'm favorably impressed with your wisdom and counsel. I'm putting you in charge of the gift to Assyria. If you do well, you will be the new palace administrator in my brother's place." He gestured to the empty seat at his right. "Tear the Temple down, if necessary, but this gift must be acceptable to the Assyrians."

Uriah nodded slightly. If his sudden promotion surprised him, his face did not betray it. His expression remained unreadable. "Yes, Your Majesty," he answered quietly.

"When everything is ready," Ahaz continued, "I will send a delegation to the Assyrian monarch, along with my personal appeal for a covenant with his nation."

Ahaz looked confident for the first time that night. He rose from his chair and began issuing orders, crossing his arms in imitation of the imposing high priest.

"We need to raise another army for the defense of Jerusalem. You're in charge of that." He gestured toward one of his advisers, who appeared horrified at the thought of producing soldiers and weapons from nothing. "As for the rest of you, begin spreading word of the coming siege as soon as you're dismissed. Make sure the city and surrounding areas are prepared as quickly as possible. It may take time for my new Assyrian allies to rally to my defense."

The task of making so many decisions seemed to exhaust Ahaz. He slumped back into his chair and propped his feet on the foot rest. "That's all we can do for now. You're all dismissed."

But before anyone moved, Uriah strode to the front again, taking charge. "Just a minute, please, Your Majesty. I'd like to make one other suggestion. Your plans should include a public sacrifice to Yahweh. We will need divine help in this crisis."

Ahaz sat up straight. "Another excellent suggestion, Uriah. I'm impressed with your wisdom. However, I don't think it would be appropriate to sacrifice to Yahweh after emptying His Temple's storehouses. I'm uneasy about that. Surely you understand." He gathered the sparse whiskers of his beard together and looked thoughtful. "No, we have already sought the help of Molech, the most powerful of all the gods. He won't desert us now, especially after I've personally sacrificed so much. So before the siege begins, we will hold another sacrifice to Molech."

Curled up in his cramped hiding place, Hezekiah had nearly fallen asleep as the meeting dragged on, but when he heard his father's words, a jolt of fear coursed through his body. He nearly cried aloud as he scrambled to his feet, his heart racing.

"Perhaps those of you who withheld your sons from Molech the last time will consider the great danger this nation is in," the king continued, glaring at his advisers. "We need Molech's great power in this crisis. We must *all* sacrifice a son this time. He's a demanding god, but surely we can father dozens of sons once Molech saves us from destruction."

Hezekiah reeled in shock as he heard his father's words. He planned to kill another son, another of Hezekiah's brothers. Or maybe *him*.

"The sacrifice to Molech must take place as soon as possible, before the siege begins," Ahaz was saying. "Uriah, I will leave all the preparations in your hands."

Uriah visibly paled as he stared at Ahaz. "I'm a priest of Yahweh, Your Majesty, not Molech."

"You're the new palace administrator!" Ahaz thundered, gesturing to his brother's empty chair. "Unless you don't want the job?"

Uriah was silent for several seconds. He seemed to have stopped breathing. Then he bowed slightly. "Of course, Your Majesty. As you wish."

"Good. Then you're all dismissed."

"No!" Hezekiah cried out, unable to stop himself. "No . . . no!" But as the advisers filed noisily out of the room, only Ahaz's valet, rushing through the anteroom to attend to the king, heard Hezekiah's frantic cries.

"Hey! What are you doing in here?" he said, taking Hezekiah by the shoulders. "You don't belong in here."

"No . . . no!" Hezekiah cried, struggling to break free.

"What's going on?—where's my valet?" Ahaz demanded. The servant picked up Hezekiah and carried him, struggling, into the council chamber.

"It's your son, my lord. I found him in the antechamber. I'll take him upstairs."

"You again," Ahaz growled. "What are you doing down here?"

Hezekiah wanted to rush forward and strike his father, to lash out against him for hurting his mother, for killing Eliab, for plotting to kill again. But he couldn't speak, couldn't move, immobilized by fear and hatred.

Ahaz's eyes darted nervously, resting on his son only briefly, as if unable to bear the sight of him. Then he lunged at Hezekiah. "Why are you looking at me like that?" he cried. "Take him out of here!"

3

The high priest, Uriah, left the palace and wandered slowly up the hill to the Temple, deep in thought. It had been
an astounding meeting. Uriah had seized the opportunity
of Prince Maaseiah's death to catapult himself from the
back row of the council chamber to King Ahaz's right-
hand side. The moment should have been the happiest of
his life. He had attained a position of enormous power in
the nation, power he had worked hard to claim for over 18
years. He should be overjoyed. Yet a deep, gnawing unrest
filled his soul as he thought of the price he would pay for
that power.

He would have to profane Solomon's Temple, plundering its gold for the Assyrian tribute. He dreaded being
responsible for that desecration. But he knew the king
would take whatever gold he wanted whether Uriah ap-
proved of the destruction or not. At least he could try to
hold the damage to a minimum.

No, the principal root of his unrest was the sacrifice to
Molech. Uriah knew what the Torah commanded: "You
shall not make for yourself an idol in the form of anything
in heaven above or on the earth beneath or in the waters
below. You shall not bow down to them or worship them."
He was Yahweh's high priest—how could he deliberately
disobey Yahweh's commandment? Yet if Uriah refused to
preside over the sacrifice to Molech, he would surely lose

his new position as palace administrator. Then he would return to being what he had always been: an impotent priest in the crumbling Temple of Yahweh, struggling to scratch out a living year after year from meager offerings. One of the priests of Molech would willingly do the king's bidding; he would be the one to gain power and preeminence as the high priest of the nation.

Uriah's jaw tightened, and he clenched his massive fists. Never! He would fight for what was rightfully his. Yahweh was the only God of Israel, and all the power belonged to His high priest, not Molech's. He strode through the gate into the Temple courtyard, determined to do what had to be done.

As he approached the holy sanctuary, Uriah gazed up at its shining golden roof, painfully aware of how badly the entire structure had deteriorated. In its prime, this Temple had been magnificent, the envy of all the nations. But now it stood forlorn, forgotten, like a deposed queen, cast aside and clothed in mere rags of her former glory. He shook his head as if to erase the pitiful sight.

Ever since he had become a priest like his forefathers, Uriah had watched helplessly as the institution he served slowly crumbled and decayed from apathy. His countrymen had neglected the Lord's Temple and the required tithes and offerings for so many years that the priests and Levites could barely maintain an adequate standard of living, much less afford repairs to the building. Most of the priests had deserted Jerusalem long ago, ignoring their regular terms of duty to pursue other means of supporting themselves and their families.

The worship of Yahweh had become stagnant, Uriah thought, stuck in a routine of traditions and rituals that had no significance or meaning for the people. Yet the chief priests and Levites remained opposed to change. This stalemate, coupled with the hopeless frustration of loving Abijah, who could never belong to him, had led Uriah to pursue a position of power in the court. He had vowed to do everything he could to bring the Temple of Yahweh and its priesthood back to a position of dignity in the nation once again. He had sat in the back row of the council chamber year after year, watching for an opening, waiting for his chance at power. Now it had come. The only obstacle remaining in his path was the sacrifice to Molech.

Uriah opened a rusting door beside the main sanctuary that led to the Temple side chambers and strode inside. He needed someone to talk to, someone to confide in who could appreciate the tremendous opportunity he had been offered and help put his conscience to rest. As he already had so many times this morning, he thought of Zechariah the Levite—Abijah's father, his former teacher and mentor. He had set the example Uriah had followed in pursuing political power. Zechariah was a brilliant man, well versed in the minutest letter of the Law, an astute politician. And although Zechariah had given up his position in court after King Uzziah's death, Uriah was drawn to him now. He was one of the few people who could understand the dilemma Uriah faced.

He wandered down the dimly lit corridors until he found Zechariah's quarters and rapped softly on the door. When no one answered, he wondered if the old Levite had retired and realized that he had not seen Zechariah in several weeks. He knocked again a little harder.

"What do you want?" a voice inside asked sharply.

"Rabbi Zechariah, it's Uriah. I'm sorry if I've disturbed you, but may I have a word with you, please?" Uriah, who had put on a show of great self-confidence and authority before the king, suddenly felt inadequate before the man he had always admired and sought to emulate.

After several minutes, Zechariah opened the door and stood before Uriah, his red-rimmed eyes displaying confusion. His white hair and beard were matted and dirty, and his rumpled, wine-stained clothes looked and smelled as if they had not been changed in weeks. The room behind the old man lay in shambles and smelled of sour wine and vomit. Uriah nearly turned away. This couldn't be the respected dignitary he remembered, the man who once sat at the king's right hand. But it was.

"Uriah . . . come in . . . come in," Zechariah stammered. He led the way into the room, staggering slightly, and cleared a place in the clutter for Uriah to sit.

Uriah followed hesitantly, struggling to conceal his shock. "I—I need to talk to you, Rabbi," he began. Shaken by the change in Zechariah, he could scarcely remember why he had come.

"I'll get some wine." Zechariah tottered over to a shelf and produced a skin of wine and two goblets. Uriah shook his head.

"No—thank you, Rabbi. It's too early for me . . . but please . . . you go ahead."

Uriah could scarcely look at the old man in his embarrassing condition. He had made a mistake to come here. He stared at the floor, groping for words, wishing he could leave. Zechariah took a few quick gulps from the wine flask; then, with a pathetic remnant of his former dignity, he pulled up a stool and sat opposite Uriah.

"What did you need to talk to me about?"

Uriah saw, as if through a dingy curtain, the respected teacher he had come to seek. He cleared his throat. "Rabbi, I have just come from a meeting with King Ahaz. I wanted you to be the first to know: I've been appointed palace administrator."

Zechariah scowled. "But—Prince Maaseiah . . . ?"

"Our army has been defeated. We've suffered enormous losses. The prince is dead."

"It's a great honor for you," Zechariah sputtered, uncertainly. "But Prince Maaseiah . . . the army . . . it's a great loss . . ." He shook his head, gazing down at his hands, folded in his lap.

"I want to accept this position. It's a tremendous opportunity, but it would mean—" Uriah could not bring himself to admit that it would mean idolatry. He realized, suddenly, that he had not come for Zechariah's help in making a decision. Uriah had made his decision in the council chamber, the moment Ahaz dangled the opportunity before him. He had come to win Zechariah's approval, as if the old Levite could somehow absolve Uriah's guilt.

"It's just that some of my duties as palace administrator may go against the teachings of the Torah. But if I use this opportunity to establish myself as an adviser to the king, I will be in a unique position to teach King Ahaz about Yahweh's law. And ultimately I can do a great deal of good."

He leaned forward on the edge of his seat, almost pleading with Zechariah for absolution. "All my life, all my ambition and striving has been with one goal in mind: to revive the role of the priesthood and make the Temple an influential force in the nation again. Now I can do that. I've worked my way up from the bottom, studying, waiting, watching for a chance like this. I'll be second in command to the king."

Zechariah stared at him blankly, as if wondering where he fit in. Uriah quickly continued. "I know there are some priests and Levites who will object to what I'm doing, and I'll need your help in winning them over. You are a man of influence here in the Temple. Surely you can understand what I'm trying to accomplish. You once held the same position in the palace—" Uriah suddenly stopped, keenly embarrassed for reminding this broken, disheveled man of the power and position he had once held and lost. "I just wanted to ask if I could have your support," he mumbled apologetically.

"My support," Zechariah echoed. He stared at Uriah blankly for a moment; then a sad, ironic smile flickered briefly across his face.

"Yes, please support me in this, Zechariah. If I make a few concessions to Ahaz and gain his confidence, I can start to teach him later on, the way you once taught King Uzziah."

Zechariah's head jerked up at the mention of Uzziah. He stared at Uriah with watery eyes. Slowly, he rose and shuffled to the shelf, picking up the wineskin and fingering it nervously. His back was to Uriah.

"You're going to teach Ahaz? Make him stop his idolatry?"

Uriah winced. "It may take some time, Rabbi, but that's what I hope to accomplish—eventually."

Zechariah raised the wineskin to his lips with shaking hands, and rivulets of wine trickled down his beard and tunic. He swallowed noisily, then made a pitiful attempt to wipe his face and beard. Uriah waited.

"You've always had more ambition than any of the others," Zechariah said at last. "I won't oppose you if you decide to accept the position." His voice carried no enthusiasm.

"Thank you, Rabbi." Uriah stood. Now anxious to leave, he inched toward the door. "There are several announcements from the king that I need to discuss with the chief priests and Levites, so I'm calling for a meeting at noon today. If you'll contact the chief Levites, I'll notify the chief priests."

Zechariah nodded but did not turn to face him.

"Thank you, Rabbi," Uriah mumbled again and hurried out of the room, closing the door swiftly as if to lock away something horrible. Then he wandered slowly through the Temple corridors, oblivious to where his feet were taking him.

His former teacher's pathetic state had unnerved him. He struggled to regain his composure, closing his eyes to summon the image of himself he had so carefully practiced, the image he had so successfully portrayed before the king: erect posture, controlled gestures, intimidating stare. Then he willed his body to conform to that image. When he felt outwardly in control again, he battled to untangle his conflicting thoughts and feelings.

Uriah could not imagine how a man as great as Zechariah had ended in such a state. But now that he had a chance to be as influential in the nation as Zechariah had once been, he would not let the opportunity pass, even if it meant violating the Torah. A nagging voice tried to remind him of the price he would pay for disobeying the Law, but Uriah chose to ignore the voice.

He climbed the stairs, impatiently brushing cobwebs off the cracked ceiling. This will all change, he thought. This Temple can be the way it once was in the days of Solomon. He would not let it crumble into obscurity.

King Ahaz returned to his chambers after the meeting, hoping to recover some of the sleep he had lost the night before. He sank into bed, still dressed in his robes, and closed his eyes, reviewing all the decisions he had made. Everything was taken care of, he assured himself. He had done the right thing. Hadn't he?

The decisions had made sense in the council chamber, but now that he was alone he wasn't so sure. What if the Assyrians didn't come to his defense? He suddenly recalled what Uriah had said about the Assyrians—that they were a vicious, violent nation—and he wondered if an alliance with them was truly the only solution.

Ahaz was exhausted, but sleep eluded him. He tossed and twisted in bed for over an hour, battling with the ensnaring bedcovers and his doubts and fears. He cursed his father for dying so suddenly, leaving him in control of the nation at the age of 20. Ahaz had enjoyed being a prince, indulged and spoiled by his father and all the court, but now he found the pressures of his reign intolerable, the burden of decisions and responsibilities unbearable.

At last Ahaz decided he had no other choice but to call on the Assyrians. Maaseiah was dead, and the thought of the conspiracy against him, the thought that he may die as well, made his loins turn to water. He kicked the bedcovers onto the floor and gave up his attempt to sleep.

He rose wearily and crossed to the latticed window, then peered out through the slats as if from a prison cell. The sun stood high in the sky, and the streets below him bustled with activity. People from unwalled villages and towns flocked to take refuge behind the massive walls of Jerusalem as news of the approaching enemy spread. An atmosphere of great tension permeated the city as it prepared for the siege.

A hot, dry breeze blew up from the Judean wilderness and rustled through the branches of the tree outside Ahaz's window. He stared at the quivering leaves, and it seemed to him that the whole city trembled as the leaves did. Fear, like a starving animal, gnawed at his insides, slowly consuming him.

He stepped away from the window, afraid to watch the bustle of activity, feeling impotent and helpless, his mouth dry and bitter. He reached for a drink and remembered the warning about his water resources. Down by the Gihon spring, a long line was probably forming as slaves and servant girls, balancing clay jars on their heads, made their way through the water gate and down the steep ramp.

Water. As crucial to his nation's defense as swords and spears once the broiling summer sun and dry desert wind sucked every drop of moisture from the land. He was keenly aware that Jerusalem had no source of fresh water within its protective walls; the Gihon spring and aqueduct lay outside them. But a solution to the problem lay beyond his limited imagination.

Ahaz abruptly decided not to remain idle, hiding in his rooms as his nation prepared for the siege. Instead, he would take an inventory of his water supplies. He needed to make a public appearance, to be visible to the people of Jerusalem, to convince them that he was confident and unafraid. That was a great king's duty in a time of crisis. And maybe he could convince himself as well. He rang for his valet.

The servant entered with head bowed low and prostrated himself like a dog about to be beaten. At first Ahaz could not imagine what had provoked such a reaction. Then he recalled his son's outrageous behavior in the council room.

"Forgive me, my lord," the valet muttered with his forehead pressed to the floor. "I don't know how the boy managed to slip past me."

"You should have been at your post. It could have been an assassin instead of my son. Even now my enemies are plotting to kill me."

"I swear to all the gods that it will never happen again, my lord. Please, have mercy."

"I should have you beaten, or maybe I should beat you myself, but there's no time for it. Get up. We've got a siege to prepare for."

"Oh, thank you, my lord. Thank you." The valet scrambled to his feet, bowing repeatedly.

"What did you do with him?"

"With your son, my lord?"

"Yes—my son! Who else are we talking about?"

"My son"—the words sounded peculiar to Ahaz, as if he had said them for the first time, and he remembered Abijah accusing him of murdering his son. It was true: he had ordered the sacrifice. But his sons did not seem like real people to him, merely nameless, faceless infants, possessions under his sovereign control—until tonight, that is. Twice tonight he had seen his son face-to-face and looked into his accusing eyes.

"I took him to his room, Your Majesty."

"Bring him here."

"But—but, he's only a child, my lord. He didn't mean any harm."

"I said bring him here."

A few minutes later the boy entered, holding the valet's hand. He bowed properly in respect, and Ahaz felt pleased. His son had been well trained.

"You are Eliab?" Ahaz guessed.

The child started, then shook his head. "I'm Hezekiah."

Suddenly Ahaz remembered. Eliab had been his firstborn. He blinked nervously, and his gaze darted around the room before coming to rest on his son again, but the boy's gaze never wavered. Ahaz tried to determine what emotion he read in his son's eyes. Fear? Yes, certainly fear—but something else as well.

"So. I find you everywhere, it seems—sleeping in my wife's chambers, inviting yourself to my council meetings. Maybe you would like to be the king?" The boy did not answer. "You are the crown prince, heir to the throne. Do you know what that means?"

Hezekiah stood like a statue, unblinking, staring at Ahaz with large, dark eyes—accusing eyes—Abijah's eyes. Then Ahaz's jaw dropped in astonishment as he suddenly deciphered the look in Hezekiah's eyes. It was hatred.

"How dare you!" He nearly slapped the child but restrained himself. "Someday you'll be in my place! Someday you'll see what it's like to be responsible, to have to face one crisis after another! You'll be the one who has to make decisions, regardless of the cost! Do you think it's so easy? Well, do you?"

Hezekiah didn't answer. But neither did he flinch or begin to cry. He remained in control of himself, and Ahaz suddenly felt foolish for losing his temper. His son had courage, Ahaz had to admit.

"Why am I wasting my breath on a child?" he muttered, shaking his head. "Look—you enjoy following me around? Then get dressed. You can accompany me on my inspection tour." He motioned to his valet. "Get him dressed. He's coming with me."

An hour later, with his son by his side, Ahaz walked south from the palace with his entourage, down the long main street of Jerusalem, inspecting the levels of rainwater in the city cisterns. The fact that they were barely half full distressed him. Swarms of curious citizens joined in the procession—skipping children, giggling servant girls, worried peasants fleeing the surrounding villages, city elders hoping to be noticed and acknowledged by the king.

At first Ahaz tried to appear dignified and older than his years, but soon the sight of so many people looking to him for strength and trusting him for deliverance began to heighten his anxiety. He felt the weight of his responsibility like an enormous burden, as if he were required to carry everyone on his shoulders. The load exhausted him—and the siege hadn't even begun yet.

When he finished examining the cisterns, he led the procession out of the city through the southeast gate to the Shiloah pool, a man-made reservoir built to hold the overflow from the Gihon spring and supply the southern sector of the city with water. From there he followed the aqueduct up the Kidron Valley, coming at last to the spring. But once he reached it, Ahaz found that, in spite of his grand procession, there was little for him to do except stand and stare into the water.

The city's protecting walls on the cliff above his head receded in the distance like a fading mirage; the gap between the walls and the spring seemed infinite. He could see no way to defend the spring against the enemy and wondered how long Jerusalem could survive without fresh water. Long enough for the Assyrians to come to his defense?—if they came at all. Ahaz's plans seemed useless to him now, like a dream that makes sense during the night but turns absurd in the light of day.

The waters of Gihon were black and cold and deep, as if no bottom existed. Ahaz stared at the spring, not really seeing it. He saw, instead, the defeat of his city and his own certain death and knew this inspection tour had been a mistake. He felt worse than before. What's more, he no longer had his brother by his side, but his son, a child barely weaned. With Maaseiah dead, Ahaz had no one to turn to with his doubts and fears. He could only hold his feelings inside, turning them around and around in his mind until they sucked his soul down like a whirlpool into the cold, dark, bottomless depths of depression. He stood immobilized. The chattering children and maidens grew still. The procession waited in awkward silence.

Dimly, he heard the rustle of robes and footsteps approaching on the path, and the crowd parted. Ahaz looked up apprehensively, as if expecting enemy soldiers, and recognized the slender, aristocratic man walking toward him, holding a small boy by the hand. His regal bearing and reddish beard confirmed his kinship to the royal line of King David. Father and son bowed in respect, then stood side by side before the king and his son. The two boys, nearly the same age, gazed at each other curiously.

"What do *you* want, Isaiah?" Ahaz spat the words contemptuously.

"This is my firstborn son, Shear-Jashub," Isaiah answered quietly. His eyes, as clear and deep as the Gihon spring, bored into Ahaz's, and he knew it was an accusation. The king's firstborn son was dead. The strange name Shear-Jashub meant "a remnant will return," just as a mere remnant of Ahaz's army would return.

"You think you're so clever, don't you?" Ahaz sneered.

"I have a word of advice for you, King Ahaz."

"Advice? I'll bet you're after a position in my court now that I've lost my three top men!"

Isaiah shook his head. "No. I have renounced my kinship to the house of David because of—"

"You were *thrown* out of the palace!" Ahaz interrupted. "And for good reason too. My father didn't want to listen to your radical, fundamentalist opinions, and neither do I."

Isaiah stepped toward Ahaz. "How can I remain silent

while my nation rushes toward disaster? Unless Judah reforms—"

"Reforms? If we listened to you, we'd end up living in tents like Abraham." Ahaz tried to laugh, but it came out forced and unnatural.

Isaiah held his head high, meeting Ahaz's gaze without flinching. "Unless this nation repents . . . ," he began quietly.

"We don't need a doomsayer, Isaiah. The people are already worried. You can't get an audience in my court, so you force your views on the common people and call it prophecy. Well, I don't want to listen to you, and neither do they."

"I have a word for *you*, King Ahaz—from Yahweh." The prophet's tone changed, and there was something in his manner, an unmistakable authority in his voice, that made Ahaz keep silent. "Be careful, keep calm and don't be afraid. Do not lose heart because of these two smoldering stubs of firewood—because of the fierce anger of Rezin and Aram and of the son of Remaliah."

"What are you talking about?" Ahaz exploded. "These 'stubs of firewood' are rapidly approaching Jerusalem with all their armies!"

"Yes, these two kings are coming against you. They say, 'We will invade Judah and throw her people into panic. Then we'll fight our way into Jerusalem and install the son of Tabeel as king.' But the Lord God says, 'This plan will not succeed. King Rezin's kingdom will not increase its boundaries. King Pekah's power will not increase.' You, King Ahaz, must stand firm in your faith in the Lord God as your head, or you will not stand at all."

"I don't know where you get your bizarre ideas, and I don't care. But I've already made plans to deal with this crisis, and I'm not changing them now."

Isaiah's piercing eyes narrowed. "You don't believe that the Lord can deliver you from the enemy, do you?

You'd rather ask the king of Assyria for help than put your trust in Yahweh."

Ahaz glared at Isaiah, wondering how he had learned of the planned alliance so quickly. "The gods belong in the temples, not in the streets—and certainly not in government."

Isaiah took another step forward. "Ask Yahweh for a sign, then," he challenged. "Let Him prove that He will indeed crush your enemies as He has said. Ask anything you like, in heaven or on earth."

"No," the king answered sullenly, staring once again into the bottomless pool. "I will not ask. I will not put Yahweh to the test." Isaiah's confidence had shaken him. If Isaiah were somehow to produce a miracle in front of all these people, Ahaz would be obligated to abandon his plans and trust in the sign.

"Hear now, you house of David!" Isaiah cried angrily. His quiet voice grew and surged, like water rushing down a dry riverbed, until it seemed to thunder and roar. "You're not satisfied to exhaust my patience; you exhaust the Lord's as well! Very well then—Yahweh himself will choose the sign: a child shall be born to a virgin and shall be called Immanuel—"

"That's ridiculous," Ahaz stormed. "How can a virgin have a child?"

Isaiah ignored the interruption. "The land of the two kings you dread so much will be laid waste," he continued. "But Yahweh will bring a terrible curse on you and on your nation and on your family. There will be terror, such as has not been known since the division of Solomon's empire into Israel and Judah. The mighty King of Assyria will come with his great army! Yahweh will take this 'razor'— these Assyrians you have hired to save you—and use it to shave off everything you have: your head and the hair of your legs, and your beard also."

Ahaz did not want to hear any more. He turned abruptly and strode toward the steep ramp that led back to the city, anxious to escape Isaiah's words. They were too horrible to consider. What if this prophet were right? What if Assyria chose to invade him instead of rescue him? He glanced over his shoulder, expecting Isaiah to pursue him, but saw only Hezekiah following behind, gazing up at him with accusing eyes. Isaiah had blended into the crowd and disappeared.

"Curse you, Isaiah!" he fumed. Again he felt alone, abandoned, defeated. "May all the gods curse you!"

With sagging shoulders and bowed head, Ahaz wearily dragged his procession back to the palace, staring sightlessly at the ground, avoiding the gawking crowds who clamored for a glimpse of their king. He sent Hezekiah away with a servant and returned to his own bedchamber, deeply depressed.

Outside his window the frantic preparations for the siege continued, but Ahaz no longer sought comfort in activity. The hole inside where fear gnawed at him felt even larger.

"I don't want to be king anymore!" he wanted to scream. "Let someone else be the king!" But his brother Maaseiah was dead, and he was alone. There was no one else. Ahaz lay down on his bed, buried his face in his hands, and wept.

—◈—

Uriah sat in the Temple council chamber, ignoring the priests and Levites who argued bitterly, and carefully planned his strategy. His head pounded from tension and exhaustion as the meeting dragged on interminably. The overcrowded room, a small version of the king's council chamber, felt damp and stuffy, the atmosphere charged with emotion.

The retired high priest, Azariah, Uriah's uncle, presided over the meeting from his place on the raised dais as the others sat in a semicircle around him. The meeting had begun with the announcement of Ahaz's decision to raise tribute for Assyria, then had quickly reached a stalemate as the priests argued over which section of the holy place should be dismantled for its gold.

Uriah closed his eyes and squeezed his throbbing temples with his fingertips. "This is what I hate," he mumbled to the priest seated beside him. "We need change if this institution is going to survive—yet these fools can't even reach a simple consensus. No wonder we're stagnating."

"Do you suppose they'll finish in time for the evening sacrifice?" the priest yawned.

"Who knows?" Uriah grumbled. "I don't know how the Temple managed to survive this long, but I can see how it will all end."

He opened his eyes and tried to concentrate on the discussion. He had not mentioned his promotion, much less Ahaz's decision to offer another sacrifice to Molech, knowing he would have to handle these subjects with great care. Let them exhaust their energy arguing over the Assyrian tribute first, he decided.

After what seemed like hours, the priests finally reached an agreement. The Temple, like a proud noblewoman taken captive, would be stripped of her finery to pay for the tribute. Azariah divided the work among the priests and was about to dismiss the gathering when Uriah rose from his place.

"Just a moment, gentlemen. There is another matter we need to discuss." The men groaned with fatigue, but Uriah took his time, choosing every word, every gesture with extreme care. He must win their support. There was no other option.

"At the emergency council meeting this morning King Ahaz asked me to replace Prince Maaseiah as palace administrator." His words were met with stunned silence. He paused a few beats and then added, "I have decided to accept the position."

He had expected applause or at least words of congratulations, but the room grew as still as a tomb. He decided to lay everything before them at once, while they were still in shock, and get it over with quickly.

"One of my first duties as palace administrator is to organize a public sacrifice before the siege begins."

"Here, at the Temple?" Azariah asked.

"No. Ahaz plans to offer another sacrifice to Molech."

"Have you lost your mind?" the Levite Conaniah cried, leaping to his feet as if he might strike Uriah. "How can you possibly sacrifice to idols? You're the high priest of Yahweh!"

"He's right," Azariah added sternly. "I don't see how you can possibly serve as palace administrator to a king who worships idols. It's out of the question. You've gone too far, Uriah."

Their protests opened the floodgate, and everyone began talking and shouting at once. Uriah's head felt as if it would burst.

"Let me finish!" he finally shouted above the chaos. "At least listen to me before you condemn me!"

Azariah began calling for silence and eventually restored the meeting to order. When everyone was seated, Uriah began to slowly circle the men, his voice calm and authoritative. As he spoke, he fixed his intimidating gaze in turn on each priest and Levite—in silent warning not to defy him. He was a natural leader; he knew they respected him and would probably follow his lead if his words were persuasive enough—and if he could silence his opponents.

"We serve a dead institution," he began. "Look around you. Even the building is crumbling down on us, and we don't have the resources to repair it. It's time we faced the truth: the men of Jerusalem are no longer willing to support this Temple or its priesthood with their tithes. Like the king, they go elsewhere for spiritual help, to the idols and shrines in the groves. Meanwhile, we barely take in enough offerings to keep our families alive. It's time to make some changes and—"

Azariah leaped to his feet, cutting off Uriah's words. "How can you talk about change? Yahweh *never* changes. The Law and the sacrifices, even the pattern for the Temple itself, were all ordained by God. You don't have the authority to change what the Almighty One has command-ed!"

"I have not finished speaking!" Uriah forced himself to take authority over his elderly uncle. "You'll have a chance to speak when I'm through!" Grudgingly, Azariah sat down again, but his face was ashen, his lips taut with anger. The tension in the room grew as Uriah continued.

"Our Temple worship has to change with the times, or it will eventually die altogether. It has stagnated because we are so bound up in tradition that we no longer listen to the people. I'm not talking about changing Yahweh's laws; I'm talking about examining our traditions. If the men of Judah are drawn to the popular religions of the nations around us, then we need to ask ourselves why. It's time to adapt our outmoded traditions to the changing times and become more flexible, instead of blindly clinging to the old ways. They're obsolete—"

Azariah could no longer restrain his anger. "Blasphemy!" he shouted. "You're speaking blasphemy!" The room erupted into noisy confusion.

Uriah watched helplessly, his fists clenched, ready to fight, and wondered how he would ever restore order again. After several frustrating minutes he began to shout, "Quiet, all of you! Shut up and listen to me! Are you going to think for yourselves or listen to a few closed-minded extremists?"

Eventually, most of the men quieted. Uriah ignored the few scattered objections and continued, his voice hoarse from the strain. "It is very important that we have the support of the king if this Temple is going to survive.

The people follow his leadership in spiritual matters—you know that. Some of you can remember how it was when Uzziah was king. This Temple was the focal point of the nation because of Uzziah." He turned to Zechariah. "Tell them how you won Uzziah's confidence and were able to influence the entire nation."

Zechariah made a shaky attempt to stand and speak, but Uriah quickly realized from the old man's glazed eyes and swaying legs that he was drunk. He turned away in disgust and hastily resumed his speech. "My esteemed colleague Zechariah has already assured me of his full support." The old man nodded vacantly and sank back into his place again.

"King Ahaz is very young and has no understanding of Yahweh's law. It is up to us to teach him and draw him back to the worship of Yahweh. Then we will draw the people back as well. King Ahaz trusts me. He has made me second in command of the nation. I'm merely using this sacrifice as a first step to draw the nation back to this Temple."

"By worshiping idols?" Conaniah shouted. "You want to revive the worship of Yahweh by sacrificing to idols? That's insane! The only way to revive Temple worship is through repentance. The men of Judah must give up their idolatry and turn their hearts back to God!"

Uriah swiftly crossed the room and stood before Conaniah, towering over him with such fury that it seemed they might exchange blows.

"This Temple has been trying to operate under your narrow-minded, outdated views long enough. Repentance!" Uriah spat. "Where has *that* gotten us? We've lost an entire generation of worshipers. The whole purpose of this Temple is to serve the spiritual needs of the people. Obviously our traditions aren't meeting those needs, or the people would come back. First we draw them back to worship. Later we can wean them from their idolatry.

"No! You're wrong!" Azariah cried, coming to Conani-ah's defense. "The purpose of this Temple is to serve Yah-weh, not the people. We sin against Him if we lead the people into idolatry."

"We're not leading them into idolatry! They're already worshiping idols!" Uriah shot back. "We can sit here and starve to death from lack of offerings, or we can adapt to the changing times and reclaim some of our former power and strength in this nation. Now is our chance! I have the king's trust and support. If I don't take a leading role in this sacrifice, then Molech's priests will. Look, I am simply making all the arrangements. Molech's priests will per-form the ritual. But the·people must be convinced that our priesthood is supreme over all the others."

"No!" Azariah answered. "We are priests of the one true God. We can't give our consent to idolatry."

"Our consent is not an issue! Ahaz is stripping the last of the Temple wealth—don't you understand that? There's nothing left! Are you going to sit here clinging to the past while the building crumbles down around you?" He slammed his powerful fist against the wall with such force that bits of plaster and dust fell from the ceiling as if to prove his words. The room was silent for a moment.

"It's getting very late, gentlemen," Uriah said at last, his voice calm and controlled. "We've debated long enough. We have to carry out the king's orders today. The tribute must be sent to Assyria before the siege begins. The sacrifice must be held immediately. We cannot waste any more time arguing. It's time to vote."

He ignored the scattered murmurs of dissent and scooped up the container of pebbles used for voting. As he passed it around, each man took one black and one white stone.

"If you wish to support me as high priest and revive our Temple worship again, put in the white stone," he or-dered. "If you wish to tie my hands with your antiquated

69

traditions and wait for the Temple to fall down around us, put in the black stone."

"Don't listen to him!" Azariah pleaded. "He's giving us no choice!"

Uriah turned on him. "That's because there *is* no choice—don't you understand that? We are the dying custodians of a dying institution! We need change! Now, vote."

"No!" Azariah hurled his stones at Uriah's feet. "I will not vote! I will not be a part of this blasphemy . . . this abomination!" He spat on Uriah and strode from the room. Conaniah and a few others followed.

Uriah held his breath, waiting to see who else would leave, but no one moved. He still had enough men for their decision to be legally binding. He quickly passed the box for the vote, listening to the dull thud of the stones as they hit the bottom. When it came around to him, he tossed in his white stone, then turned the box over and dumped its contents in the middle of the circle.

"Count them," he ordered.

He could tell by the mixture of black and white that the vote would be close. Two scribes rose and began separating and counting the stones as Uriah watched tensely. If they voted against him, he would have to resign as high priest. His authority over the priests and Levites and his power to make changes in the Temple would come to an end. But if he won, today would be a new beginning.

"Twenty-three black," the first scribe announced.

"And twenty-eight white," the second one added. "The vote has gone in your favor, Uriah."

They passed the container to collect the unused stones, and the men silently filed out, their faces filled with exhaustion from the emotional strain of the meeting. When he was alone, Uriah sank into his uncle's seat on the dais, staring at the stones still piled in the center of the room.

He had won. He had done it. He had a new position

of power with the young king, and now the priests and Levites had supported his leadership as well. His whole life had shifted in the past few hours and had finally come into focus. He knew he should be elated, but instead his victory left him with a hollow feeling inside that he was afraid to examine too closely.

He would wait until the sacrifice to Molech was over, he told himself. Maybe then he would feel differently. Maybe then he could silence the quiet voice that haunted him.

His mother's screams jolted him awake. Hezekiah opened his eyes and the nightmare returned. Like the rumble of an approaching storm, soldiers poured down the hallway toward his room. They were coming again—for him.

The last time they had come Hezekiah had not known the horror that awaited Eliab, but this time he knew. He needed to run, he needed to hide, but there was no place to hide. His mother's screams grew louder, closer.

Maybe this was just a dream. Maybe he would wake up. But when he saw his brother's empty bed next to his, he remembered the stench and the roar of the flames, and he knew it was not a dream.

The soldiers flung his door open and pulled him from his bed. Strong hands tried to force the tunic over his head. Hezekiah remembered Molech's gaping mouth and his brother falling and falling, headlong, into the inferno. He remembered and fought against the soldiers with all his strength, but they picked him up effortlessly, almost amused at his futile struggle, and carried him away.

The hallway outside his room was shadowy and dim, but he saw dozens of soldiers in the flickering torchlight, and his mother on her knees, clinging to the high priest's feet as she pleaded with him.

"Oh, my lord, please! Please don't take him too!" Her eyes were wild, frantic, her face chalky with fear.

Hezekiah struggled to go to her, but one of the soldiers held him tightly. "Mama!" he cried. "Mama, help me!"

"Please, Uriah, please!" she begged. "They've already killed my Eliab. Isn't that enough? Please don't kill Hezekiah too! I beg you! For my sake, for my father's sake! Have mercy on him!"

"Take her out of here," Uriah said quietly.

"No—no!" she screamed pitifully as a knot of soldiers surrounded her and pried her hands from Uriah's feet. Hezekiah huddled closely to his younger brother Gedaliah, and they cried in vain for their mother. Her agonized screams faded in the distance.

"Which one is the firstborn?" Molech's priest asked.

Hezekiah and his half-brother Amariah were nearly the same height and only a few months apart in age. But Hezekiah knew that he was older than Amariah. As the eldest son of King Ahaz, he was next in line on the royal throne of King David. He was also next in line for the fire.

"This one."

Hezekiah felt Uriah's huge hand rest briefly on his head. He was going to die like Eliab had died. He gazed up at Uriah, and the burly high priest seemed like a giant to him. Their eyes met, and Hezekiah, too terrified to speak, pleaded wordlessly for his life. Uriah turned away.

"Let's get it over with," the giant man said. His voice was barely a whisper.

Hezekiah couldn't walk. When one of the soldiers picked him up he fought desperately to break free, but the more he struggled the tighter the soldier's hands gripped him. He was carried through the halls and down the darkened stairways, kicking, flailing, clawing at the arms that encircled him, screaming in terror. By the time they reached the procession waiting in the courtyard, Hezekiah felt bruised and exhausted, too numb to struggle anymore.

The early-morning sun hurt his eyes after he emerged

from the dimly lit palace corridors, but as his eyes adjusted he could see that everything was nearly the same as the last time: the huge, gawking crowd of people; the richly attired priests and nobles; the white-robed children, chosen to appease the monster's burning rage. And leading them all—his father, King Ahaz. Only the endless rows of soldiers were missing.

The procession started down the hill through the city streets to the Valley of Hinnom again as they walked to the throbbing beat of the priests' drums. Each pounding stroke felt like a fist pounding deeply in Hezekiah's stomach. After a while the soldier carrying Hezekiah set him down and ordered him to walk, but Hezekiah's legs trembled so violently with fear that he had to be supported on either side by soldiers. They pushed and dragged him through the streets, and he stumbled along until they finally reached the southern gate.

In the distance a thin column of smoke snaked ominously into the sky. Hezekiah froze. Ahead of him the jagged cliffs marked the entrance to the valley of death. He couldn't move. But the soldiers jerked him roughly by the arms and propelled him forward again as his feet dragged against his will.

As if sensing their approaching fate, some of the children started to wail, while the priests began their chant to drown out the pitiful cries: "Molech . . . Molech . . . Molech . . ." The throbbing cadence, echoing off the cliffs and the city walls, seemed to swell as the procession inched closer to the site of the sacrifice. They were almost to the monster—and there was no escape.

Suddenly Isaiah pushed his way through the crowd, stepping in front of Ahaz to block his path. The prophet's eyes flashed with anger, and his whole body shook with rage until he seemed about to burst apart. He shouted above the pounding drums in a voice that penetrated to the soul.

"Hear, O heavens! Listen, O earth! For the Lord has spoken: 'I reared children and brought them up, but they have rebelled against me. The ox knows his master, the donkey his owner's manger, but Israel does not know, my people do not understand.'"

"Get out of my way!" King Ahaz growled, shoving Isaiah aside. He continued walking, his eyes fixed on the fire god ahead of him. But Isaiah kept his pace, walking backward to face Ahaz, shouting to be heard above the din.

"Ah, sinful nation, a people loaded with guilt, a brood of evildoers, children given to corruption!" He spread his arms wide to implicate the entire crowd. "They have forsaken the Lord; they have spurned the Holy One of Israel and turned their backs on him."

Again, Isaiah tried to stand in Ahaz's path, but the king, his face red with rage, shoved him aside—harder than before. Isaiah stumbled and nearly fell.

"Oh, my people, haven't you had enough of punishment?" Isaiah cried, fighting to regain his balance and keep up with Ahaz. "Will you force me to whip you again and again? Must you forever rebel? . . . Your country lies in ruins; your cities are burned; while you watch, foreigners are destroying and plundering everything they see, [while] you stand there helpless and abandoned . . ."

By now Uriah had elbowed his way to the head of the procession to stand beside Ahaz. He towered over Isaiah, but the prophet showed no fear as he met the high priest's gaze.

"Your hands are full of blood," Isaiah accused. "Wash and make yourselves clean. Take your evil deeds out of my sight! Stop doing wrong, learn to do right!"

"Get out of the way, Isaiah, or I'll have you arrested!" the king threatened. Then he turned and joined the priests of Molech as the procession moved, step by step, toward its destination.

Isaiah made no more attempts to follow the king but

stood by the edge of the road pleading desperately with the people as they filed slowly past him.

"'Come now, let us reason together,' says the Lord. 'Though your sins are like scarlet, they shall be as white as snow; though they are red as crimson, they shall be like wool. If you are willing and obedient, you will eat the best from the land; but if you resist and rebel, you will be devoured by the sword.' For the mouth of the Lord has spoken."

Isaiah's efforts seemed futile. The chanting crowd filed blindly past him, following the king's example, ignoring Isaiah's words and turning their faces away from him as if from a leper.

Finally, the fire that radiated from Isaiah and ignited his words seemed extinguished. His shoulders sagged, and he stood beside the road with tears in his eyes, watching the crowd stream past, oblivious to him.

As Hezekiah observed, he felt a glimmer of hope for the first time since he was awakened that morning. But when he saw his father shove Isaiah aside, the last door of escape seemed to slam shut in Hezekiah's face. All hope was gone. Now he would die.

As the soldiers dragged Hezekiah past the place where Isaiah stood, the fire suddenly returned to the prophet's small frame. Isaiah looked up, staring straight into Hezekiah's eyes, and his gaze seemed to penetrate deep inside him, stripping him naked.

"Don't be afraid," Isaiah told him, "for Yahweh has ransomed you. He has called you by name. You belong to Yahweh. When you go through deep water, Yahweh will go with you. And when you ford mighty rivers, they won't overwhelm you. When you pass through the fire, you won't be burned. The flames will not hurt you. For Yahweh is your God. The Holy One of Israel is your Savior."

The soldiers tightened their grip on Hezekiah's arms, propelling him forward once again. He turned his head, trying to keep Isaiah in sight, waiting for Isaiah to snatch him from the soldiers' grasp and rescue him, but the prophet vanished from view.

Over and over Isaiah's words throbbed in Hezekiah's ears to the pounding beat of the drums. "When you pass through the fire, you won't be burned . . . for Yahweh is your God . . ." Over and over he repeated them to himself, as if they possessed the power to protect him from what lay ahead.

The mob formed a circle around the smoking monster, as close as the billowing heat allowed. In front of Hezekiah, the priests and their attendants, carrying the children, mounted the steps of the platform. Beyond sat the mighty fire god Molech, his brazen image glowing, his mouth open, waiting. When Hezekiah saw the roaring monster, his legs buckled and he collapsed, paralyzed with fear. One of Molech's priests scooped him up. Hezekiah tried to struggle, tried to fight, but the priest pinned his arms to his sides and carried him up the steep steps of the platform. Once again he faced Molech.

The high priest of Molech began to chant the ritual of sacrifice, but Hezekiah heard none of it. He was aware of only the intense heat on his face and the outstretched arms reaching for him. Isaiah's words still echoed over and over in his mind to the rhythm of the drums and the pounding of his heart: "When you pass through the fire . . . Yahweh is your God . . ." The priest holding him tightened his grip, as if sensing that Hezekiah's instincts screamed for him to flee.

Now the chanting crowd reached a frenzied, deafening pitch. The moment of sacrifice was near. Hezekiah could no longer hear his own screams above the noise of the crowd, the beating of the drums, and the roar of the flames. The words of Isaiah that he had repeated over and over to himself began to blur, and in his terror he remembered only one word: Yahweh.

The monster's huge brass eyes stared down at him,

the tongues of flame darted hungrily from its gaping mouth. Molech's priest finished his prayer. He turned and started walking toward Hezekiah.

"YAHWEH! YAHWEH!" Hezekiah screamed the words in terror, over and over again.

The priest reached out for the king's firstborn son. He reached past Hezekiah and grabbed Amariah. Hezekiah saw the wrong son being hurled into the fire god's arms. He heard his half-brother's screams of agony as he rolled toward the open mouth. He watched Amariah die in the flames instead of himself.

As the roaring crowd continued its cry for more, Hezekiah stood dazed. Another child was thrown into the flames, and another and another until the nauseating stench filled the air, stinging his eyes, burning his throat, gagging him.

Then it was over.

The words of Isaiah resounded in Hezekiah's mind once again: "When you pass through the fire, you won't be burned . . . for Yahweh is your God."

Then Hezekiah fainted in a heap on the platform.

—◈—

The throbbing cadence of drums faded and died with the last of Molech's victims, and the crowds returned to their homes in somber silence to finish preparing for the siege. As Uriah walked beside King Ahaz through the city gates and up the hill to the palace, he wondered how the king felt about what he had just done.

Uriah had been a priest all his life. He had sacrificed thousands of animals and was no stranger to bloodshed. But none of his sacrificial victims had ever looked at him the way Ahaz's son had. No dumb beast had ever shown such terror.

Uriah had thought it would be only an empty ritual—another sacrifice like all the many others he had presided over. But he had never witnessed human sacrifice before, and he was not prepared for the overwhelming revulsion he now felt.

For a brief moment, when Isaiah had blocked the king's path, Uriah had found himself praying that Ahaz would listen to him, that he would stop the horrible carnage before it began. But the king had ignored the prophet's words and carried Uriah's careful plans to their horrible conclusion.

It was still early morning, but Uriah stumbled wearily through the city streets and up the hill as if he had worked a full day of heavy labor. He reached the palace numb and exhausted. As he accompanied Ahaz down the corridors to his chambers, he heard anguished cries of grief and mourning through the open windows of the king's harem and shuddered. What had he done? How could he ever face Abijah again? She would never forgive him.

"She'll get over it," Ahaz grumbled, as if reading Uriah's mind. "As soon as the next one is born, she'll forget."

Uriah fought the urge to punch him. Ahaz talked about Abijah as if she were a cow that quickly forgets her weaned calf. But Uriah remembered how desperately Zechariah's daughter had pleaded for her child's life, and he knew she would never forget. Nor, he guessed, would Zechariah. Suddenly his teacher's pathetic condition made sense; these victims were his grandchildren.

When they reached the king's private chambers, Uriah waited for Ahaz's orders, struggling to keep his stony features unreadable, his seething emotions hidden from view.

"Well, it's over," Ahaz sighed. "I think everything went well, don't you? And I was glad to see that some of the city elders have finally realized how serious our situation is and have offered up their sons too." Uriah mumbled a vague reply.

"I believe Molech will hear us this time," Ahaz continued, as if trying to convince himself. "He's a very powerful god, you know. He asked for a great sacrifice, and so his power must surely be very great."

Uriah did not answer. His anger at the king's superstitious ignorance came close to the flash point. He had little patience with the stupidity of idolatry and was eager to begin the monumental task of teaching Yahweh's laws to Ahaz, beginning with the first commandment. But not today. Today Uriah was too physically and emotionally drained to do anything.

"I guess there's nothing we can do now except wait for the invasion," Ahaz said, and his voice trembled. His confidence in Molech abruptly vanished, and his fear became transparent. "How long do we have, Uriah? How long before the siege begins?"

"A day perhaps. Certainly no more than two days." Uriah tried to sound calm, to instill a measure of confidence in the panicky king.

"Are we prepared? Can we withstand it?" His face wore the pathetic look of a beggar pleading for alms. Uriah fought back his revulsion as he recognized the king for what he was: a coward. Only a coward would send his children to their deaths in order to save his own life. He drew a deep breath.

"Yes, Your Majesty," he answered stonily. "Defensively, our city is well situated. The enemy will grow tired of the siege long before we will."

But Ahaz was not convinced. He paced the length of his room, wringing his hands anxiously. Uriah longed to escape from him, to run as far from the palace as he could and never return. He knew, however, that he would have to support Ahaz and be his strength through this crisis, and he wondered where he would find the energy. He was already exhausted.

"Your Majesty, if I may be excused, there are many things I need to do."

"Yes, I suppose so," Ahaz replied absently. Uriah hurried away before the king changed his mind. He left the palace through the royal portico and headed up the hill to his quarters in the Temple. He knew he should supervise the preparations for the siege, but he felt numb and sick, as if he had swallowed a heavy stone.

When he reached the Temple courtyards, everything seemed quiet and still, the air clean and pure. The outer courtyard felt open and spacious, the view of the surrounding mountains unhindered by jagged cliffs. The scene was a stark contrast to the narrow, confining valley where Molech sat enthroned, the silence welcome after the frenzied clamor of Molech's ritual, the air sweet after the stench of burning flesh.

Uriah paused at the gate to the inner courtyard to steady himself and gazed at Yahweh's sanctuary. It was as familiar to him as his own face. Yet today, for some reason, it seemed alien and remote, like a scene from a dream. A faint breeze rippled the water in the huge brazen laver where the priests washed, the water gleaming like molten silver in the sunlight.

Wash and make yourselves clean. The memory of Isaiah's words rippled through his mind. *Your hands are full of blood.* Uriah gazed down at his hands. When he ministered in Yahweh's Temple, they would run red with the sticky blood of his victims. Today they felt filthy, though they remained unstained.

He looked up at the huge brazen altar dominating the center of the courtyard, its fires slowly burning, consuming the lamb from the morning sacrifice. But as Uriah stared at it, the lamb seemed to take the form of a child in the shimmering heat. He shuddered and shook his head to clear away the image, then turned abruptly to leave, nearly colliding with Zechariah, who staggered blindly into the courtyard. The old man lost his balance, and as Uriah grabbed him by the shoulders to steady him, he smelled wine on his breath.

"I have to stop him . . . ," Zechariah mumbled. He appeared agitated, his bloodshot eyes wild with fright.

"Stop who?" Uriah shook him, his voice sharp. He feared that Zechariah meant him, that he was coming, too late, to stop him from killing his grandchild.

"King Uzziah . . . I must stop Uzziah . . ."

"Uzziah's dead," Uriah said, shoving him in disgust. "And you're nothing but a pathetic drunk." Uriah's anger and self-loathing boiled over as he lashed out at Zechariah. "I admired you so much. I wanted to be like you. You had the most brilliant legal mind the priesthood had seen in generations, and now you're talking to a king who's been dead for years. You're a disgrace to the tribe of Levi. How could you turn your back on everything you believed in?"

Zechariah did not answer. He stared into the distance, watching the birds fluttering and chirping around the roof of the Temple.

"I'm taking you back to your room," Uriah finally said. "Stay there until you're sober." He spun Zechariah around and led him back to his chambers, half dragging, half supporting him.

Pity, guilt, and grief raged inside Uriah, but he carefully hid them behind his anger, the only emotion he dared express without losing control, without breaking down.

"Look at this room!" he cried. "The whole building's falling apart! I'm tired of begging for the tithes that are rightfully mine, tired of going hungry year after year, tired of scraping and pleading. I swear to God I'll win back the power and recognition our priesthood deserves and restore this Temple to its former glory, no matter what it takes. I was counting on your help to do it, Zechariah, but if all you can do is drink, then stay out of my way."

He gave Zechariah a hard shove, and the old man stumbled, losing his balance, collapsing to his knees in a heap on the floor. Several minutes passed as he lay without moving. Finally Zechariah looked up. His eyes were no longer vacant but filled with despair, the weak man looking to the strong one for answers.

"Oh, Uriah—oh, please—," he moaned. "Can I ever find forgiveness for what I've done?"

In the silence of the room an icy chill passed through Uriah's veins as he remembered the sacrifice to Molech, as he remembered what *he* had done. Then the room grew colder and colder as Zechariah's agonized cries filled the air.

"O God, please! . . . let me die . . . let me die . . . let me die!"

Abijah wept when they brought her son to her and placed him in her arms. Somehow he had been miraculously spared, and she wondered if Uriah had intervened. Hezekiah's hair and clothing reeked of smoke, but she held his sooty face between her hands and, as if in a dream, kissed him over and over, washing away the grime with her tears. Hezekiah clung to her, and she saw in his eyes all the horrors he had witnessed.

"Yahweh," he whispered. "Yahweh . . ."

At first Abijah did not understand the name he repeated hoarsely again and again. Then she recognized it as the God her father worshiped: Yahweh.

"Hush, baby. You're safe, now. Everything's going to be all right."

But as she gazed at her trembling child, she wondered if he would ever be the same. The winsome, curious boy who brightened the palace corridors with his laughter slipped away like fine silk through her fingers. She clung to his body as if the force of her love could bring him back.

"Yahweh . . ."

Watching Eliab die had changed him into a terrified child who awoke screaming night after night, afraid to sleep again and risk the nightmare's return. But today's sacrifice had severed the last cords of her son's love and trust. And she didn't know how to bind them together again.

Part of Abijah wanted to retreat from reality as well. Her life had veered from its natural course of marriage and family to descend on a path that led to Sheol. She had married royalty, a descendant of King David, a man capable of killing his own children.

"They will never take you away from me," she cried, crushing Hezekiah to her. "Never." But she knew it was an empty vow that she was powerless to keep.

Maybe she should pray. Maybe she should call on Yahweh, the God Hezekiah asked for. But He was the God who had married her to Ahaz? Her father's devotion to Yahweh won her the honor of marriage to the royal family?

She had never asked anything of God before. She had learned early in life not to harbor wishes and desires of her own. Once, when she was a child, her father had brought home a little gray dove in a wooden cage. Its crippled foot had made it unsuitable as a sacrifice.

"I want one too," she had said when she saw her brothers playing with it. Abijah's mother had slapped her across the mouth, the only time she had ever been struck.

"You want nothing," her mother cried, "except what your father wants for you; what you want doesn't matter!"

Abijah had accepted that, had grown up knowing it would always be so.

"Do you want to marry Prince Ahaz?" her father's student Uriah had once asked her.

"I'm not allowed the luxury of choosing," she had replied. "Surely you know that."

"Because your father promised King Uzziah?"

"No, because I'm a woman. I will be given in marriage—given, like a present. Do presents have the luxury of choosing to whom they will be given?" There had been no bitterness in her voice. She had merely stated the truth.

"And you accept that, Abby?"

"Of course," she shrugged. She saw the tender concern on Uriah's face.

"Haven't you ever wanted something so badly that you were willing to fight for it?" Uriah asked.

She hadn't answered his question. She hadn't understood it then. But now she did. And something inside her, an inner strength she didn't know she had, told her to fight for Hezekiah. She must not let him slip away.

"Come back to me, sweetheart. Please, come back." She took his stiff little hands in hers and clapped them together. "Sing with me, baby—Reuben, Simeon, Levi . . ." It was the rhyming song he had loved to sing that named the 12 sons of Israel.

"Yahweh . . . ," Hezekiah sobbed.

Fight for him, the voice seemed to shout.

For the remainder of the day Abijah fought for her son, trying every means she could think of to draw him back to a world he no longer wanted to be part of, a world he feared and mistrusted. The hopelessness of her battle exhausted her. His body remained stiff with fear. His eyes stared sightlessly.

As the sun began to set, she carried him to the window, but he would not look out. It was nearly time for the evening sacrifice. Then darkness would fall, and the long, nightmare-filled night would begin for both of them. She rocked him gently and felt a sob shudder through him.

"Yahweh . . ."

Where had Hezekiah learned that name? she wondered. What part did the ancient God of her father play in this nightmare? She might never know.

"My lady, you've been holding him all day. You've eaten nothing." Compassion filled her maidservant's eyes. "Let me hold him a while. Perhaps I can get him to eat."

In the distance a shofar sounded, announcing the evening sacrifice, and Hezekiah jumped.

"Yahweh!"

Abijah, who had been told what to do all her life, who had never been forced to make a decision, decided in that moment what she must do for her child.

"Hezekiah, Mama has to leave you, but I'll come back in a little while. I promise. You'll be fine. Sarah will take you now."

She nearly changed her mind as he screamed for her to stay, but she covered her head with her shawl and hurried out of the palace, nearly running along the royal walkway to the Temple.

Few worshipers had gathered for the evening sacrifice—a dozen men, a handful of women—and she scanned the faces of the priests and Levites, looking for her father.

As the worshipers fell to their knees, Abijah clutched the wall that separated the women's court from the men's court, as if clutching the hem of Yahweh's garment, beseeching Him.

"You know I've asked nothing of You before, Lord," she wept. "And I ask nothing for myself now, but for my son. He cries for You, Lord . . . Help him . . . Bring him back. Show me what to do, God . . . Show me how to help him."

She didn't notice that the service had ended, nor did she notice the white-robed priest approach, and his voice startled her.

"Would you like to make an offering, my lady?"

Abijah hastily wiped her tears. "No—I—"

The priest crossed his arms and glanced around the courtyard impatiently, as if anxious to finish his duties.

"My—my father is Zechariah, the Levite," she stammered. "Do you know where he is? Could—could you take me to him?"

The priest frowned slightly, then nodded. "Come this way."

Abijah didn't know why she had asked for her father. She only knew that her son needed help, needed Yahweh. And Yahweh was her father's God. She would willingly give Hezekiah up, entrusting him to Yahweh's care, if only He would save him. She hurried to keep pace with the priest as he led her into the dark hallways of the Temple's side chambers, praying that Ahaz would never discover what she was doing.

—◆—

When Zechariah opened his eyes, he was alone, sprawled on the floor of his room. He had no memory of how he got there. What hour was it? What day? He could not recall. Then he saw the empty wineskin and remembered that Abijah's child, his grandson, was dead. How she must hate him! He remembered praying to die. But Yahweh had not answered his prayer.

He slowly pulled himself to his feet, leaning against his cot for support as the room tilted and swayed. Through the cracks of his shuttered window he saw the sun rapidly sinking in the western sky. He had slept in a drunken stupor all day.

Now he was sober again. The numbing effects of the wine had worn off, leaving him powerless to face his guilt and failure. He wanted more. He tore through his disheveled room in search of a drink, but the wineskins were all empty, and he was too shaky to go for more. Zechariah collapsed to his knees and covered his face in shame.

If he could go back and unravel all the mistakes he had made, he would gladly do it. But he could never go back. And now his grandson had paid for those mistakes with his life.

He punishes the children and their children for the sins of the fathers to the third and fourth generations. "No . . . ," he moaned. "No, please—no more, Yahweh! Have mercy on me, O God—have mercy on me!"

The sound of a trumpet blast announced the evening sacrifice, startling him as if the voice of God rang out in accusation. Moments later the haunting strains of the Levitical choir drifted into his room. Familiar words of Scripture collided and clashed in his tortured mind with memories of Molech's sacrifice; he mumbled the words aloud to drive away the painful images:

> *Out of the depths I cry to you, O Lord;*
> *O Lord, hear my voice.*
> *Let your ears be attentive*
> *to my cry for mercy.*
>
> *If you, O Lord, kept a record of sins,*
> *O Lord, who could stand?*
> *But with you there is forgiveness . . .*

Zechariah stopped. He had sung the words of this psalm all his life without hearing them. Could they be true? Would the Almighty One really stoop down to the sin-filled pit where he lay and forgive him?

Molech's image suddenly reared before him, and his fiery grimace seemed to mock the psalmist's words. Zechariah continued reciting to drive the image away: "I . . . I wait . . ."

> *I wait for the Lord, my soul waits,*
> *and in his word I put my hope.*
> *My soul waits for the Lord*
> *more than watchmen wait for the morning,*
> *more than watchmen wait for the morning.*

Forgiveness: could God's forgiveness end this bitter cycle of sin and punishment and death for Zechariah's children and his children's children? His soul wanted that, longed for that, more than watchmen wait for the morning.

A beam of dying sunlight penetrated the shuttered

window, a finger of light pointing accusingly at Zechariah. He shut his eyes, reciting, to escape it:

> *O Israel, put your hope in the Lord,*
> *for with the Lord is unfailing love*
> *and with him is full redemption.*
> *He himself will redeem Israel*
> *from all their sins.*

Full redemption: that was the bridge leading back across the bottomless chasm of sin, back to God. And God himself would provide that bridge. Zechariah fell on his face before God, pleading for forgiveness for what he had done.

> *Have mercy on me, O God,*
> *according to your unfailing love;*
> *according to your great compassion*
> *blot out my transgressions.*
> *Wash away all my iniquity*
> *and cleanse me from my sin.*
>
> *For I know my transgressions,*
> *and my sin is always before me.*
> *Against you, you only, have I sinned*
> *and done what is evil in your sight.*

He understood now. His life, dedicated and consecrated to God, had been lived only for himself. That was his greatest sin—wasting the life that belonged to God. Zechariah cried out, praying King David's prayer of repentance from the depths of his heart and soul.

> *Cleanse me with hyssop, and I*
> *will be clean;*
> *wash me, and I will be whiter than snow.*
> *Let me hear joy and gladness;*
> *let the bones you have crushed rejoice.*
> *Hide your face from my sins*
> *and blot out all my iniquity.*

"Then . . . then . . ." Zechariah stopped, stumbling

over the words. Outside, the sun had sunk below the western hills. The light was gone.

"Then . . . then . . ." What? What could he possibly promise God to atone for all of his sins?

> *You do not delight in sacrifice, or*
> *I would bring it;*
> *you do not take pleasure in burnt*
> *offerings . . .*

The blood of a thousand lambs and goats could never bring Eliab back or give Zechariah another life to live again. He struggled against the pain in his heart to remember the rest of the psalm.

> *Restore to me the joy of your salvation . . .*

Then . . . then . . .

> *Then I will teach transgressors your ways,*
> *and sinners will turn back to you.*

"O God!" he pleaded. "Forgive me! Forgive me and give me another chance. Let me make up for the wrong I have done. I *will* teach transgressors Your ways, Lord. Please, give me another chance to serve You . . . please . . ."

In the distance the shofar sounded, signaling the end of the sacrifice. The evening benediction settled over Zechariah peacefully. The images of Molech had fled.

As he lay on his face on the floor, he heard a soft knock on his door. He rose to his feet shakily and stumbled across the room. Who could it be? Had he forgotten something? Was he supposed to be on duty at the Temple?

His daughter, Abijah, stood in the doorway, her lovely face tear-streaked, her eyes red with sleeplessness. He searched it for hatred or reproach, but she fell into his arms.

"Abba, please help my Hezekiah," she begged. "Night after night he dreams about the sacrifice to Molech. His fear is destroying him, Abba."

"Help him—?" Zechariah stammered. "I—I don't know how—"

"He cries for Yahweh, your God, over and over again." Yahweh—his God, the God of forgiveness and cleansing. "Please, Abba! Please come!"

Zechariah released her and wrung his trembling hands. He felt so helpless, so unworthy. He couldn't go. He didn't know how to help. And he desperately needed another drink.

But as he looked past Abijah through the open door, he suddenly saw a slender bridge stretching out before him, reaching back across the gulf, back to God. He knew then that Yahweh had heard him, that Yahweh was offering forgiveness. He grasped his daughter's hand tightly and followed her out of the room, closing the door firmly behind him.

Zechariah walked down the hill to the palace, back to where it had all begun. As if unraveling a tapestry that had gone awry, he went back to where his mistake had been made. He would start all over again, with the twisted mess he had made of his life coiled at his feet like tangled piles of wool. He would begin anew, not with King Uzziah in the splendor of the royal throne room, but in the palace nursery, with this small boy with the wide, frightened eyes. Hezekiah clung to Abijah, staring through Zechariah as if he were not there. The only word he spoke was "Yahweh," whispered with a voice hoarse from screaming.

I've done this, Zechariah thought. This is my fault. Don't be like the other nations, the Torah said. They sacrifice their children to idols. But he had not heeded the warning.

Eventually Hezekiah fell asleep in Abijah's arms. Exhausted, she laid him in his bed.

"I'll watch over him," Zechariah told her. "Get some sleep." She left, and he sat down on the empty bed beside Hezekiah's.

What could he possibly do for his little grandson? Where and how should he begin? Was he strong enough to fight off Ahaz's soldiers if they came back? Zechariah knew he would gladly die before he would let them sacrifice another child for his sins.

Gradually the oil lamps burned lower, and the room darkened. A gentle night breeze blew through the open window, bringing cooler air after the hot, dry day. The night was quiet and still, except for the sound of Hezekiah's deep, rhythmical breathing.

Zechariah's hands trembled. He needed a drink. He thought about all the wine in the palace wine cellars below him. He knew where to find the chief wine steward. If he just slipped downstairs for a moment, he could bring a flask of wine back with him. He rose to his feet.

Suddenly a cry shattered the stillness. For a moment it startled Zechariah, and he couldn't remember what he was supposed to do. Then he saw Hezekiah in the bed next to him, screaming in terror, and he remembered.

He lifted the trembling child in his arms. The boy clung to him, sobbing. His little body seemed so small, so vulnerable.

Zechariah's eyes filled with tears. He felt a heavy weight of guilt for the part he played in Hezekiah's nightmare. But he didn't know how to help him.

"Yahweh . . . ," Hezekiah sobbed. "Yahweh . . ."

"Shh . . . shh . . . ," Zechariah soothed as he stroked the boy's curly head. "Yahweh's here with us—Yahweh's here."

Then, not knowing what else to do, Zechariah began reciting softly, stirring up the nearly forgotten words from the dusty chambers of his memory. "Yahweh is my light and my Savior—whom shall I fear? Yahweh is my strength and my life—I don't need to be afraid."

Almost imperceptibly, he felt Hezekiah's stiffened body relax, heard his sobs die to soft whimpers. Zechariah swallowed the lump in his throat and continued, his deep voice soothing and calm: "For in times of trouble, Yahweh will keep me safe in his shelter. Yahweh will hide me in the secret place where he dwells and will set me up on a high rock. . . ."

At dawn, when the flickering oil lamps finally burned out, Hezekiah lay asleep in his grandfather's arms. But Zechariah continued to recite as the first soft rays of sunlight lit the room: "Yahweh is my shepherd. He will supply all my needs. . . . Even when I walk through the valley, in the shadow of death, I won't be afraid. For Yahweh is with me . . ."

7

As the sun dipped below the rim of the western hills, Uriah listened unconsciously for the trumpet announcing the evening sacrifice. Then he remembered. There would be no trumpet. The trumpet had not sounded for six weeks, since the day the Aramean armies poured into the valleys surrounding Jerusalem and placed the city under siege. So far the city's steep cliffs and thick walls had kept the enemy at bay, but supplies and tempers were growing short. With no wood for the fire, no lambs for the offering, the daily sacrifices in Yahweh's Temple had ceased.

Uriah felt tense and exhausted as he walked to the throne room. Forced to act as a buffer between the king, isolated in his palace, and the real conflict taking place outside, Uriah averaged a mere three or four hours of sleep a night.

Inside, the leisurely splendor of the throne room stood in stark contrast to the realities of siege warfare outside. Uriah had difficulty adjusting to the change. He entered wearily and bowed low before the king.

Ahaz slouched on his massive ivory throne, studying the checkered shadow on the floor cast by the setting sun as it slanted through his latticed window. He acknowledged Uriah's presence with a limp wave of his hand.

"Your Majesty, I—," Uriah began.

"This cursed weather," Ahaz groaned. "I can't take

this heat." The servants, languidly fanning the king with dried palm branches, began waving them vigorously.

"Yes, it's very hot, Your Majesty. I've come to report that—"

"I'm tired of just sitting here, tired of this stifling throne room, tired of watching all these useless advisers of mine scurry around all day whispering and arguing."

The knots of men scattered around the throne room froze, eyeing the king with alarm. Ahaz, in spite of his claim to boredom, made no effort to move off his throne.

"I'm sick of this cursed siege. Six weeks already! Six weeks of sitting cooped up in this city waiting for help to arrive. When are the Assyrians going to come to our rescue?"

Uriah glanced at his smaller throne beside the king's, wishing he could sit down, but Ahaz offered no invitation. The sun's heat pressed against Uriah like a wall, and he longed for a cup of cold water from the Gihon spring. The only water available, from the cisterns, tasted warm and stale.

"I'm sure help will come any day now, Your Majesty. The tribute we sent has surely reached the Assyrian king by now."

Uriah remembered the long, winding caravan that had been hastily sent to Tiglath-Pileser, loaded with the last of the Temple's wealth. He had stood on the tower of the north gate with Ahaz and watched the camels depart, nodding their way slowly down the road, calmly chewing with their crooked jaws. That was the last time Ahaz had left the palace. A day and a half later, thousands of enemy troops had arrived to begin the siege.

Every day the king sent Uriah to the top of the walls to survey the enemy encampments, but Ahaz steadfastly refused to look for himself. Messengers raced in and out of the throne room with the latest news of the enemy's attempts to storm the gates, but Ahaz would not observe the fighting or offer words of encouragement to his meager troops. He had vowed not to leave the palace until it was over.

"I'm cut off from the rest of the world," Ahaz grumbled. "I don't even know what's happening to my nation—or if I have a nation left."

Uriah saw the king slipping into depression, and he longed to get away from him. "Your Majesty, the fighting is over for the day. With your permission, it is time to prepare the daily reports."

Ahaz nodded absently, blotting the sweat off his face with a linen towel. "The fighting is over for the day," he repeated dumbly to his advisers. "Go and prepare your reports." The counselors filed slowly from the throne room, whispering furtively among themselves.

"Uriah, you stay behind," Ahaz added. "You will join me for dinner in the banquet room."

Uriah bowed slightly, gritting his teeth. "As you wish, Your Majesty."

Ahaz's servants appeared, scurrying around him, adjusting his robes and train, escorting him with exaggerated pomp from the throne room. The air was slightly cooler in the open courtyard as the evening breezes blew in from the Judean hills, but they carried with them the scent of smoke and destruction from the valley below. Uriah followed King Ahaz along the covered walkway, dreading the task of trying to lift Ahaz's spirit.

In the enormous banquet room, only one table of many dozens had been set for the evening meal. Ahaz and Uriah, seated on cushions at opposite ends, seemed lost in the vastness. As servants glided silently in and out, bringing platter after platter of rich food, Uriah stared in amazement at the exquisitely embroidered tablecloth, the shimmering silver bowls and plates, the platters heaped with delicacies: roasted lamb, cooked lentils and beans, cucumbers, melons, pomegranates, fig cakes, olives, grapes, cheese, and bread. Uriah would consider such a meal extravagant in prosperous times, but with his nation suffering, his city under siege, the meal became grotesque. He fingered his silver goblet, wondering why Ahaz had plundered the silver from the Temple if the palace held all of this. But he knew better than to question Ahaz. The impulsive young king could strip him of his new position as easily as he had awarded it.

Uriah pushed aside his bewilderment and bowed his head to recite the blessing. But before he could begin, Ahaz interrupted, loudly slurping the slimy juice from a pomegranate. Uriah hesitated, wondering how to remind the king of Yahweh's law, but Ahaz reached across the table for a handful of olives and stuffed them into his mouth.

"Why aren't you eating?" Ahaz growled.

Uriah mumbled a hasty prayer under his breath and looked around for the pitcher of water for the ritual handwashing. Ahaz stopped chewing and glared at him.

"Now what are you looking for?"

"Nothing," Uriah mumbled. It's because of the siege, he told himself. Water is scarce. The handwashing doesn't matter.

A servant appeared at Uriah's side with a platter, heaped with juicy chunks of lamb. Since no daily sacrifices were being offered at the Temple, Uriah knew that the animal had been slaughtered as one of Ahaz's many sacrifices to Baal. And judging by the blood pooling along the edges of the platter, it had not been slaughtered according to the Law, either. As the high priest of Yahweh, Uriah was forbidden to eat such defiled food. But, as if in a dream, he found himself grimly piling the rich slices of meat onto his plate.

First a drop, he thought, then a small trickle, and finally in a flood, the laws and precepts he had faithfully followed all his life washed away before his eyes while he did nothing to prevent it.

He tried to remember his larger goals—restoring the Temple, empowering his priesthood. Nothing else mattered. Nothing else was important. Certainly not vain, empty rituals that had lost their meaning centuries ago.

"Eat, Uriah, eat," Ahaz urged. "You've put in a full day's work. You deserve it."

Uriah picked at his food, pushing it around on his plate without eating much. He had just come from the infirmary, where he had seen today's casualties, and he had no appetite. Their cries of pain still sounded in his ears.

"Uriah, I want to ask you something." Ahaz motioned for him to lean closer. "The other advisers aren't here now, so tell me the truth. How are we really holding up against the siege?"

Uriah studied Ahaz for a moment while the king continued to stuff food in his mouth as if he had asked about the weather instead of the state of his nation. He wondered if he should give Ahaz the truth or lie to him, cheering him with half truths and false hopes as he had done for the last six weeks. Uriah was sick of the charade. Ahaz needed to hear the truth.

"Your Majesty, our greatest threat isn't the enemy on the outside. Jerusalem's walls and steep slopes are a formidable barrier. They can withstand a great deal."

Ahaz grunted and spat three olive pits onto his plate.

"The greatest threat in siege warfare is always morale. People start to panic when they see their water supplies decreasing and—"

"I thought I said to post guards at the cisterns and ration the water supplies!" Ahaz shouted, spitting small bits of food from his over-full mouth.

"That's being done, Your Majesty, but—"

"By all the gods in heaven, this is the limit! Defending this city from the enemy is bad enough, but now you're telling me I have to use my precious manpower against my own people? Curse them all!" He threw his bread down and pushed away his plate. Too late, Uriah realized that it had been a mistake to give Ahaz the truth. The king grabbed his wine goblet and gulped noisily, then signaled for more.

"I'm sick to death of this siege! We should have sent the tribute to Aram and Israel instead of to Assyria. Maybe they would have left us alone. We could have thrown in a few thousand slaves too, if that's what they're after. Do you think it's too late to buy their favor?"

Uriah tried not to show his irritation at Ahaz's stupidity. "They never would have been happy with tribute, Your Majesty. They want it all: the whole nation of Judah. Besides, there's no tribute left to send." He deliberately kept his gaze on Ahaz, ignoring the silver-laden table in front of him.

Ahaz grunted and returned to his plate of food, chewing in silence for several minutes.

"How do you like your new living quarters, Uriah?" he asked abruptly. "Is everything satisfactory?"

"Everything's quite satisfactory, Your Majesty." Uriah suppressed his astonishment at the king's change of topics.

"Good, good. I wanted you in the palace, close at hand in case I need you. They were my brother Maaseiah's quarters, you know."

Ahaz stopped eating. His face contorted in pain as he let out a long moan. "Why did I let him go into battle? Why didn't I send somebody else?" He grabbed the front of his tunic with both hands and tore it, then beat his breast with his clenched fist. "He didn't even get a decent burial."

Uriah knew how much Ahaz still mourned for his brother and silently marveled at the fact that the king had never shown the slightest remorse over the loss of his sons. The memory of those children huddling together, gazing at him in terror, made Uriah shudder.

"You've suffered a great loss, Your Majesty," he forced

himself to say. "I am honored that you chose me, but I know I can never replace Prince Maaseiah."

Uriah's platitudes seemed to pacify Ahaz. He grunted and began eating again.

"By the way," the king added, his mouth full of bread, "I understand you're not married. How did you manage that?"

Instantly Uriah thought of Abijah. She should have been his wife, not Ahaz's.

"I'm not sure, Your Majesty," Uriah shrugged. "No time to look for one, I guess." He wondered if Ahaz ever took the time to talk to Abby the way he used to. Did he know anything at all about her? Did he know that she loved to eat fresh bread dripping with date honey? that lilies made her sneeze? that she was afraid of spiders? Did Ahaz notice the way the corners of Abby's mouth turned down slightly just before she smiled? Or didn't Abby smile anymore?

"Well, if you ever get lonely, just let the servants know," Ahaz continued. "They'll arrange to have a few concubines sent to your quarters."

"Thank you, Your Majesty." Uriah tried to appear grateful, but everything about this dinner disgusted him: the lavish opulence, the wasted food, the inane small talk. Ahaz was a fool, discussing concubines when his city was under siege. Uriah could no longer stand the sight of him. He studied his plate, toying with his food while the king ate noisily.

The sudden crash startled Uriah. He looked up as Ahaz hurled a second platter to the floor.

"You're lying to me!" Ahaz cried. "We're all going to die, aren't we?"

Uriah wondered how much longer he could disguise the hatred he felt toward the king. "It will all work out, Your Majesty," he said calmly. "The Assyrians will come."

"But that's the trouble," Ahaz cried. "Remember what Isaiah said? What if they don't come as allies?"

"They will, Your Majesty. I'm sure of it. Don't listen to Isaiah. He's a fool."

"I don't want any more food." Ahaz pushed his food away and rose ponderously from his cushions. "I'm going to the council chamber and wait for the reports."

Uriah scrambled to his feet and followed the king out of the banquet hall and across the open courtyard. The air felt cooler now that the sun had set, and the first few stars flickered in the sky above their heads. Uriah wished he didn't have to go inside. He longed to walk slowly up the hill to the Temple mount and enjoy the stars' dazzling brilliance from the highest point in the city. Instead, he followed the king into the dreary council chamber and closed the door behind them.

Ahaz took his place on the dais and waited while the servant refilled his wine glass. He drained it in one gulp and wiped his lips with the back of his hand. Uriah tried to recall how many times Ahaz had drained his cup during dinner, but they were too many to count.

"Let's get this over with," Ahaz growled. "Somebody start."

The king's army chief rose to his feet, shuffling through his scrolls with quick, nervous gestures. "Our casualties have been light today—only 24 men killed and 17 wounded. But our supplies of weapons are getting dangerously low, and we don't seem to be recovering very many weapons from the enemy. They make sure every shot hits its mark. None are wasted."

As he droned on in a boring monotone of statistics, Uriah noticed that Ahaz was not listening. When the chief finished his report and sat down, several minutes passed in silence as Ahaz gazed unseeingly into space. Uriah decided to take over, nodding to Ahaz's defense minister.

"We'll hear your report next."

"The enemy concentrated their assault against our most vulnerable area, the northwest gate," he began, making no attempt to disguise his anxiety. "We sustained only minor damage, but their repeated attempts to set the gates on fire were almost successful. We managed to douse the flames, but our water supplies are becoming critically low. In fact, there was nearly a riot at Solomon's Temple today when a mob tried to break through the gates to draw water from the brazen laver."

Ahaz threw down his wine glass and shouted a curse. He was drunk, and his words came out slurred. "Do I have to take a sword and guard every cistern in this city myself? Doesn't anyone ever listen to me? I told you from the start of this cursed siege to post guards at all the cisterns and to ration the water!"

"But, Your Majesty, every available soldier is needed to defend the walls—"

Ahaz shouted another curse. "No wonder we're in such a sorry state! I give orders that nobody bothers to follow!" He turned on his defense minister in a rage. "Get out! Get out of my sight right now!"

The atmosphere was tense as the minister gathered up his things and hastily left the room. Uriah turned to Ahaz.

"Your Majesty," he said soothingly, "you shouldn't have to listen to this. It's upsetting you." He took Ahaz's arm and pulled him to his feet, then led him like a child to the door. "I'll finish hearing the reports for you, and we can decide what measures need to be taken in the morning, after you've rested. A weary king will be no help to his nation, my lord."

It did not take much to convince Ahaz. He stumbled from the room with an injured air, allowing Uriah to steer him to his chambers.

"Send my servants in here with some more wine," he slurred when he reached his chambers. "You have no idea what unbearable pressure I'm under."

"Get some rest, Your Majesty. I'll take care of everything."

As Uriah turned to leave, Ahaz clutched his arm. "Are

sacrifices being offered night and day?" he asked urgently. "To Baal . . . Asherah . . . Molech . . . all the gods?"

"Well, Your Majesty," Uriah hedged, "there is very little wood, and we can't spare many animals because of the siege—"

"Check on it!" he cried. "Make sure none of the gods are being offended!"

"I'll see to it, Your Majesty. Rest well."

As he hurried away, Uriah wondered what he would do if Ahaz ordered another sacrifice to Molech. When he thought of Ahaz's sons cowering in fear, his revulsion for the king was so great that he wanted to keep walking, past the council chamber, out of the palace, back to the Temple of Yahweh on the hill high above the city. But the king's advisers were waiting for him in the council room. He was second in command.

He passed a trembling hand over his face and straightened his shoulders, then strode into the council chamber to take his place as head of the royal court.

—◈—

When Ahaz opened his eyes, thin slivers of sunlight were streaming through his shuttered windows, intensifying the throbbing pain that hammered behind his eyes. He groaned and tried to sit up, but his stomach churned as the room spun.

"Your Majesty?"

The voice startled him, and the sound echoed loudly through his head as he tried to focus on a blurred figure standing in his doorway.

"Who is it?—what do you want?"

Uriah entered, and as he approached the king's bed, Ahaz groaned and covered his eyes to stop the pain. "More bad news of the siege, no doubt?" he mumbled, remembering the unfinished reports from the night before. "Just go away. I can't take this anymore."

But Uriah's stony features, usually unreadable, were curiously cheerful. "Your Majesty, they're leaving!"

"Who's leaving? What are you talking about?" Ahaz's mouth tasted sour and dry. He searched for a drink of wine and spied a half-empty goblet on the table beside his bed.

"The armies outside the walls have broken camp. They're retreating."

Forgetting the wine, Ahaz threw aside the covers and scrambled out of bed, struggling to comprehend Uriah's words. As they slowly penetrated his foggy brain, he wondered for a brief moment if this were a cruel joke calculated to send him over the brink of sanity. He grabbed the front of Uriah's tunic with both hands and tried to shake him, but the priest's powerful frame didn't budge.

"Are you telling the truth?" he shouted up at him.

"Yes, Your Majesty," he replied calmly. "It's the truth. Come to the wall and see for yourself."

Ahaz released his grip and eased onto the edge of his bed. "They've come at last," he said incredulously. "It worked! The Assyrians came to our defense."

"Yes—they're probably attacking Aram from the north. The Arameans obviously received word of an invasion and have gone back to defend their own land. It's over."

Ahaz breathed a deep sigh of relief as he felt some of the strain lift from him for the first time in months. It was over. He had survived. Now he could return to his accustomed lifestyle and leave all the day-to-day decisions to Uriah.

"No one will dare attack my country now." He licked his parched lips with a dry, thick tongue. "Molech answered my prayers, Uriah. I paid a great price for Molech's favor, but it was worth it, wasn't it?"

Uriah remained silent. Ahaz could never decipher the high priest's thoughts, and his stony silences made Ahaz nervous. He waved his hand, dismissing Uriah.

"Thank you for the news. You may go."

When he was alone again, Ahaz sat on the edge of his bed, silently planning the feast of celebration he would hold. He smiled as tantalizing visions of revelry danced before him, but his smile faded as he recalled his cousin Isaiah's words: "Your hands are full of blood . . . you will be devoured by the sword."

Ahaz's mood darkened. He reached for his wine goblet and glanced at his shaky hands as if expecting to see blood on them. He took a gulp, but the warm wine tasted like vinegar, and he spewed it out in disgust. The wine in the jug tasted sour as well, and he threw it to the floor, cursing the fiery prophet who intruded on his thoughts like an unwanted guest.

Gradually, Ahaz became aware of shouts coming from the courtyard below his window. He crossed the room and cautiously peered out between the wooden slats. News of the retreat seemed to be spreading like a grass fire throughout Jerusalem, and the relieved citizens were pouring from their shuttered homes into the streets to celebrate.

The siege was over, he told himself. Nothing was going to spoil his mood today, least of all Isaiah, whose prophecies of doom had obviously proved worthless. He rang impatiently for his servants. It was time to get dressed. He must lead his nation in a celebration of victory.

Zechariah pulled the heavy curtains into place over the window of Hezekiah's bedchamber and trimmed the wick of the oil lamp. It sputtered to life, casting flickering light in the darkened room.

"Grandpa?" Hezekiah said sleepily. "Will you sing for me?" He gazed at his grandfather with solemn brown eyes, and Zechariah felt his heart constrict. How he had grown to love this child in the past few months!

At first they had clung to each other, each one needy in his own way. But in time, with the siege over and the threat of Molech a mere memory, bonds of love had replaced the cords of need.

"Yes, Son. Close your eyes, and I'll sing for a while."

"OK," he yawned.

Zechariah sat on the edge of Hezekiah's bed. He closed his eyes and hummed softly for a moment, his body swaying slightly in rhythm; then he began to sing.

"I love you, O Lord, my strength. . . ."

His deep bass voice was rich and mellow, the melody slow and haunting.

"The Lord is my rock, my fortress and my deliverer; my God is my rock, in whom I take refuge—"

"Grandpa?" Hezekiah interrupted. Zechariah stopped short in surprise.

"What is it, Son?"

"Can Yahweh close His mouth?"

"What? Why do you ask about Yahweh's mouth, child?"

Hezekiah sat up in bed, peering intently at Zechariah. "Because Molech never closes *his* mouth. I think he must get tired of holding it open, Grandpa." He spread his mouth wide and made a menacing face in an imitation of the fire god. "Is Yahweh's mouth like that too? Can Yahweh close His?"

Zechariah's delight in his little grandson and his deep love for the child welled up inside him and burst forth in laughter. His life had been arid for so long that he couldn't recall the last time he had laughed. He only knew it felt good, like the first cup of cold water after the long siege had ended.

"No, Son," Zechariah replied at last, "Yahweh's mouth isn't open all the time like Molech's."

"What does Yahweh look like, Grandpa? Can you show me His statue sometime?"

Zechariah stroked Hezekiah's curly hair, thick and silky beneath his hand.

"There is no statue, Son. One of Yahweh's commandments is that we must never try to make an image of Him."

"Why not?"

"Well, because Yahweh is so . . . so . . ." He searched for the right words to describe God, gesturing helplessly. "We could never put all of Yahweh's greatness into a mere statue. Besides, no one has seen God. No one knows what He looks like. We only know that we are made in His image."

Hezekiah fidgeted, as if it required a physical struggle to comprehend. "But Grandpa, how do you know that Yahweh is real if you can't see Him?"

Zechariah was speechless. The simple question struck him like a hammer blow. The joy he had felt a moment ago vanished, replaced by fear. He was a Levite. He had once counseled the king. And now he couldn't even answer a child's simple question. He was terrified to try. Zechariah pulled on his beard in frustration.

"Hezekiah," he said softly, "you need to go to sleep now. You would keep me up all night with your questions."

"But Grandpa . . . ," Hezekiah pleaded, tugging on Zechariah's sleeve. Zechariah cut him short.

"No, Son," he answered sharply, then regretted it. "Go to sleep, and I promise . . . I promise . . . we will talk about Yahweh in the morning." He motioned for Hezekiah to lie down, then smoothed the covers into place around him. "Good night," he whispered and turned away to avoid his grandson's probing eyes.

"Good night, Grandpa."

Filled with shame, Zechariah cleared his voice to sing, but suddenly Yahweh seemed far away again, the gulf between them unbridgeable. His voice trembled slightly as he sang.

"He is my shield and the horn of my salvation, my . . ."

He stumbled over the words, momentarily confused, Hezekiah's question still haunting him.

". . . my stronghold. I call to the Lord, who is worthy of praise, and I am saved from my enemies . . ."

He continued singing in the darkness, his body rocking gently in rhythm with the verse. Because it was a nightly ritual, he knew the words, but they were empty words to him. His inadequacy and failure haunted him. He no longer knew the answers.

Before long he became aware that the pattern of Hezekiah's breathing had changed. He was asleep.

". . . In my distress I called to the Lord; I cried to my God for help . . ."

O Yahweh, I'm calling to You for help now, Zechariah prayed silently. *Hezekiah asks how I know You are there. What shall I tell him? O Yahweh, help me!*

". . . From his temple he heard my voice; my cry came before him, into his ears . . ."

God? Do You really hear my cry? Please help me.

In the fading lamplight, Hezekiah's dark hair had a coppery cast. As Zechariah tenderly brushed a curl away from his face, he felt his love for Hezekiah like a deep ache. The boy's soul had been healed, his nightmares forgotten. But he had never asked questions about Yahweh before.

As he sat in the silent darkness, Zechariah felt the weight of his love for Hezekiah twist into a knot of pain in his soul. In desperation, he fell on his face to the floor.

Almighty God, have mercy on this small boy. Send someone to teach him about You. Please don't let him walk in the ways of Ahaz. Lord, don't punish him for the sins of his father—and grandfather. Mold him into Your servant, Lord. Hear me, I pray.

The stars moved silently across the heavens as the city slept. A cool breeze rustled past the heavy curtain, and the oil lamp sputtered, then died. Zechariah never noticed. With his forehead pressed to the cold stone floor, he cried out to God throughout the long night, praying as he had not prayed for many years.

Please send someone to teach him, Lord. I can't do it. You had mercy on me before and answered my prayer. I asked for forgiveness, and You gave it to me. Now I ask for Your help again, although I am not worthy to call on You. Please—please, teach him Your laws. Let him grow up to serve You, I pray.

At dawn, as the sun inched from behind the Mount of Olives in the east, Zechariah lay exhausted and still. He had no words left to pray. The knotted burden of his heart had been released. In the darkened room he could barely see Hezekiah's bed a few feet in front of him, but he heard him breathing softly.

Then in the silence, from somewhere deep inside Zechariah's soul, Yahweh spoke.

"You will teach him, Zechariah."

No, I can't, Lord, I can't! I failed with Uzziah, and I don't

want to fail again. Not with Hezekiah. Not with him. I love him,
God. I love him, and I can't . . . I can't . . .

But the voice of Yahweh spoke in his heart once again
to still his protests.

"Sing the rest of the psalm."

That was all.

Zechariah began to tremble. His heart raced as he
struggled to recall which psalm he had sung to Hezekiah
earlier that night.

"My God turns my darkness into light. With your help
I can advance against a troop; with my God I can scale a
wall. . . . It is God who arms me with strength and makes
my way perfect."

A tear slipped down Zechariah's cheek and glistened in
his beard. Yahweh had spoken to him again. He tried to remember the last time he had heard that powerful, tender
voice speaking to his heart. It seemed like a lifetime ago. He
had been a young man then, like Uriah, newly appointed by
King Uzziah to be palace administrator. His first love had
been the Law—God's holy, precious Torah. But through the
years another mistress slowly took its place—his pride:
pride in his own achievements and in the recognition he received before the entire nation.

Now he understood why he had failed with King
Uzziah. He had relied on his own knowledge, his own
strength, and it was not enough. He had stopped seeking
God's strength and wisdom. Zechariah covered his face in
shame.

Forgive me, Yahweh. Forgive my foolish pride.

The sun rose steadily to the top of the Mount of Olives
and crept over the ridge, flooding around the edges of the
curtains. Hezekiah stirred slightly and sighed in his sleep.
Zechariah rose to his feet and gazed at his grandson.

He resembles his mother so much, Zechariah thought.
He has Abijah's curly dark hair, her soft brown eyes, and
smooth, tawny skin. Ahaz was ruddy and fair, like the

house of David, but Hezekiah was not like him. Zechariah closed his eyes in prayer.

Make him different in spirit, too, Yahweh. Help me to teach him about You. Help me. Give me wisdom.

Fear began to knot within him again, but Yahweh's wisdom spoke louder than his fear as he recalled King Solomon's proverb:

"Trust in the Lord with all your heart and lean not on your own understanding; in all your ways acknowledge him, and he will make your paths straight."

Thank You, Zechariah said softly. *We will teach Hezekiah. You and I, Lord—we will teach him.*

―◈―

When Hezekiah awoke, blinding sunlight was streaming into his room. He sat up, rubbing his eyes sleepily, and saw that his grandfather had thrown open the curtains that covered his window.

"The heavens declare the glory of God," Zechariah sang. He gestured expansively toward the sun and sky, the green and brown hills that rolled away toward the horizon. "The skies proclaim the work of his hands." He folded his strong arms across his chest as if nothing more needed to be said.

Hezekiah stared at his grandfather in surprise, too sleepy to comprehend.

"Listen, Son, last night you asked how I know that Yahweh is really there. I have only to look and see all the marvelous things He has created. The *heavens* declare His glory."

Zechariah crossed the room and gently urged Hezekiah out of bed, dressing him in his robe and sandals as he talked.

"The sun, the moon, the stars, the rolling hills and valleys around us—all speak to us of God's glory. Yet the greatest miracle of all is that we are made in His image.

Come on, Son. Today I will teach you about Yahweh, our God."

Hezekiah could not imagine what had brought about such a change in his grandfather. But he sensed that they were about to embark on a great adventure, and he felt restless to begin.

In the dazzling sunlight, Zechariah's face seemed almost radiant. Yahweh must look like my grandfather, Hezekiah thought: tall and strong, with a flowing white beard and magnificent robes. His eyes must be wise and kind, too; his face noble and dignified like my grandfather's.

The city seemed to stretch and yawn, rousing from its slumber as Zechariah and Hezekiah left the palace hand in hand, walking down the hill through the streets. The air was smoky with the first fires of the day and filled with the sound of grinding hand mills and crowing roosters.

In the marketplace, a merchant shouted threats at his sleepy servant, hastily piling goods for the first customers. Zechariah stopped at a market stand and bought two barley buns and a handful of dates. Hezekiah ate them and spit out the pits while they walked.

As they approached the valley gate, Zechariah pointed to the shrines King Ahaz had set up along the streets. "All these altars are for worshiping false gods," he told Hezekiah. "They are merely statues, made by human hands and human imaginations. There is only *one* God, Hezekiah. You know Him by the name of Yahweh, the God of salvation."

The little images appeared harmless to Hezekiah, but he shuddered at the thought of facing Molech's blazing image again.

"Where are we going, Grandpa?"

"I want to take you outside the city where we can see Yahweh's creation."

When they reached the valley gate, they left the

walled city, following the course of the aqueduct up the Gihon Valley to the spring. Hezekiah recognized it as the route he had taken with his father the first time they had met Isaiah. Terraced olive groves and vineyards swirled down the rocky slopes of the mountains to the east, their branches drooping under the weight of ripening fruit. A herd of goats clambered over the rocks beneath the city walls, scrambling to find the sparse clumps of grass that grew among the stones. When Zechariah reached the spring, he stopped.

"Hezekiah, have you ever seen the wind?" The boy shook his head. "Then how do you know it's there?"

Hezekiah looked at his grandfather curiously and shrugged. "'Cause I can feel it blowing on me."

"Ah!" Zechariah nodded. "You've never seen the wind, but you know it's there because you know what it does—how it ripples through the golden seas of wheat or whistles through the tree branches. And you can feel it cooling you on a hot summer day. It is the same with Yahweh. You and I have never seen Him, but we can see where His hand has touched our lives, like when He saved you from Molech. And we can hear Him speaking to our hearts, like when He spoke to you through His prophet Isaiah. And if you reach out to Him, Hezekiah, you will feel His touch on your life and on all that you do. He's the Creator of life, the Creator of everything there is."

Zechariah spread his arms wide and shouted to the hills and fields, "Hear, O Israel! Yahweh is God—Yahweh alone! Love Yahweh your God with all your heart and with all your soul and with all your strength!"

He looked down at Hezekiah, and they grinned at each other as the goats on the hillside bleated enthusiastically in response to Zechariah's shouts.

"Those words are the 'Shema,' our covenant with Yahweh. You must learn those words and never, ever forget them: 'Hear, O Israel. Yahweh is God—Yahweh alone.'"

Zechariah and Hezekiah sat by the water's edge and looked up at the steep cliffs and the walls of the city high above their heads. They formed a powerful stronghold against the enemy, and Hezekiah felt vulnerable outside them. Molech lived in the valley outside those walls. He inched closer to his grandfather for reassurance and closed his eyes as he tilted his face toward the sky. The sun warmed his cheeks, and he again thought of Molech. Molech's strength and power were tangible to him. Yahweh, whose arms he couldn't see, offered no such evidence of strength.

"Grandpa, is Yahweh strong?"

"Yes, Son. He is."

"But is He really, *really* strong?"

"Yahweh is all the strength you'll ever need. That's what your name means in Hebrew, Hezekiah: 'The Lord is my strength.'"

"But if you can't see Yahweh, how do you know how strong He is?"

"Don't be fooled by strength you can see. Yahweh often hides His power in the simple things, the weak things, and so His strength often seems foolish in man's eyes. Shall I tell you a story about Yahweh's power?"

Hezekiah nodded eagerly and nestled close to his grandfather. In his grandfather's arms he felt protected, secure. Still, he longed for the reassurance of Yahweh's strength and further proof of His mastery over Molech.

"Our enemies once had a champion warrior," Zechariah began, "a giant named Goliah who stood more than nine feet tall. All of our soldiers were terrified of him."

Hezekiah remembered the huge high priest who had led the sacrifice to Molech. As Zechariah told the story, Hezekiah's imagination cast Uriah in the giant's role.

"Now your ancestor King David was just a boy like you, but he volunteered to fight the giant and—"

"Did David have a sword, Grandpa?"

"No, all he had was a shepherd's sling and five smooth stones, but—"

"Was he scared?"

"He had faith in Yahweh! He shouted to Goliath, 'You come against me with sword and spear . . . but I come against you in the name of the Lord Almighty!'"

"Who won, Grandpa? Who won?"

"Yahweh won! David's stone hit Goliath right in the middle of the forehead, and the giant crashed to the ground. Goliath made a mistake when he sneered at the size of his opponent. David had Yahweh on his side, even though no one could see Him, and Yahweh can defeat even the strongest enemy!"

"What else did Yahweh help David do? Tell me another story!"

Zechariah laughed and hugged Hezekiah. "When David grew up, he decided to conquer the city of Jerusalem so he could build a temple for Yahweh. But Jerusalem was a strong fortress, and it belonged to the wicked Jebusites. They taunted David, saying, 'You'll never get inside these walls!' But—"

"David got in, didn't he, Grandpa!"

"Yes he did." Zechariah laughed. "You see, Jerusalem has one weak spot. Its water supply is outside the city walls. Remember how we had to ration water during the siege?"

"It tasted bad too."

"Yes it did. The Jebusites decided to dig a secret water shaft from the city down to this spring so they could draw water from it during a siege. But Yahweh led David to the secret tunnel, and some of his men climbed up it. That's how David's army got into the city."

"Is the tunnel still here, Grandpa?"

"I don't think so. That was hundreds of years ago. David probably sealed it up so his enemies wouldn't crawl through it."

The day grew hot as the sun inched higher in the sky. Reluctantly, Zechariah rose to his feet.

"I guess we'd better head back, Son."

But Hezekiah needed to know one more thing about Yahweh. He summoned his courage to ask it. "Grandpa, does Yahweh want sacrifices too?"

Zechariah squatted down to face him. "Yes, Yahweh also asks for sacrifices, but He forbids us to kill our own children. We sacrifice lambs or—"

"Does Yahweh eat the lambs like Molech eats people?"

"No, Son, He doesn't eat them. He—"

"Then why does Yahweh want them?"

"Because when we sin we deserve to die. But Yahweh allows us to sacrifice a lamb, instead. The lamb dies in our place."

"Amariah died instead of me, Grandpa. I was really the firstborn son."

Zechariah drew him close. "Yes, your brother is gone. But I thank God that you're alive!"

"Will you tell me more stories about Yahweh tomorrow?"

"Yes, I'll tell you dozens of stories tomorrow." They started walking up the steep path toward the water gate. "Come on, Hezekiah—say the Shema with me this time. 'Hear, O Israel . . .'"

"Louder, Grandpa." Hezekiah beamed. "Make the goats bellow again!"

"HEAR, O ISRAEL," Zechariah shouted. "YAHWEH IS GOD—YAHWEH ALONE!"

Uriah stood at the window, staring down at the figures waiting in the courtyard below. The Judean soldiers looked hot and disgruntled after standing in the courtyard fully armed for almost an hour, waiting for King Ahaz to descend the palace steps so the journey could begin. The horses stamped the ground impatiently and strained at their bits, while behind them the caravan of slaves and pack mules stood loaded and waiting, the mules tossing their heads and pulling at their tethering ropes.

The Assyrian soldiers heading up the caravan seemed the most restless of all as they waited silently in their ranks. They had arrived in Jerusalem without warning to summon King Ahaz to a meeting with their emperor, Tiglath-Pileser. Ahaz's enemy, Aram, had been destroyed; he was to follow the Assyrian soldiers to the ruined capital of Damascus immediately.

Uriah sighed and turned away from the window. Ahaz's dawdling seemed deliberate as he took his time, choosing robes and finery for his trip, changing his mind every few minutes, ordering his servants around in circles. Whenever he caught their eye, Uriah glared at the servants, hoping to frighten them into moving faster, but his efforts were useless. Ahaz would not be rushed. Finally, Uriah reached the end of his patience.

"Your Majesty, the caravan has been waiting—"

"Let them wait. I'm not ready."

"But the journey to Damascus will be a long one, and you should make the most of the daylight hours—"

Ahaz turned on him angrily. "I am about to leave on a very important diplomatic mission. I'll be meeting with the great Emperor Tiglath-Pileser. I will *not* be rushed." He turned back to finish primping in front of his bronze mirror.

"But, Your Majesty, the Assyrian ambassadors arrived more than a week ago to summon you. You really should—"

"Don't you see?" Ahaz interrupted excitedly. "I'm finally getting the international recognition I deserve. The emperor of the most powerful nation on earth wishes to meet with me." He smiled at himself in the mirror. "We are allies. We'll be sitting in counsel together—discussing the nations of the world, signing treaties as equals, pledging our support to one another. I must look my best." He adjusted the folds of his embroidered robe and turned sideways, admiring himself.

Uriah stared at the king in disbelief, wondering how Ahaz could possibly imagine that he would sit as an equal with the king who had just rescued him from invasion. He had to make Ahaz face the truth.

"Your Majesty, you've formed an alliance with Assyria, but that doesn't mean—"

"You've heard the reports of what our Assyrian friends have done for us. They've conquered Aram and deported their population. And then Israel surrendered rather than meet the same fate. Now the Assyrians want to meet with me."

"That's my point, Your Majesty." Uriah crossed to Ahaz's side, pleading with him. "With such obvious power and military strength, surely you can't possibly think—"

But Uriah knew Ahaz wasn't listening. He interrupted to bark a new set of orders at his exhausted servants, then added, "I will always be remembered as one of Judah's greatest kings."

Uriah gave up trying to reason with him and returned to the window, reminding himself that for a few weeks he would be rid of Ahaz and in control of the nation. He folded his arms serenely across his chest, but his jaws were tightly clenched.

At last Ahaz decided he was ready. A trumpet fanfare announced his arrival, and he descended the palace steps in a flurry of regal pomp. Nobles and elders bowed before him in obeisance as Ahaz surveyed the waiting caravan with pride. The Assyrian soldiers, sent to escort him to Damascus, stood in tight, well-disciplined ranks, ready to lead the procession. Behind them, Ahaz's personal chariot stood harnessed to a team of six horses. It would carry Ahaz, his driver, and the valet who would attend to his personal needs. Pack mules and slaves carried equipment for the journey, as well as more gifts for the Assyrian king. The remainder of his own Judean soldiers, meager as they were, served as rear guard.

A large crowd had gathered in response to the trumpet call, and they greeted Ahaz enthusiastically, shouting, "Long life to the king!" Ahaz, who loved all the regal trappings and pomp, beamed and waved, savoring each moment.

But as he mounted his chariot, a voice suddenly shouted above the murmuring crowd: "Your Majesty! King Ahaz! Wait!"

From the steps of the palace, Uriah saw the king's good mood turn to rage as Isaiah pushed his way through the crowd toward the chariot. Uriah groaned and bounded down the steps, elbowing his way through the mob to stop Isaiah.

"Guards!" Ahaz roared. "I won't have him ruining this day with his useless cries of doom and ruin. I won't listen to you, Isaiah. Is Jerusalem destroyed? Has the enemy defeated us? No, because your words were nonsense! I've entered into a covenant with Assyria. I've made an agreement with Tiglath-Pileser. Nobody can defeat us now. You're nothing but a false prophet." Ahaz turned away and slouched into his chariot.

"Therefore hear the word of the Lord, you scoffers who rule this people in Jerusalem," Isaiah cried. He stood beside the king's chariot with dignity, his voice steady, authoritative. "You boast, 'We have entered into a covenant with death, with the grave we have made an agreement. When an overwhelming scourge sweeps by, it cannot touch us, for we have made a lie our refuge and falsehood our hiding place.'"

"I said I don't want to hear any more!" Ahaz's pale face flushed with rage. He signaled to his driver, but the chariot could not move until the ranks in front of him moved.

"So this is what the Sovereign Lord says," Isaiah continued shouting, loud enough for the gathered crowd to hear. "'Hail will sweep away your refuge, the lie, and water will overflow your hiding place. Your covenant with death will be annulled; your agreement with the grave will not stand.'"

When Uriah reached him, he grabbed the prophet by the arms, dragging him away from Ahaz's chariot. But they made little progress in the crowded street, and Isaiah continued to shout as they struggled.

"The understanding of this message will bring sheer terror. The bed is too short to stretch out on, the blanket too narrow to wrap around you."

"You're a *fool!*" Ahaz shouted. "You don't know what you're talking about—beds that are too short! I have an important journey ahead of me, a trip that will have lasting significance for this nation long after you're gone."

"Stop your mocking," Isaiah shouted back, "or your chains will become heavier; the Lord, the Lord Almighty, has told me of the destruction decreed against the whole land."

Isaiah's words and the tone sent a chill through Uriah's veins. His grip on the prophet went slack, and Isaiah shook himself free and walked away into the crowd.

Ahaz's signal to start finally reached the head of the caravan, and the black-bearded Assyrian soldiers set off at a brisk pace. The crowds parted to let them pass, and the people cheered and bowed as their king rode by. But their shouts rang hollow in Uriah's ears even after the procession disappeared from sight.

—◈—

A cold, damp rain fell over Jerusalem, and low-hanging clouds shrouded the nearby Judean hills from view. The chilly morning air penetrated to the bone, but Hezekiah didn't care about the weather as he skipped through the wet streets, splashing his sandals in the puddles, splattering muddy water over his ankles and feet.

"Please hurry up, Grandpa," he begged, running in giddy circles around Zechariah. "We're going to be late and miss the morning sacrifice."

"We'll be on time, Son. Don't worry."

"I want to see all of it!"

"We're almost there now. See that wall?" He pointed. "That's the top of the Temple enclosure." Hezekiah skipped with delight and tugged on his grandfather's hand. "Please hurry!"

"I can't climb any faster. This damp air makes my old bones ache."

"You promised to take me to the Temple a long time ago!"

"I know, I know," Zechariah chuckled. "But we had to wait for the right time. I'm not sure King Ahaz would approve of my taking you to Yahweh's Temple. But since he's in Damascus—"

A delicious thrill in sharing a secret with his grandfather tingled through Hezekiah—even more so from the thought that Ahaz would not approve.

"Why doesn't he want us to come here? 'Cause he worships Molech?"

"Well, yes. That's part of it."

"Doesn't he worship Yahweh too?"

"He can't do both. Remember? 'Yahweh is our God—Yahweh alone.'"

"Will you take me inside the Temple after the sacrifice, Grandpa?"

"Well, remember now—only the priests can go into the holy sanctuary . . ."

"But we can go inside where you live, can't we?" Zechariah had told him that Yahweh's Temple was the most wonderful place on earth, and Hezekiah wanted to see it all.

"Yes, I'll show you everything I can, Son." He gave Hezekiah a quick pat on the head, and the boy darted off in search of another puddle.

As they passed through the gate into the Temple courtyard, Zechariah pointed to the two massive pillars that supported the porch of the sanctuary. "Look. Those are the bronze pillars I told you about. Do you remember their names?"

Hezekiah squinted in thought. "One is Boaz, and the other is . . . um . . . what is it again, Grandpa? I forgot."

"The other is Jakin: 'Yahweh establishes.' And Boaz means 'In Him is strength.'" Zechariah gave a sigh, almost a groan, and Hezekiah looked up at him. "I wish you could have seen these pillars before your father had them stripped. They used to be overlaid with brass and covered with magnificent carvings."

Ugly wooden scaffolding, hastily assembled to strip off the bronze metal work, stood beside each pillar, making the Temple's facade look crowded and unsightly, not at all the magnificent structure Hezekiah had expected to see.

"Why did he take them all apart, Grandpa?"

"Your father needed beautiful presents to give to the king of Assyria, and he knew the most beautiful treasures in the nation were here in Yahweh's Temple."

A handful of priests and Levites emerged from a Temple side door and walked solemnly to the center of the courtyard, where the great altar stood. Hezekiah looked around. Thousands of people followed the procession to the Valley of Hinnom, but only a small knot of men attended this sacrifice at the Temple.

"Where are the rest of the people?" he asked Zechariah. "Why don't they come to Yahweh's sacrifice?"

Zechariah sighed. "Because the people of Judah have turned away from worshiping Yahweh. They worship many false gods now, and they don't seem to know the difference. It's up to the king to lead the way, for the people will follow his example, but your father has turned his back on Yahweh."

"Why, Grandpa?"

Zechariah shook his head. "I don't know, Son. I guess, in a way, I'm to blame, and I'm sorry—"

Hezekiah scowled, wondering how his grandfather could be to blame. He was about to ask about it when a plump little man hurried over to greet Zechariah, followed closely by a boy several years older and a head taller than Hezekiah.

"Zechariah, my friend! Oh, praise His name—it's so good to see you!" The little man seemed surprised, delighted, and his merry brown eyes beamed with joy. The two men embraced. "I've been so worried about you, Zechariah. But you look wonderful! Wonderful!"

"I am a new man, Hilkiah, thanks be to God. And I want you to meet my grandson, Prince Hezekiah."

"This is my son, Eliakim. We're honored to meet you." Hilkiah dropped to his knees, bowing, and pulled his startled son down beside him.

Their actions surprised Hezekiah. He rarely left the palace and was not used to having grown-ups or other children bowing before him. When they stood up again, the adults were soon engrossed in conversation, ignoring the two boys. Eliakim studied Hezekiah for several seconds and then began firing questions at him in rapid succession, giving Hezekiah scarcely enough time to answer between them.

"Are you really a prince?"

"Yes."

"Then King Ahaz is your father?"

"Yes."

"Where is he?"

"In Damascus."

"Why did he go there?"

"To see another king, I think."

"What does it feel like to be royalty?"

"I don't know."

"Abba says kings and princes have royal blood. Do you?"

"I guess so."

"What does it look like?"

"It's red."

"So's mine. Why is yours any different, then?"

"I don't know," Hezekiah shrugged. He had never thought about being different before. But then, he had never met other children besides his brothers or cousins.

"Are you going to be the king someday?"

Hezekiah hesitated, unwilling to admit he was the firstborn.

"Maybe . . . ," he hedged.

"You'll get to stand on that platform by the pillars. What are you going to do when you're the king?"

Hezekiah answered with a shrug.

"I never saw you here before. Are you going to come to the evening sacrifice too?"

"Maybe."

"Abba and I come every day, morning and evening. I have to watch from out here, though, because I'm not old enough yet. But after my next birthday I can go into the inner court and worship with all the other men."

Hezekiah envied this boy who was almost a man. He wondered what it would be like to have a father like Hilkiah who brought him to Yahweh's Temple twice a day. Suddenly the shofar sounded, and Hilkiah said good-bye and hurried off to join the other men at the inner court. Eliakim followed him as far as the gate.

"We'll have to watch from the outer courtyard too," Zechariah reminded him. He squatted down beside Hezekiah and rested his hand on his shoulder, pointing to the activities taking place.

"First the men have to cleanse themselves at the brazen laver. They confess their sins to Yahweh and wash to make themselves symbolically clean. That laver used to stand on a base of 12 brazen oxen. Ah—they were so beautiful! They stood taller than you, and three faced east, three west, three north, and three south. They were magnificent!"

"What happened to them?"

"Your father took them as well," Zechariah sighed, "to give to the Assyrian king. Look now. See how the men are washing? They must wash their feet so they can walk uprightly before God, and their hands so that all the works of their hands will be clean in His sight, and their lips so that they will speak only words that are pure. Now they can go before the altar. Come on. Let's move over here so we can see better."

He took Hezekiah's hand, and they walked to the other side of the courtyard. Hezekiah saw no statue, no open mouth or waiting arms—only a huge, unadorned square altar looming ahead of them, twice as high as Zechariah's head. The air above it shimmered. When a gust of wind suddenly blew the smoke in their direction, Hezekiah felt the heat from it on his face, and he drew back in fear.

"I want to go home," he said.

"It's OK, Son," Zechariah assured him. "You don't have to be afraid."

Hezekiah gripped Zechariah's hand tightly, fighting his fear and the strong memories that the sacrifice stirred.

One of the priests held a young bullock by a rope. The blade of a knife glinted in the priest's hand. As the bullock twisted and strained on the rope in an instinctive effort to flee, Hezekiah identified with the bullock, remembering the weight of the soldier's hands on his shoulders, remembering his brothers, Eliab and Amariah. He blinked back tears.

"I want to go home," he said again.

Zechariah knelt to face him, tenderly taking Hezekiah's hands in both of his. "Yahweh isn't like Molech, Son. There is nothing to fear in His Temple. See how the men are laying their hands on the bull's head? The bull will take their place now and bear all their sins. Blood has to be shed to atone for sin, but the bull's blood will be shed, not yours or mine."

When the last man lifted his hand from the bullock's head, the priest swiftly slit the animal's throat. The bullock went limp as the basin held by a Levite slowly filled with red-black blood. Hezekiah felt dizzy and sick. He closed his eyes so that he wouldn't have to watch.

Then above the murmur of animals and voices, the hissing and crackling of the flames, Hezekiah heard his grandfather's familiar voice as he joined in singing with the Levitical choir. The deep, rich tones comforted Hezekiah, and he opened his eyes and looked around. The Levite musicians had assembled on the steps of the sanctuary with their instruments, and Zechariah sang along with them:

> *O Lord, how many are my foes!*
> *How many rise up against me!*
> *Many are saying of me,*
> *"God will not deliver him."*

When Hezekiah looked at the bullock again, not much remained. The priest had swiftly cut it into pieces, and as the worshipers formed a circle around the great altar, one of the priests walked up the ramp to the top with the offering of the bullock's fat. Another priest sprinkled the bullock's blood around the base of the altar as the Levites sang:

> But you are a shield around me, O Lord;
>> you bestow glory on me and lift up my head.
> To the Lord I cry aloud,
>> and he answers me from his holy hill.

The worshipers dropped to their knees, then fell forward together, their foreheads touching the wet pavement's stones. It was the same way people sometimes bowed before Hezekiah's father.

> I lie down and sleep;
>> I wake again, because the Lord sustains me.
> I will not fear the tens of thousands
>> drawn up against me on every side.

All eyes focused on the priest who stood ready to present the sacrifice.

> Arise, O Lord!
>> Deliver me, O my God!
> Strike all my enemies on the jaw;
>> break the teeth of the wicked.

The priest placed the offering on the altar and stepped back. Seconds later, a pillar of flame soared high into the air above the altar. Although they stood a dozen yards away, Hezekiah jumped back in surprise.

"He is here!" all the men shouted. "He answers!"

The God he couldn't see had demonstrated His power. *No wonder Yahweh has power over Molech,* Hezekiah thought. *Yahweh is also a God of fire.*

Even though Zechariah assured him that Molech wasn't real, Hezekiah secretly feared the monster who had killed his two brothers. After seeing Yahweh's power in the pillar of fire, though, Hezekiah was nearly convinced that this unseen God was indeed stronger than Molech.

"From Yahweh comes deliverance," all the men sang. "May your blessing be on your people."

The priests placed the remainder of the bullock on the altar, but no dramatic flame shot skyward this time, no mighty roar—only a plume of smoke and the hissing and snapping of coals. The fragrance that drifted from Yahweh's fire smelled pungent yet sweet. The worshipers dispersed, and within minutes the courtyard stood deserted. The morning sacrifice was over.

The ceremony was far different from what Hezekiah had expected, and he felt disappointed. But in the next moment he forgot about it, anticipating his long-awaited tour of the Temple.

"Can we see the doors made of gold now?"

"Ah—the golden doors to the holy place. Yes, come on, then." They crossed the silent courtyard to the portico of the sanctuary and squeezed past the skeletal form of scaffolding to peer through the grating at the huge double doors to the holy place. But they were no longer overlaid with gold. They stood stripped naked, the bare wood gouged and scarred.

"They're not gold at all!" Hezekiah cried. He felt cheated, robbed.

"I'm sorry, Son. I didn't know. I guess Ahaz took that too. Ah, Yahweh—forgive him."

Hezekiah's disappointment felt like a fist in his stomach. He quietly followed Zechariah around to a side door and into the maze of chambers and storerooms in the Temple, but his enthusiasm for the tour had vanished. Zechariah tried to point out a few things along the way, to raise Hezekiah's interest once again, but everything appeared dingy and drab to him. He saw no splendor—only cracks and cobwebs. When they came to a large storeroom, Zechariah seemed shocked to see the nearly empty shelves. He looked around as if in a dream, then picked up a tarnished silver cup and tried in vain to polish it against his sleeve.

"This was the treasury for the sacred vessels used in the sacrifices. This room used to be full . . . and now . . . I guess everything was sent to Assyria . . ." His voice trailed off, and he stared blankly at the empty shelves as if forgetting that Hezekiah was there.

The boy tugged on his grandfather's sleeve. "What will the other king do with all of it, Grandpa?"

"I'm not really sure. Melt everything down, I suppose. I've also heard that heathen kings use holy vessels like these for drinking wine at feasts to their false gods. It hurts me to think of Yahweh's sacred things used in such a way."

Zechariah closed the door to the storeroom and led the way down the hall. "I saved my favorite place for last: the Temple library."

They entered a long, narrow room with a row of deep windows set high on one wall. Below the windows and on the opposite wall as well were dozens of niches carved into the thick, plastered walls, filled with hundreds of scrolls, their wooden handles protruding into the room. More shelves filled with scrolls were arranged in rows in the middle of the room, and between them were benches and tables where scribes and scholars could work. But only one scribe sat at his desk, patiently copying the faded Hebrew letters from an ancient scroll. The room had a fragrant smell of leather parchment and wood, instead of the damp mustiness of the other rooms.

"These scrolls contain all the laws that Yahweh gave our nation." Zechariah's pride glimmered in his eyes. "And they also tell the history of our forefathers all the way back to Adam and Eve. Yahweh's truth is one thing that your father can never change or destroy." He smiled triumphantly, but Hezekiah made no reply. "You're disappointed in the Temple, aren't you, Son?"

Hezekiah shrugged and stared mutely at his mud-spattered feet. Zechariah squatted down in front of him and planted his hands on Hezekiah's shoulders.

"I'm very sorry for misleading you about the glory of this Temple. Until today I guess I was blind to how much it has deteriorated. My vision was clouded over by memories—memories of how magnificent it all was during the golden age of King Uzziah. But that was more than 25 years ago. I'm sorry, Son. Today I am seeing it through your eyes—how it really is, not how it used to be."

"I wish it was still beautiful, Grandpa. Why did my father have to wreck everything?" He frowned.

"Come. Sit down over here." He led Hezekiah to one of the work tables, where he watched as Zechariah scanned the stacks of scrolls. When he found the one he wanted, Zechariah sat down beside him and carefully unrolled it.

"You know, Yahweh isn't surprised that your father's enemies attacked him all at once. In fact, Yahweh caused it to happen. This scroll is from the Torah and was written before the children of Israel moved to this land. May I read you some of it?" Hezekiah nodded but didn't look up, idly kicking his sandal against the table leg.

"'After you have had children and grandchildren and have lived in the land a long time—if you then become corrupt and make any kind of idol, doing evil in the eyes of the Lord your God . . . you will quickly perish from the land that you are crossing the Jordan to possess.'"

Hezekiah didn't understand. He looked up at Zechariah questioningly.

"The reason your father had to strip the Temple," Zechariah explained, "is because our enemies attacked us from every side. They destroyed entire cities and carried thousands of people away as captives. It happened just as Yahweh said it would, because the people have turned away from Him to worship idols. Your father gave Yahweh's gold to the Assyrian king so he would save us from our enemies. We're supposed to be servants of Yahweh, but now we are servants of Assyria instead."

Hezekiah felt a shiver of fear. "Will Yahweh go away and stop being our God?" he asked quietly.

"Well—let me read the rest of this, and maybe you can answer that question yourself: 'But if from there you seek the Lord your God, you will find him if you look for him with all your heart and with all your soul. When you are in distress and all these things have happened to you, then in later days you will return to the Lord your God and obey him. For the Lord your God is a merciful God; he will not abandon or destroy you.'"

"He'll forgive us, Hezekiah," the old man said softly. "He loves us and will forgive us if we'll only turn back to Him. I know with all my heart that this is true."

Hezekiah stopped kicking the table leg, and they sat in silence for a moment. "You know, Son, someday you will be the king of Judah and—" Zechariah stopped. "No. You're much too young to understand the responsibilities that lie ahead. We've talked enough for today."

Hezekiah struggled to understand all that his grandfather had said, but disappointment clouded his comprehension.

"Grandpa?" he asked at last, "couldn't Yahweh kill all our enemies and save us? Then my father wouldn't have to spoil His Temple. Couldn't Yahweh do that?"

"Certainly He could! Don't you remember the story I told you about how Yahweh helped David defeat Goliath?"

"Yes," Hezekiah nodded.

"And remember Joshua and the battle of Jericho?—and how Yahweh caused the sun to stand still so Joshua could defeat the five Amorite kings? Of course! Yahweh could defeat *all* of Judah's enemies."

"Then why didn't He, Grandpa?"

"Because, Hezekiah," Zechariah sadly shook his head, "because we didn't ask Him to."

→○≫ 10

The hot desert wind swirled across the road in a sudden
gust, raising a cloud of soot and dust. King Ahaz closed his
eyes to shield them from the dirt and to block out the scene
of utter desolation lying before him. The magnificent city of
Damascus stood in ruins. Thick stone walls that had once
offered protection now displayed gaping holes through
which jackals ran furtively, scavenging for whatever they
could find in devastated storerooms and kitchens.

As far as the eye could see, black Assyrian tents
spread across the charred plain, surrounding the city like a
low-hanging cloud, revealing no trace of the rich vineyards
and olive groves that once graced the fertile river valley.
Blackened stumps remained where thick forests of syca-
mores and carob trees once stood.

Before riding ahead to the encampment, the escort of
Assyrian soldiers halted Ahaz's procession a short distance
from Damascus and left him to wait in the searing heat, with
only the canopy of his chariot to protect him from the blazing sun. Ahaz rubbed his gritty eyes and sighed impatiently.

The Assyrian soldiers had set a brisk and exhausting
pace, and the long journey had wearied Ahaz. Every bone
and joint in his body ached from the jolting ride, and he
desperately wanted to bathe and lie down in a cushioned
bed. But as he gazed at the desolate city in front of him, he
knew that his accommodations couldn't possibly be luxuri-

ous. He ordered his valet to fan him and sank back in his chariot with a groan while closing his eyes.

Several minutes passed before the valet roused him. "Your Majesty, someone's coming."

Ahaz stood, watching nervously as three chariots approached and halted amid a choking pall of dust and soot. A tall, dark-skinned Assyrian wearing a short military tunic and armed with sword, bow, and spear emerged from the lead chariot. He wore his crisp black hair and squared-off beard perfectly curled in the distinctive Assyrian style. Ahaz dismounted and bowed low before him.

"I am Ahaz ben Jotham, King of Judah and Jerusalem," he announced, assuming this to be the great monarch Tiglath-Pileser greeting him as a friend and ally. The Assyrian responded with a few mysterious sentences, then ordered a tall, gaunt Hebrew in the chariot behind him to come forward and translate.

"You needn't bow—this is the Rabshekah, the Assyrian monarch's representative," the translator explained. Ahaz reddened, embarrassed by his mistake. "The Rabshekah will deliver the tribute that you have brought to the storehouses of Tiglath-Pileser. He will also take command of the Judean soldiers and weapons that you have brought him as a gift."

Ahaz paled. "Wait . . . wait a minute," he stammered. "There must be some mistake. These soldiers are my only remaining army. I didn't intend them as a gift. Can you explain that to the Rabshekah?"

The Hebrew gave a short laugh, and his lips twisted in a cynical smile. "I don't think you want me to do that. The vassal nations of Assyria aren't allowed to have armies. You won't need them any more. You're under Assyrian protection now."

The translator's impudence infuriated Ahaz, and he had to suppress the urge to slap the man's smirking face.

"You'd better tell your troops to follow the Rabshekah," he continued. "Then you must follow me."

Trembling with impotent rage, Ahaz turned to his captain. "Order your men to follow the Rabshekah," he said, then he watched in numb silence as his army marched away with the Assyrian escort. He wondered fleetingly if his men would ever be allowed to return to their homes and families again, then suddenly realized his humiliating position. After leaving Jerusalem with a grand procession, he would be forced to a disgraceful return with only his personal chariot and a handful of servants and bodyguards.

He stood rooted in the middle of the road until the last of his army marched away to the distant Assyrian camps. Then, when the dust settled once again, the Hebrew interpreter broke the uneasy silence.

"I shall take you to your tent now."

"Tent? My *tent?*" Ahaz repeated. His humiliation turned to outrage at being accorded only a tent for his accommodations, but he quickly suppressed his anger. Without an army, he was scarcely in a position to protest. Wearily, he mounted his chariot, and the interpreter crowded in beside him, pointing the way for the driver. Ahaz stared morosely at the Damascus ruins as the chariot jolted down the dusty road.

"I am Jephia, son of Shemaiah, of the tribe of Naphtali," the Hebrew interpreter said. "Your tent is not too far."

Ahaz continued to stare unseeingly at the horizon. "What brings you to Damascus?" he asked disinterestedly, his voice flat and hollow.

Jephia stared at him. "What brings me to Damascus?" he repeated incredulously. "You're obviously very naive when it comes to the Assyrians, King Ahaz ben Jotham." Again, his lips twisted in a mirthless grin. "The Assyrians captured me when they invaded Israel. I'm their slave, brought to Damascus to serve as an interpreter for the Rabshekah."

Ahaz felt his cheeks flush, and he quickly looked away. "I saw evidence of the Assyrian invasion on my journey through Israel," he mumbled.

"Yes, our king wisely surrendered and paid tribute to spare Israel the total destruction that Damascus received. Most of my countrymen won't suffer deportation, at least for now. But my nation is a vassal state of Assyria, and that means—" Jephia stopped abruptly and laughed with contempt. "That means we are *all* slaves. Here is your tent, King Ahaz."

The chariot drew up to a small encampment outside the ruined city walls. Ahaz's tent, consisting of four large rooms, was much bigger than he had expected and well supplied with food, wine, and, to Ahaz's great amazement, a portable bath.

"I will stay with you and see to your needs," Jephia told him, bowing slightly.

"When will I have an audience with the Assyrian emperor?" Ahaz saw Jephia suppress a smile, and it infuriated him. "That is why I have come here!" he shouted. "We have a treaty to sign. We are allies."

Jephia responded to his outburst calmly, his chin held high. "When the other vassal kings have arrived, Tiglath-Pileser will summon all of you at once. You must stay here until then."

Ahaz's servants usually cowered before him in fear, and Jephia's lack of respect galled him. The man's manners were outwardly correct, but Jephia lacked a deferential attitude, and every time he used the word "vassal" there was a hint of sarcasm barely concealed beneath the surface. If Jephia wouldn't cower and shake in his presence, Ahaz decided he didn't want his assistance. He turned his back to Jephia and summoned his own valet.

"I would like to bathe and then rest a while." He smiled with satisfaction as the man leaped into action, bustling around the tent to wait on him. "You are excused," he told Jephia coldly. The interpreter bowed slightly and left.

Several tedious days passed as Ahaz rested from his

journey, but he soon became bored. He had plenty of excellent food and wine but nothing to do except grow more impatient and nervous as he waited for the Assyrian monarch's summons. Yet he was determined not to ask Jephia about the delay. He hated Jephia's cynical smile and the way he explained everything as if Ahaz were a child.

Then at last a message arrived at Ahaz's tent, and he called Jephia to interpret it. As the interpreter silently read the message, one eyebrow rose slightly.

"The Rabshekah sends for you. All the other vassal kings have arrived. I am to conduct you on a tour of Damascus—then you will meet Tiglath-Pileser."

"Finally!" Ahaz sighed. "I'll need some time to get ready and—"

Jephia shook his head. "You don't understand. You must come at once." His voice held a stern note of warning that Ahaz did not miss. Ahaz glared at Jephia for a moment, then turned and hurried into his tent, changing into his finest robe as quickly as he could.

He reappeared a few minutes later, and they mounted his chariot, then rode in silence to the city. Ahaz had not yet seen the ruins of Damascus up close, and he struggled to conceal his shock and horror. A forest of rotting corpses, impaled on tall stakes, stood planted along the road leading to the main gate.

"The emperor would like you to meet the chief elders of Damascus," Jephia smirked. "They were impaled alive and left to die, watching the destruction of their city and the violation of the women."

Ahaz shivered and gazed straight ahead, avoiding the grisly, hollow-eyed stares. A crudely lettered sign tacked above the gate read, "This is the fate of the enemies of Assyria." Two huge mounds of human heads stood on either side of the gate.

"The scribes take a head count, and the soldiers are paid accordingly," Jephia explained. Ahaz fought desperately to keep from vomiting at the nauseating stench, holding a linen handkerchief over his mouth.

"They could have picked a better place to leave all this—this gore!" he sniffed in disgust. "We shouldn't have to look at this."

Jephia stared at him, shaking his head. "You still don't understand, do you, King Ahaz ben Jotham?"

"Understand what?" Ahaz answered petulantly.

"Why do you think all these corpses were left here? Why do you think you were invited to Damascus?"

"We are allies—"

"No!" Jephia interrupted sharply. "This is not going to be a meeting of 'allies,' as you so naively believe. This is a carefully orchestrated warning to all subservient nations like yours. Tiglath-Pileser knows that any vassal king who sees this devastation and cruelty will never entertain thoughts of rebellion against him. He doesn't want your friendship, King of Judah. He wants your fear and submission."

Ahaz shook his head as if he could shake aside Jephia's words. "No . . . no . . ."

"He wants your tribute, King Ahaz—now and for the rest of your life! He knows that no matter how much he demands, you will beat it out of the backs of your people rather than see Jerusalem end up like this!"

Ahaz stood paralyzed. He wanted to scream at Jephia and call him a liar, but as he stood before the gate, watching the other vassal kings approach through the forest of impaled bodies, he knew that Jephia told the truth. He felt like a fool for not seeing it before. He leaned against the side of his chariot, shaken and dazed. Then, with agonizing clarity, he recalled Isaiah's parting words: "We have made a lie our refuge."

"I've seen enough," Ahaz said quietly. But Jephia shook his head.

"You will see it all."

Ahaz rode through the rubble-strewn streets of Damascus in gloomy silence, the sights around him a vague blur. But Jephia continued with his grim narration, pausing to point to a small group of naked men and women with shorn heads, who were picking aimlessly through the wreckage of gutted buildings.

"These are the survivors of another city in a distant part of the Assyrian empire, deported here to rebuild Damascus while their own land is rebuilt by strangers. That is the Assyrian way."

"The Assyrian way," Ahaz repeated softly. He was beginning to understand the full extent of Assyria's brutal power and military might. His nation's sovereignty would be swallowed up, becoming a mere puppet kingdom in the vast Assyrian Empire. And there was nothing he could do but pay homage.

"That mound ahead is where the temple once stood." Jephia gestured toward a man-made hill, the highest point in the city. "We will have to walk from here. The streets are choked with debris from the temple."

Wearily, Ahaz climbed from the chariot and followed Jephia, weaving around massive stones that had once been part of the Aramean temple. He was grimy with sweat and the sooty dust that seemed to cover the entire land. He paused to catch his breath, mop his face, and watch the other vassal kings as they made their way up the slopes of the temple mound.

"Why are we all assembling here?"

"You will pay homage to the Assyrian gods at the altar on top, acknowledging that they are superior to Yahweh, the god of your land."

Ahaz nodded mutely, too numb to argue, and followed Jephia to the top of the hill. Not one stone of the former temple remained upon another, and the paved courtyard was bare except for a massive bronze altar standing in the center. Figures depicting the gods of Assyria decorated all four sides, but the central figure on each panel was Assur, the archer riding astride a winged sun.

Ahaz and the other kings gathered around the altar while priests brought 10 bulls forward to be sacrificed. They began chanting the ritual, which Jephia dutifully translated for him.

"All praise to Assur, who has led us to victory
over our enemies.

All praise to Assur, who has wielded his judgment
over them.

All praise to Assur, who has made Assyria the most
powerful nation in all the earth.

All praise to Assur and his representative among
us, Tiglath-Pileser."

Then the assembled kings bowed in homage, and Ahaz, filled with superstitious dread, knelt in the dust beside them, proclaiming: "Yahweh, the God of Judah, bows before Assur."

He remembered his grandfather, Uzziah, and the punishment inflicted on him for his blasphemy and almost wished that Yahweh would strike him dead and end his misery.

The ceremony continued in a dizzying whirl of chanting and bloodshed until the combined heat of the midday sun and the giant altar nauseated Ahaz. He wished it would end. He wanted to lie down alone in his tent and try to weave the fraying strands of his life back together. But when the ritual finally ended, Jephia turned to him with a contemptuous smile.

"Now you will meet your 'ally,' Tiglath-Pileser."

Ahaz looked at his robes, filthy with sweat and dust. "Like this?" he groaned.

Jephia merely smiled and led the way through the rubble to King Rezin's former palace, the only major building in the city that stood intact. A huge dais and throne had been erected on the palace steps, and the visiting kings were assembling on the street below it. Resplendent on his throne, with slaves fanning him in the oppressive heat, sat the Assyrian monarch, Tiglath-Pileser. He wore a long fringed tunic of richly embroidered purple silk and a tall, conical cap intricately decorated with golden threads. His blue-black hair and beard glinted in the sun, like the jewels that adorned his fingers and wrists, and his black gimlet eyes were cold and piercing.

Ahaz stood below the throne in the dizzying heat, wishing he could lie down somewhere and cool his parched throat with a drink of wine.

"What happens now?" Ahaz whispered to Jephia.

"First, a procession of the captives. Then all the vassal kings will take part in a ceremony of obeisance." Jephia pronounced the word "vassal" with his usual contempt, but it no longer bothered Ahaz. He understood.

The procession began with soldiers from the Assyrian army, and Ahaz watched as row after row of black-bearded warriors passed before him, their dark eyes staring straight ahead, their weapons glinting in the sun. The mounted cavalry followed the foot soldiers, each man heavily armed, then more soldiers in chariots. As the battering rams and siege towers paraded past, Ahaz remembered the fierce beating Jerusalem's walls had suffered during the siege a few months before. The weapons used then paled in comparison to this Assyrian arsenal. Jerusalem's aging walls would topple in a matter of months under their assault.

In wave after wave the Assyrian army passed, until it seemed to Ahaz that the entire population of Judah must have passed before him. Then came the captive booty of Damascus, heaped in golden piles on horse-drawn carts. Ahaz had never seen so much wealth, and his head spun with envy. Prisoners of war staggered behind the riches that had once belonged to them, led by King Rezin and his nobles and princes. They wore only chains around their ankles as their captors led them through the streets by bridles that pierced their nostrils and lips. Rotting, decapitated heads hung suspended on cords around their necks like royal diadems.

Ahaz's queasy stomach churned in revulsion, but he knew he didn't dare avert his eyes from the procession. Choking back bitter gall, he struggled to keep from retching.

When the captives reached the palace steps, King Rezin and his noblemen knelt before Tiglath-Pileser's throne. The emperor rose gracefully, brandished a sword, and, oblivious to his cries for mercy, ruthlessly cut out Rezin's tongue and gouged out his eyes. Then Ahaz watched in horror as the Assyrians staked Rezin and his nobles to the ground by their wrists and ankles and slowly flayed them alive. Masters of torture, the Assyrians removed all their victims' flesh without killing them, prolonging their suffering as long as possible.

At the sound of their agonized screams, a fear like he had never known overcame Ahaz. He quickly pushed to the rear of the crowd, fell to his knees, and vomited. He longed more than ever to be back in his palace in Jerusalem and away from the Assyrians and their horrible butchery. He wished he had never called upon their bloodthirsty king for assistance, and as the heaving finally subsided, he remembered Isaiah's warning: "We have entered into a covenant with death."

He wiped his eyes and mouth and rose shakily to his feet, aware that he had to return and watch the rest. He looked up and saw Jephia waiting for him, and for the first time he saw a hint of compassion in the interpreter's eyes.

After an eternity the tortures ended, but the cries of the dying men echoed in Ahaz's mind. Now, one by one, the vassal kings and their attendants lined up to pay homage to Tiglath-Pileser, assembling in order of importance and power. Deeply humiliated, Ahaz found himself among the least important. As he waited in line, trembling with fear, he wondered how he had imagined himself sitting with the Assyrian monarch as an equal, signing treaties, discussing the nations of the world.

At last he walked forward, his knees threatening to buckle beneath him. "I am Ahaz ben Jotham, King of Judah and Jerusalem, your humble servant and vassal." His own voice sounded unfamiliar. Then he fell prostrate before the king with his forehead pressed to the ground, the dust of Damascus filling his nostrils and throat. He fought the urge to cough.

Finally, Ahaz felt the touch of the royal scepter, and he rose on shaking knees. He did not wipe the dirt from his forehead and robes, for he understood who he was now—a pathetic puppet king, sworn to serve the Assyrians for the rest of his life. And if he rebelled or failed to send tribute, his fate would be the same as King Rezin's.

"Is it over now?" he asked Jephia pathetically. "Can I go back to my tent?"

Jephia shook his head. "The king invites you to a banquet in his honor. I'm afraid you can't refuse the invitation."

Through a maze of marble hallways, the Assyrians led the way inside King Rezin's former palace to a huge banquet hall, lavishly decorated with exquisite tapestries representing the many nations of the vast Assyrian Empire. Musicians sang and played their instruments, exotic dancers whirled in rhythm, while hundreds of naked slaves stood beside the laden tables, ready to serve the kings.

Ahaz found his seat at the lowest-ranking table. Meat dishes, fine breads, vegetables, and fruits of all kinds lay spread before him, but the food repulsed him. Haunted by the cries of the tortured men, he felt only an unquenchable thirst.

Near his table, two slaves poured wine into a huge laver while two more ground a mixture of leaves and seeds into a fine powder and stirred it into the wine. Ahaz longed for its familiar numbing power. When the slaves finally served it, he gulped down great draughts of it. The hovering slaves replenished his cup as fast as he emptied it.

It was meant to be an extravagant feast, but Ahaz couldn't enjoy it. He couldn't forget the horrors he had witnessed that day or the withering dread he had felt in the presence of the Assyrian king. A wave of nausea engulfed him, and he stared glumly at the linen tablecloth as the noise and merriment roared in his ears.

Gradually the wine began to take effect, and the room seemed to sway slowly with the music. Ahaz liked the sensation at first, but as he stared vacantly at the wall he was startled to see that the figures on the tapestries had somehow come to life and were dancing in front of him. He shut his eyes to blot out the strange image, but bright lights and flashing colors appeared before him in the darkness, swirling crazily, and he feared that his head would shatter into a thousand pieces.

He quickly opened his eyes but had trouble focusing them. As he fumbled for his glass of wine, his hand suddenly detached from his wrist and floated through the air toward it. He grabbed the glass with both hands and gulped another drink, fighting desperately to control his splintering mind. The glass slipped from his grasp and crashed to the floor.

"What's happening?" he cried, clutching his head. His voice seemed to come from a distant corner of the room.

"It's the wine," Jephia told him. "The Assyrians mix powerful drugs with it and allow the gods to take them on a journey into the world of the spirits. It is part of their worship."

Ahaz moaned. He didn't want to journey to the spiritual world. If he could journey anywhere, he would like it to be home. He covered his face with his hands, trying to recall Jerusalem's familiar sights—his palace, Solomon's Temple, the rock-strewn valleys and terraced hillsides surrounding the city. But in his vision the prophet Isaiah suddenly loomed before him, screaming, "You will be devoured by the sword!"

Ahaz uncovered his eyes, and the prophet vanished. His detached hand reached for the new glass the servants brought him, and he took another drink. "I'm losing my mind!" he groaned.

"It is useless to fight the power of the drugs," Jephia smiled. "Let the spirits carry you away, King Ahaz."

Ahaz realized Jephia was right. He yielded to the control of the drugged wine. As he did, his mind suddenly came into focus, and it seemed as if he could think more clearly than he ever had before. In a blinding flash of revelation, he understood Isaiah's words: the wealth of Judah would be devoured as he struggled to meet the Assyrian tribute demands, tribute that would fund the Assyrian sword.

He closed his eyes, and the prophet reappeared in a swirling flash of color. "The understanding of this message will bring sheer terror," Isaiah screamed at him. "The bed will be too short to stretch out on, the blanket too narrow to wrap around you."

Ahaz knew what that prophecy meant too. He opened his eyes, seeking to escape from the prophet's words in the only way he could: he drank the remaining contents of his cup.

Swaying and flashing, the room before him swirled as the potent mixture took effect. Then gradually, all the horrible events of the day began to fade and blur into a past that he could scarcely remember. His fears shrank to manageable proportions, and a wonderful feeling of euphoria overwhelmed him. He wanted that feeling to last forever. He wanted more wine.

As the waiting servants refilled his glass again and again, the only fear that troubled Ahaz was the fear that his cup might run dry.

11

Zechariah awoke from a deep sleep to find Hezekiah standing over him. "Grandpa . . . Grandpa," he called, shaking him.

He opened his eyes, blinking to focus them. "What is it, Son?"

"Grandpa, what's that noise? Listen." The sound of hammers ringing against stone drifted into the room from the courtyard below.

"It sounds like they're building something, Son. Sounds nearby too." He yawned, still fuzzy with sleep, and swung his feet to the floor. Hezekiah eyed his slow movements with the impatience of youth. "You don't have to wait for me, child. Go on—have a look. Tell me what you see."

Hezekiah darted to the window, tugging on the heavy curtains until they opened, then stood on his tiptoes and peered down into the courtyard.

"Grandpa, you're right!" he shouted. "They're building something—down there. Come and see."

Zechariah shuffled to the window and boosted Hezekiah for a better view.

"What are they making, Grandpa?"

"I have no idea."

They watched as workers removed paving stones from the center of the palace courtyard and dug a foundation. More workers labored to haul huge limestone blocks to the site. The base of the cleared area was small, but judging from the number of stones, the finished building was going to be tall. A tower, perhaps? Was Ahaz preparing to worship the heavenly bodies in addition to all the other gods he worshiped? Zechariah shivered.

"Oh—look how high the sun is already!" Zechariah suddenly exclaimed, pointing toward the Mount of Olives. "We'll have to hurry, or we'll be late for the morning sacrifice." He pulled his robe on and smoothed down his hair and beard, then helped Hezekiah finish dressing.

"Don't forget this, Grandpa." He handed Zechariah his prayer shawl. "Can we go see the new building first?"

"There's not enough time. We're late as it is."

They hurried through the palace hallways and out to the street. Zechariah pulled his prayer shawl over his shoulders as he walked. The sound of ringing hammers should have receded in the distance behind them, but as they walked up the hill, Zechariah was surprised to hear their sound in the Temple courtyard as well. It was a sound that definitely didn't belong there, and he began to jog, a trickle of fear running like sweat down his spine. As soon as he passed through the Temple gates, it was as if the earth had shifted from under him and the familiar landscape of the Temple's inner court had tilted askew.

"What are they doing, Grandpa?" Hezekiah asked, but Zechariah barely heard him.

Overnight, with sledges, pulleys, and a team of oxen, the altar of Yahweh had been moved from its God-ordained position in the courtyard. Now a huge, new altar was being constructed in its place. Zechariah hoped he was dreaming, that he would awaken to find everything returned to the way Solomon had built it 300 years ago.

But as he moved closer, he was horrified to see that the brass side panels for the new altar were decorated with figures of animals and idols and strange foreign symbols in blatant defiance of Yahweh's commandment against making images. In the center of each panel was the god Assur, standing astride a winged sun. Zechariah stared in horrified disbelief.

The presiding Levites and priests emerged from the Temple's side door in a frightened huddle, as if fearful of the wrath of God, and gathered around the altar of Yahweh that now stood on the north side of the courtyard.

Zechariah felt Hezekiah tugging on his sleeve. "Grandpa, why is it all changed?" His eyes were wide with fear.

"That's what I'm going to find out. Wait right here, Son." He left Hezekiah standing by the gate to the inner court and hurried over to the priest who was preparing for the morning sacrifice.

"What is that abomination doing in Yahweh's Temple?" he cried, pointing to the new altar being built. "Idolatry? Here? This is blasphemy! Who ordered this?"

The priest glanced around nervously and answered Zechariah in a hushed whisper. "King Ahaz did. He sent the plans for it from Damascus and ordered Uriah to build it before he returns."

"And Uriah agreed to this?" he asked in astonishment.

The priest shrugged helplessly. "All the sacrifices will be offered on the new altar when it's finished. Yahweh's altar will be used only for seeking guidance."

"He can't do that!" Zechariah shouted, and the men gathering to worship turned to stare at him. "Where's Uriah?" he demanded.

"Probably still at the palace—"

Zechariah strode back across the courtyard, through the gates, and down the hill to the palace. With every step he took, his shock transformed to anger.

"Grandpa? Grandpa, wait—what about the sacrifice?" Zechariah was only vaguely aware of Hezekiah trotting behind him.

When they reached the palace, Zechariah hurried

through the hallways to Uriah's chambers, his anger burning hotter every minute. He stopped to catch his breath when he reached Uriah's door and noticed Hezekiah staring up at him.

"Go to your room and wait for me, Son," he ordered as he pounded on the door. Hezekiah stepped back a few feet but remained in the hallway, watching.

Uriah's door opened a crack. "Yes? What do you want?" a servant asked, peering out.

Zechariah barged past him. "Where's Uriah? I want to speak with him. Where is he?"

Uriah appeared, followed by several wary servants. "What are you doing here, Zechariah?"

"I want to talk to you. Preferably alone." He gestured toward the beautiful young concubine who had followed Uriah into the room.

"He's probably drunk," Uriah muttered to his servants. "Take him back up to the Temple." He turned to leave as his servants closed in around Zechariah.

"I'm not drunk, Uriah. Call them off."

The high priest stared gravely at Zechariah, then motioned to his servants. "All right—let him go. Give us a few minutes alone." The two men waited in silence until the servants disappeared, their eyes locked in angry combat. "What do you want?" Uriah asked coldly.

"You have no right to do this!" Zechariah shouted. "And neither does Ahaz!"

"You'll have to tell me what you're talking about, Rabbi." Uriah's tone was condescending.

Zechariah struggled to contain his anger. "I'm talking about that . . . that . . . abomination you're building!"

"That 'abomination,' as you call it, is actually quite ingenious. The Babylonians invented it to keep track of the time." He gestured to the construction in the palace courtyard, just visible outside his window. "The tower will have stairs that spiral down the side, and as the sun moves higher or lower in the sky, the tower will cast a shadow on the stairs. Each stair represents an increment of time—"

"I don't care about that! I'm talking about the heathen altar you're building in Yahweh's Temple!"

"I don't need to explain my decisions to you."

"I am a Levite, Uriah. And what you do in Yahweh's Temple is my concern." He stared up at the tall priest unflinchingly, and Uriah's expression softened slightly with respect.

"Listen," he sighed, spreading his huge palms wide as he attempted to placate Zechariah. "I'm trying to centralize our religion at the Temple. The king has altars all over the city, and it's confusing to the people. The new altar will draw everyone back to the Temple—"

"To worship idols? In Yahweh's holy place? This time you've gone too far! You're bringing idolatry right into the Temple!"

"Only at first. Look—you know as well as I do that hardly anyone comes to the Temple anymore. The morning and evening sacrifices are poorly attended. But if we can draw people back, eventually they will come to see Yahweh as supreme over their idols. I'm doing it for the good of the Temple."

Zechariah slowly shook his head. "Maybe you can convince the others to listen to you, but not me. No, Uriah. You're lying to them and to yourself." They glared at each other until finally Uriah looked away.

"I can't tell King Ahaz what to do," he said quietly. "He ordered me to build the altar. I have to do whatever he says."

"I thought that was why you took this position—so you could teach him Yahweh's laws."

"I'm trying to. But I need more time."

"You'll never change Ahaz by working *for* him. You have to fight *against* him. Take a stand, Uriah. Show him he's wrong. You must resign."

"Resign?" Uriah gave a short laugh and began pacing

nervously in front of Zechariah. "And then what? He'd make me resign as high priest of the Temple too. Then maybe I could take up farming? Or serve as priest in some remote village out in the desert somewhere? No. I'm not going to resign. Not now."

"Not after you've tasted luxury," Zechariah finished for him. Uriah stopped pacing and glared at him.

"That has nothing to do with it."

"Doesn't it? You can't lie to me, Uriah. I know better than anyone else what you're going through. I've lived here too—remember?"

Uriah looked away. "Yes, I remember."

"And we're very much alike, you know: the same drive, the same burning ambition to succeed. Yes, I understand you very well. You've worked long and hard to get where you are, and now that you're at the top you sometimes have to do things that compromise your faith. Believe me—I know. But you can't go back. It's a long way down to where you've crawled up from, isn't it?—a long way down. And when you hit the bottom again, you're afraid you'll shatter into a thousand pieces, like I did. So rather than fall, you'll make a few concessions to your faith. A little here, a little there, and every time you compromise, something inside your spirit dies a little."

"This is nonsense." Uriah folded his arms across his broad chest, but he didn't look at Zechariah.

"Is it? Can you honestly stand there and tell me you didn't die inside when you watched those children burn to death? Because if you can, then it's already too late. You're already dead."

Uriah stalked away to stare out the open window, but when he spoke, his voice was so soft Zechariah could barely hear him.

"Please. Go away and leave me alone."

"Uriah, resign!—now, before it's too late. Make them stop building this altar. Help me oppose Ahaz's idolatry."

Uriah swiftly turned to face Zechariah. "Are you forgetting that Ahaz is the king? He'll have you executed."

"Yahweh dealt with King Uzziah, and He'll deal with Ahaz too. But you'll face Yahweh's judgment along with the king if you compromise with him. Believe me—I know what I'm talking about."

As the old man gazed at his former student's troubled features, he sensed the conflict raging in his heart. But then, even as he watched, Uriah's face hardened again. His jaws locked as he thrust his chin forward defiantly, and he seemed immovable, as if carved from stone.

"I'm not going to become a fanatic, Zechariah. I can do more for Yahweh here, in a position of authority. I know how to handle Ahaz. That's where you went wrong. You didn't know how to control King Uzziah."

"If you have so much control, then put a stop to this altar."

"I've already explained it to you. The altar will draw the people back to the Temple, back to Yahweh. I don't see it as a threat. Why are you so resistant to change?"

It seemed to Zechariah that the high priest's heart, like his countenance, had turned to stone. He shook his head.

"I thought I could reach you. I thought I could make you see the truth. But I guess it's too late. All this has blinded you—dulled your senses." He gestured to Uriah's opulent living quarters with a heavy sigh. "I'm not sure I would have listened to the truth either," he added, almost to himself.

They stared coldly at each other for several moments, knowing that neither one would give in. Then as Zechariah turned to leave, he saw Hezekiah standing by the open door listening, and his anger returned. If Ahaz and Uriah continued to rebel against the God of their fathers, his grandson would have no future, no nation to reign over. Zechariah knew it was up to him to stop them. He gathered Hezekiah into his arms, then turned to point an accusing finger at the high priest.

"You're serving the wrong king, Uriah."

—◈—

A week after his confrontation with Uriah, Zechariah awoke with the firm conviction that he must do the will of God. As the shofar announced the morning sacrifice, he donned his Levitical robes, unworn for many months, and placed the turban on his head.

"Grandpa, why are you wearing that kind of robe?" Hezekiah asked as he watched him dress.

"This is what Levites must wear when we serve in the Temple, Son."

"But you said we wouldn't go to the Temple anymore until they got rid of the new altar."

"I know I did. Come here, Hezekiah. We need to talk." Zechariah crouched beside him and put his arm around Hezekiah's shoulder. "The men who put that altar in Yahweh's Temple have done a very evil thing. And I made a promise to Yahweh that I would speak against such evils and teach transgressors God's ways. Do you understand?"

"I guess so."

"Now that your father is back from Damascus, he is planning a special sacrifice this morning on the new altar. What he's about to do is wrong. So I must keep my promise to Yahweh and tell the king and all the other men of Judah that it's wrong."

"Can I come too, Grandpa?"

"No, Son—not this time."

"Please? I'll be real quiet. No one will know I'm there—"

"No," he said sternly. "You must promise me that you will stay here. Promise?"

"OK," he answered reluctantly. "I promise."

"Good boy."

"Grandpa? When you're done telling them, will you come back here to teach me my lessons?"

Zechariah hesitated. "Well, your father is very unpredictable. I'm not sure how he will react—"

"Please, Grandpa?"

Zechariah hugged him tightly. "Yes, of course I'll be back. I may be a little bit late, but I'll be back."

"I love you, Grandpa."

Zechariah held him close a moment longer. "And I love you too." He slowly rose to his feet and touched Hezekiah's cheek. "I must go now or I'll be late."

The dew covering the pavement stones dampened the hem of Zechariah's robes as he hurried up the hill to the Temple and through the gates to the inner courtyard. The other Levites and priests bustled around, making sure everything was in order as Uriah, dressed in the mitre and ephod of the high priest, supervised. Avoiding him, Zechariah headed around the perimeter of the courtyard to where the Levitical singers had assembled on the Temple porch. They stared at him in surprise as he approached in his ceremonial robes.

"Zechariah—what are you doing here?" his friend Shimei asked as he joined them.

"I'm taking part in the sacrifice today."

"But aren't you past the age of retirement?"

"Yes. But I'm going to sing anyway."

He offered no other explanation, and no one pressed him further as the blast of the trumpets signaled the arrival of King Ahaz. He arrived by the processional route through the main gate, and a great crowd of people swarmed behind him, filling the courtyards. A hushed whisper crackled through the assembly like a grass fire as they caught their first glimpse of the magnificent new altar. Then the whisper died away as the Levites began to sing.

While Ahaz led the way to the brazen laver, Zechariah watched the ritual closely, waiting for the right moment to speak. He continued to sing the service as the priests slew the sacrifices and the men assembled around the new heathen altar. At first Zechariah saw no major changes. Uriah conducted the ritual the same way he had on Yahweh's altar.

But when the time came for Uriah to ascend the ramp with the sacrifice, King Ahaz stepped forward from the crowd and walked to the top of the altar, followed by Uriah and the priests, carrying the offerings.

"Dear God, help us all!" someone beside Zechariah whispered.

Shimei stopped singing. "Is he going to make his own offering?" he asked in amazement.

Zechariah began to tremble. "No, he isn't," he told them calmly. "Because I'm going to stop him."

Shimei grabbed his arm. "Have you lost your mind?"

"No, I made a promise to Yahweh."

He shook free of Shimei's grasp and pushed his way to the front of the Temple porch. The singing stopped as Zechariah's deep voice carried across the courtyard with authority.

"King Ahaz, stop! What you're about to do is a grave sin. Listen to me, all you men of Jerusalem. Only the anointed priests of Yahweh can come before Him to present sacrifices. They are the intermediaries between God and man. That's why Yahweh brought judgment on King Uzziah. And He'll bring judgment on you too, if you commit this act."

Ahaz turned to Uriah, his face red with rage. "Get him out of here!" The high priest quickly descended the altar stairs, signaling to the Temple guards—but Zechariah continued to shout.

"Yahweh will not tolerate this blasphemous altar in His holy Temple. He has commanded: 'You shall not make for yourself an idol in the form of anything in heaven above or on the earth beneath or in the waters below. You shall not bow down to them or worship them . . .'"

The guards reached Zechariah first and seized him by

the arms. "What are you doing?—let go of me!" he cried, struggling as they dragged him down the steps of the porch. But before they could remove him from the court-yard, Isaiah pushed through the crowd and stood at the base of the altar.

"I will call on Uriah the priest and Zechariah the Levite as witnesses," he shouted. He unrolled a scroll and held it aloft for all to see. It read "Quick to the Plunder—Swift to the Spoil."

"When the prophetess conceived and gave birth to a son, the Lord said to me, 'Name him Quick to the Plun-der—Swift to the Spoil. Before he can say papa or mama, the riches of Damascus and the plunder of Samaria will be taken away by the King of Assyria.' These two witnesses can testify that they heard me speak this prophecy the day my son was brought here to the Temple for his circumci-sion. My son is still just a baby, and you have seen with your own eyes, King Ahaz, the fulfillment of that prophe-cy."

Ahaz did not speak or move, but seemed to shrivel where he stood, like a piece of fat in the fire.

"Now Yahweh speaks another prophecy to His peo-ple: 'Because this people has rejected the gently flowing waters of Shiloah and rejoices over Rezin and the son of Remaliah, therefore the Lord is about to bring against them the mighty floodwaters of the River—the king of Assyria with all his pomp. It will overflow all its channels, run over all its banks and sweep on into Judah, swirling over it, passing through it and reaching up to the neck.'"

He pointed his scroll at Assur's brazen image on the new altar. "Its outspread wings will cover the breadth of your land."

The courtyard was silent and tense except for the crackling of the altar fire. Ahaz, who had stood stunned, suddenly shook himself, as if coming to his senses.

"Somebody stop him!" he shouted. "Stop him!"

Isaiah stuffed the scroll inside his robe and vanished into the crowd before Ahaz could descend the altar steps.

"I said stop him!" he sputtered. But the murmuring crowd drowned out his words. He drew his robes around himself as if they could protect him from Isaiah's words and stormed across the courtyard, out of the Temple gates. Uriah raced after him, shoving people out of his way.

"Your Majesty, wait—we haven't finished the sacrifice!" Uriah called.

———◈———

King Ahaz, shaking uncontrollably, didn't stop as he hurried down the royal walkway to his palace. When Uriah finally caught up to him, Ahaz turned on him angrily.

"The next time my sacrifices are interrupted, I'm holding you responsible. I never want to see Isaiah or hear his words again. Do you hear me? Never again!"

"I'm sorry—"

"And you'd better get your priests and Levites under control too, or I'll have to find a new high priest!"

"I'm sorry, Your Majesty. I don't know why Zechariah—"

"Get rid of him." Ahaz shuddered as he recalled Zechariah's words. He had been a child when his grandfather Uzziah had been stricken with leprosy, but he remembered the day, and his father's grief and anger, very well. His father, King Jotham, had never worshiped in Yahweh's Temple again.

"Zechariah's a fool, and I never want to see him again."

"But he's your father-in-law—"

"I know who he is. Get rid of him."

"I'm sorry about what happened today, Your Majesty. I'll take care of everything. We'll hold another sacrifice tomorrow, and I assure you nothing will go wrong."

But Ahaz wasn't listening. Isaiah's vivid description

of the deluge of Assyrian soldiers had overwhelmed him, and he felt as if he were drowning. He had rejected Isaiah's advice at the Gihon spring; he had ignored his warnings before leaving for Damascus. Both times Isaiah's prophecies had been fulfilled. What if he was right this time?

Fear paralyzed Ahaz. In a nightmare vision he saw Jerusalem besieged by thousands of Assyrian troops, battering rams mercilessly pounding the city walls, his nobles and advisers impaled alive on stakes in the Gihon Valley. And he saw himself being flayed alive like King Rezin. He knew only one way to escape from this vision: he fled to his chambers and ordered some wine, mixed the Assyrian way—to help him forget.

—◆—

As the king hurried back to his palace, the milling crowd filtered out of the courtyard in stunned confusion.

"It's over—let me go," Zechariah told the guards. After they released him, he watched the people leaving and felt a sense of satisfaction and victory. He had done the right thing. This time Yahweh had won.

Elated, he returned to his rooms in the Temple, changed his clothes, then folded his ceremonial robes carefully and placed them on his bed. Today was probably the last time he would ever wear them. But he had stopped the king. He had kept his promise to God.

He sighed and thought back over his long career as a Levite. There were many things he was ashamed of, many things he regretted, but Yahweh had forgiven him and entrusted him with other duties now. He must teach Hezekiah.

He would say good-bye to all his friends, then move out of the Temple for good. He could not serve Yahweh in a Temple polluted with idolatry. He left his robes on the bed and quickly rummaged through the room, hurriedly packing his personal belongings.

As he stuffed the last of his scrolls and keepsakes into

a small wooden chest, he glanced around the room, dismayed at the mess he had made with his hurried packing. But he had no time to straighten up. He had promised Hezekiah he would return for his lessons. That was his most important task.

Suddenly his door flew open, and Uriah filled the doorframe, his dark face unnaturally pale, his anger raging dangerously out of control.

"Your actions at the sacrifice have outraged the king! Maybe you were once a highly respected rabbi, but that gives you no right to interrupt the sacred observances when you feel like it!"

Uriah towered over him like a stone giant, but Zechariah remained calm. "I have sworn an oath to be faithful to Yahweh, and I will keep that oath, speaking out whenever my God is blasphemed."

"Why start now?" Uriah asked in exasperation. "Why all of a sudden? Why didn't you protest when Ahaz sacrificed to Molech? You were there, Zechariah."

"I know. And I'm ashamed of what I have done, and what I haven't done, in the past." He stepped closer to Uriah, defiantly. "But my past is forgiven. And I will no longer stand by while you lead the entire nation into idolatry. I won't let you do it. I will join with Isaiah and preach against what you are doing every chance I get."

The muscles in Uriah's face rippled as he clenched his jaw. "You will never get that chance, Zechariah, and neither will your friend Isaiah," he said with quiet control.

"Are you threatening us?" he asked in surprise. Uriah didn't answer. "When did we become enemies, Uriah? You were my finest student. My protégé. When did you join the opposing side?"

"Rabbi, I have great respect for you . . . this is very hard . . ." Again, Zechariah sensed the struggle in Uriah's soul. "Look—we don't have to be enemies. You're entitled to hold opinions that are different from mine. Promise me that you won't cause any more public disruptions, and you'll be free to believe whatever you like in private."

For the first time that day Zechariah felt fear. "And if I don't promise?"

"Then you'll be in rebellion against the king."

Zechariah knew Uriah was begging for a promise of silence, and he knew Ahaz would go to extreme measures to guarantee that silence. But he also knew that he could never turn his back on God's forgiveness. He remembered his little grandson Eliab and knew that he feared the wrath of God more than Ahaz's threats. He slowly shook his head.

"I can't promise to be silent."

"Then you're a *fool!*" Uriah's stony efforts to control his rage began to crack. "I'm warning you: the king won't stand for it!"

"He'll have to kill me to silence me."

"That's what he's planning! Don't you understand? Why are you being so stubborn, Rabbi? Give up! You can't possibly win against the king!"

"Maybe not, but at least I'll die with a clear conscience. Will you?" He stared up at the high priest without flinching, and Uriah's rage boiled over.

"Curse you, Zechariah! Why can't you forget your holy crusade for Yahweh and go back to this?" He scooped up an empty wineskin lying on the littered floor and shoved it into Zechariah's hands, then stalked from the room, slamming the door behind him. A cloud of dust filtered down from the plastered ceiling.

The confrontation left Zechariah shaken. He sat on his bed for a long time, staring at the wineskin and replaying the scene as if he could somehow alter it and convince Uriah of his error.

Then he remembered Hezekiah. Zechariah had promised to return to the palace hours ago. Lifting his trunk by one end, he dragged it across the room. But when he opened the door, two Temple guards stood in his path.

"What are you doing here?" he asked in surprise.

"I'm sorry, Rabbi, but we have orders to make sure you remain in your rooms."

"Orders? What are you talking about? I have business at the palace." He tried to push past them, but they stood firm.

"Uriah's orders. Rabbi, please. You must cooperate with us. We can't let you leave."

Dazed, Zechariah stared at them in disbelief, then finally went back inside and closed the door, unable to accept the reality of what was happening to him. He had never expected Uriah to carry out his threat so soon.

God had given him a second chance, and he had been obedient. Surely God would honor and protect him for his faithfulness. Why was he being held prisoner?

He thought again of Hezekiah. He had scarcely begun teaching him God's Law. There was so much the boy had to learn. And he loved him. Dear God, how he loved him!

But with two guards outside his door, there was no way Zechariah could go to Hezekiah. He picked up the empty wineskin and hurled it against the door in frustration. It burst at the seams, splattering the remaining dregs of crimson wine across the floor and walls. Then Zechariah sank to his knees and buried his head in his hands.

"Why, Yahweh?" he cried. "Why? How have I failed You?"

Zechariah was still praying hours later when he heard the door open. He looked up to see his friend Hilkiah, the little merchant, standing in the doorway uncertainly. The dark forms of the guards loomed behind him in the passageway.

"Zechariah?—how are you feeling, my friend?" His round, jovial face was furrowed with concern.

Zechariah scrambled to his feet. "Hilkiah, please come in," he begged.

Hilkiah eyed the guards briefly. "All right—but they

told me I can stay for only a minute." He closed the door. "Zechariah, I think you should know . . ." He glanced around uncomfortably at the disheveled room and the puddle of splattered wine. "Uriah has told everyone that you've gone insane."

Zechariah was stunned. "Insane? Is that what he's saying? Because I dared to speak out against his idolatry? You don't believe him, do you?"

"No, no, no! Of course not! You're my friend. I should believe Uriah? May the Holy One strike me dead! All my life I've been faithful to Yahweh—blessed be His name. You know that, Zechariah. I hate what they've done to His Holy Temple, and I'm proud of you for speaking out, my friend. I'm just sorry you're here. Such a place! I've come to ask how I can help you. Is there anything you need?"

"Yes, please!" Zechariah clutched Hilkiah's arm in desperation, but he knew he must force himself to stay calm. He loosened his grasp. "Please—my grandson Hezekiah is waiting for me at the palace. I told him I'd come back, but I don't know how long Uriah is going to keep me here. Can you deliver a message for me?"

Hilkiah's eyes widened with fear. "To the palace? Ah, my friend, I don't know how I can do that. I don't have access to the prince. And who can I trust there? I could end up getting you in even worse trouble. Please—I can't promise something like that, Zechariah. I'm sorry."

Zechariah sighed and rubbed his eyes. "You're right. Never mind."

"I'm sorry. I'm so sorry."

"No. It was impossible. I guess there's nothing else you can do for me. Go home, my friend, before they lock you up too." As Hilkiah opened the door, the two soldiers glanced inside.

"Wait a minute!" Zechariah shouted. He quickly crossed the room and leaned against the door to close it. "Listen," he whispered urgently. "You must get a message to Isaiah. He's in danger as well. Have they arrested him yet?"

"No, I don't think so. He disappeared before they could."

"Then you must reach him and warn him. He has to leave Jerusalem. They will silence him too, the next time he prophesies."

"Well, I'll try—" Hilkiah looked doubtful.

"Hilkiah, please! Swear to me that you'll do it!"

"Very well, my friend. With the Holy One's help, I will go to Isaiah and warn him . . . somehow . . ."

"Thank you, Hilkiah. May God go with you."

"Shalom, my friend."

They quickly embraced, then the door closed behind Hilkiah with a hollow thud. Once again, Zechariah was alone with his doubts.

Why, Yahweh? he whispered. *Why?*

12

Hilkiah rolled over on his bed, changing positions for what seemed like the hundredth time that night. His tired body craved sleep, but his mind refused to be silent. The night was oppressively hot and sticky, his tunic soaked with sweat, and he felt as if he could scarcely breathe. At last he gave up trying to sleep and crept up to the roof, hoping for a cool breeze.

Hilkiah's house, among the city's wealthiest homes, stood high on the city mount below the palace. It clung to the hillside, and from his rooftop Hilkiah looked down on the roofs of the other houses from a dizzying height.

As the full moon shone high above the surrounding mountains, Hilkiah saw the clear outline of the Temple wall on the hill above him. He groaned and looked away, knowing why he couldn't sleep. Every time he closed his eyes, he saw his friend Zechariah pleading with him to warn Isaiah. Hilkiah had promised to do it, and he knew he would never sleep peacefully until he did. But how could he? He pulled on his beard in frustration.

"Ah, God of Abraham, I can't," he whispered.

He wondered if Zechariah realized what a dangerous thing he had asked him to do. Visiting Zechariah at the Temple had been risky enough, but if he was seen with Isaiah now, he could be accused of conspiracy. His own life would be in danger.

Hilkiah believed that Zechariah and Isaiah were right.

The heathen altar didn't belong in Yahweh's Temple. And he knew he should have the courage to fight against it like they did. But how would his young son Eliakim survive if his father were imprisoned in the Temple?—or executed as a traitor to the king?

A year ago during the hot, sultry summer months, a fever had crept through the city from house to house, stealing away Hilkiah's beloved wife and two youngest children. All that he and Eliakim had left were each other.

He looked up at the Temple again. In a few hours it would be time for the morning sacrifice on the new altar. Imprisoned in the Temple, Zechariah couldn't stop the ceremony this time or prevent King Ahaz from presenting his own offering. But Isaiah would probably try, and the guards would be waiting for him. He wouldn't slip away this time. Hilkiah thought of his son sleeping peacefully in the house below and shivered involuntarily. Then he had another thought. Isaiah had a family as well—two small sons with strange prophetic names. He took a deep breath and exhaled slowly.

"God of Abraham, help me." He turned to the stairs that led from the roof to the street, determined to warn Isaiah.

"Where are you going, Abba?" The sudden voice startled him.

"Oh, Eliakim!" he gasped. "What are you doing up here in the middle of the night?"

"I couldn't get to sleep," he frowned. Eliakim's thick black hair was tousled and damp with sweat.

"I know. I know. It's hot, isn't it?" He rested his hand on his son's shoulder, and his heart swelled with love. A slender, handsome boy, Eliakim was nearly as tall as Hilkiah. "Why don't you get a mat and you can sleep up here?"

"It's not because of the heat." Tears sprang to Eliakim's dark eyes, and he twisted away to hide them from his father.

"What's wrong, Son?"

"I'm mad about what happened yesterday." He drew

a breath and exhaled angrily. "It wasn't fair. They ruined my birthday."

"I'm sorry, Son. I didn't realize you were so upset." Hilkiah tried to draw him into his arms, but Eliakim pulled away.

"I'm finally a man, finally old enough to go to the sacrifices at the Temple with the other men, and those two crazy men ruined the whole thing!"

"Now wait just a minute!" Hilkiah said sharply. "Those two men were right. They *should* have stopped the sacrifice. What the king was about to do was *wrong*. He's not supposed to offer his own sacrifice. According to the Torah, only the priests do that."

Eliakim looked skeptical. "Well, none of the other priests tried to stop him—not even the high priest."

"Grown-ups don't always do the right thing, Eliakim—even when they know what the Torah says." Hilkiah recalled his indecision a few moments ago and winced. "Anyway, I was going to tell you in the morning, but I may as well tell you now: we won't be going to the sacrifices at the Temple anymore."

"Abba! No! Why not?" Eliakim gazed in stricken despair.

"I'm sorry. I know how much you looked forward to being old enough to go, but they've brought idols into the Temple, and we can't take part in idolatry."

Eliakim's tears threatened to spill onto his cheeks. "But aren't the sacrifices important? Aren't we supposed to go?"

"Yes, they're important. But we're supposed to go out of love for the Eternal One—blessed be His name—and to worship Him as the one true God. Otherwise, it's just an empty ritual. When they put that pagan altar in His Temple, the Holy One of Israel withdrew His presence from that place. It's a heathen ritual now, a meaningless ceremony to false gods. We have no reason to go anymore."

"But I want to go! It's not fair!" Eliakim fought back tears. He was trying to be a man, but he was also a very disappointed child.

"We must always say our morning and evening prayers, but we'll say them at home from now on—just you and me."

"It's not the same thing. Can't we please go once in a while?—just so I can see what it's like?"

"No, Son; we can't," Hilkiah said sternly. Eliakim's reaction crushed him. He had tried to teach him what the Torah said, had tried to instill in him a love for God, but Eliakim seemed interested only in the outward rituals at the Temple. He wondered where he had failed.

"Eliakim, listen to me. It takes more than a birthday to make you a man. If you always go along with the crowd even when they're wrong, you're a coward, not a man, no matter how old you are. But if you really believe that something is wrong, then you must have the courage to stand up for what you believe. That's what those two men did yesterday, and that's what I'm trying to do. Do you understand?"

Eliakim didn't reply. He kicked at the packed clay rooftop with his toe.

"Listen, Son: the Levite who spoke out yesterday is Zechariah, an old friend of mine. Do you know what happened to him after the sacrifice? He's being held under arrest at the Temple, and they're telling everyone he's crazy. He could probably promise to keep quiet about his beliefs, and maybe they'd let him go free. But I know my friend, and he won't do it. That takes courage, Son. That's being a man."

Eliakim looked up at him, and his voice trembled slightly. "Are you going to start protesting, Abba?"

"No. I don't have the authority and influence that Zechariah has. It would do no good for me to protest." Although he could justify his decision, Hilkiah felt ashamed of himself. "But there *is* something I *can* do that might help."

"What, Abba?"

"The other man who spoke out yesterday is Isaiah. He was born to the house of David, but I believe he is also an anointed prophet of the Eternal One. His prophecies have been a thorn in the king's flesh for a long time, but today Ahaz reached the end of his patience. They're going to arrest him the next time he prophesies. Zechariah begged me to warn Isaiah. He must leave Jerusalem."

"Let me warn him, Abba!"

"Absolutely not! It's too dangerous."

"Then it's dangerous for you too."

"Yes, but I'm an adult—"

"So am I!" Eliakim shouted.

Hilkiah felt trapped. If he convinced his son of the risk involved, the boy might beg him not to go. But he couldn't let Eliakim do it. "I'm the one who promised to go, Son," he said at last.

"Abba, I'm not afraid. Please, let me show you that I'm a man. Let me do something as an adult. You said I should have courage, right? Please—let me go."

"I don't know—"

"I'm smaller than you, and I can run faster and hide in the shadows better. Besides, they wouldn't arrest a boy, would they?"

Hilkiah knew his son had a point. And he knew that Eliakim longed to prove he was a man. He hesitated until the boy made his final, decisive argument.

"Abba, you taught me that the God of Abraham would always protect me if I did His will. Won't He protect me now too?"

Hilkiah drew his son into his arms. Maybe he hadn't failed after all. Maybe his son had learned about faith instead of ritual.

———◆———

Eliakim walked at a brisk pace, afraid that his courage

would disappear unless he hurried. He had never walked alone through the city at night, and every strange new sound startled him. Every familiar landmark looked eerily unfamiliar. Once he grew used to the hollow sounds of his sandals slapping against the paving stones, though, a sense of pride filled him. He was finally proving he was a man.

The full moon illuminated the narrow, twisting streets, and Eliakim had no trouble following his father's directions to the quiet street where the prophet lived. A dog barked in a nearby courtyard, and he jumped, then glanced around furtively, certain that his pounding heart could be heard. He paused in the shadows to catch his breath, then crept carefully up to the last house on the street—Isaiah's house.

Eliakim wondered why Isaiah didn't live in the palace or at least among the houses of royalty high on the hill if he was from the house of King David. Instead, Isaiah lived in a humble stone dwelling stuffed so tightly against the others that it couldn't even catch a cool breeze.

When he reached the front gate, Eliakim saw the faint glow of an oil lamp inside and wondered why it had been left to burn all night. He rapped lightly on the gate and waited, hoping someone would answer before his knocking awakened the neighbors. A moment later the door opened, and Eliakim recognized Isaiah, the man who had read the scroll at the sacrifice.

"I am Eliakim, son of Hilkiah, the merchant," he said breathlessly. "And I have a message for you from Zechariah the Levite."

Isaiah didn't seem surprised to see Eliakim. He nodded curtly in greeting and led the way through the gate, crossed a tiny courtyard, and entered the prophet's one-room house.

On one side of the room stood a small cooking hearth cluttered with clay pots, and beside it a single, homemade table littered with scrolls and the dimly burning oil lamp. Across the room on straw mats Isaiah's wife slept with their baby son nestled close to her. Another child slept on a mat by her feet. Eliakim thought of his own mother and younger brothers who had died, and he swallowed hard.

"Please sit down." Isaiah motioned to a wooden stool beside the table. "Can I offer you anything?" He gazed intently at Eliakim, and his clear, penetrating eyes made Eliakim feel as if he stood before him naked.

"No, thank you, Rabbi. I've only come to bring you the message from Zechariah." Nearly breathless and tongue-tied, he was awed by the presence that seemed to surround the prophet, and he hoped that his words sounded coherent. "Zechariah is under arrest at the Temple because of what happened yesterday at the sacrifice."

Isaiah frowned slightly but said nothing.

"Zechariah says that you are in danger too and that you shouldn't prophesy anymore. He said you must leave Jerusalem right away."

Isaiah nodded slowly. "Yes, Zechariah's right," he whispered. "Yahweh is so faithful."

Isaiah's reaction puzzled Eliakim. After his father's speech about standing up for what you believe in, he had expected Isaiah to reject the warning. He was disappointed that the prophet gave in so easily.

Isaiah rested his hand on Eliakim's shoulder. "You were sent by Yahweh, and I thank you for coming. I also heard the voice of God warning me to leave, but I've been sitting here all night arguing with Him. I'm not afraid of Ahaz. And I'm willing to face imprisonment like Zechariah for Yahweh's sake."

Eliakim glanced at Isaiah's sleeping family.

"Yahweh knows every breath they take," the prophet said, as if reading his thoughts. "If I left now, I would appear to be a coward, afraid that my God couldn't protect me or my family. But I'm not afraid. That's why I've been wrestling with God all night. A few minutes ago I prayed, asking Him to show me that leaving Jerusalem was His will. And then you came."

Eliakim stared in amazement. Isaiah's intimacy with Yahweh seemed awesome. Hilkiah talked to the God of Abraham all the time, but as far as Eliakim knew, God had never talked back. Isaiah sounded as if he had regular conversations with the Holy One, and Eliakim wondered how he had attained such a relationship with Him. He remembered pouting about not being allowed to go to the Temple to see the heathen rituals and felt ashamed.

The baby stirred and started making sucking noises in his sleep. Isaiah looked over at him and sighed.

"So I guess I'll be leaving Jerusalem." He glanced around the room as if mentally starting to pack. "But it isn't fear that makes me leave. Yahweh has other plans for me. I know that I will be starting a community of prophets, to train and teach some of the younger ones, but beyond that—well, Yahweh will show me."

Eliakim stood up and edged toward the door. Hours seemed to have passed since he left home. "Rabbi, I should go now. Abba will be worried."

As Isaiah led him through the door and across the small courtyard, Eliakim wanted desperately to apologize for wanting to go to the Temple for the wrong reasons. He felt certain that the next time Isaiah talked to Yahweh, He would tell the prophet what kind of boy he really was. But Eliakim couldn't find the right words to say.

When they reached the street, Isaiah rested his hand on Eliakim's shoulder and fixed his searching gaze on him once again.

"Eliakim." He pronounced the name slowly, respectfully. "Your name means 'Yahweh will establish.'" Then the tone of Isaiah's voice changed to one of authority and power, and Eliakim's heart began to pound.

"In that day I will summon my servant, Eliakim son of

Hilkiah. . . . He will be a father to those who live in Jerusalem and to the house of Judah. I will place on his shoulder the key to the house of David; what he opens no one can shut, and what he shuts no one can open. I will drive him like a peg into a firm place; he will be a seat of honor for the house of his father. All the glory of his family will hang on him."

Then, much to Eliakim's surprise, the prophet embraced him warmly. "Shalom, Eliakim. May Yahweh's peace go with you."

"And with you, Rabbi," Eliakim breathed.

Hezekiah sat cross-legged on the carpet, gazing sadly out his window at the new Babylonian clock tower in the palace courtyard. He idly counted the steps that spiraled up the side until they disappeared from view behind the tower, then counted them as they spiraled down the other side again. He had watched all morning as the shadow slowly inched its way up to where it now stood on the top step. Another lonely morning had come and gone, and still his grandfather had not returned.

"Hello there. Are you Hezekiah?" He heard a cheerful voice behind him and quickly turned around.

A tall, lanky stranger with wavy black hair, dark skin, and a pleasant smile stood gazing down at him. He appeared to be in his early 30s, yet he had no beard, and his clothes were in a style Hezekiah had never seen before. He carried an untidy pile of scrolls that threatened to topple from his arms any minute, and Hezekiah remembered all the scrolls in the Temple library. Maybe this stranger would take him to his grandfather.

"Yes, I'm Hezekiah," he answered hopefully.

"Well, I am Shebna," he said with a slight accent. "I am very glad to meet you. I have been hired by King Ahaz to be your tutor." Shebna smiled broadly, showing a straight, even row of white teeth. Hezekiah did not return his smile. The stranger had been sent by King Ahaz, not by his grandfather after all.

"I already have a teacher," he said at last.

"You do? But King Ahaz assured me that I was your very first tutor."

"No, my grandpa's teaching me. I'm waiting here for him."

"Oh? King Ahaz did not mention anything about your grandfather. What is it that your grandfather teaches you?"

"About Yahweh and His Torah. I'm learning to recite the Shema too. Do you want to hear it?" He wanted to impress this stranger with what a good job his grandfather was already doing, so he would leave.

"All right," Shebna nodded, without enthusiasm.

Hezekiah sat up very straight, concentrating on the words. "Hear, O Israel. Yahweh is our God—Yahweh alone. Love Yahweh your God with all your heart and with all your soul and with all your strength."

"Your grandfather has taught you well."

"He's a Levite," Hezekiah answered proudly.

"Hmm. I see. So has he taught you about anything else besides Yahweh and the Torah?"

Hezekiah looked puzzled. "Well, no—"

"That is good. I like to teach my students in my own way, from the very beginning. And now I am going to be your teacher."

Hezekiah wanted his grandfather. His fear and suspicion heightened. "Will we learn about Yahweh?"

The tutor looked uncomfortable. "No. I am not a Jew. I am Egyptian. I do not believe in Yahweh."

Hezekiah's eyes grew wide. "Do you worship Molech?"

"No, I do not worship Molech either—how did we ever get into this?" he muttered. "Look, I am going to be very honest with you right from the start. I do not believe in any gods at all, even the gods of my own nation, Egypt. I think they are all up here—," he said, tapping his high forehead, "in the minds of men. People make up gods to explain all the things they cannot understand. For example, if there is a drought, they say, 'The gods must be angry.' But I believe that there are droughts simply because it has not rained. That is all. I do not believe in the supernatural. I seek knowledge, not myths."

Hezekiah glowered at him. "What is the matter?" Shebna asked him. "Why do you make that face?"

"Yahweh is real! He's like the wind—that's why you can't see Him. My grandpa didn't make him up!"

"Very well. We will not talk of Yahweh anymore. King Ahaz knows all about my views on religion, but I am not here to teach you about that." He smiled his broad, even smile again. "Would you like to start your lessons today? I am anxious to see what kind of a student you will be. Can you read?" Hezekiah shook his head. "Would you like to learn how?"

"I want my grandpa." Tears welled in his eyes.

Shebna gave a forced smile and sprawled out on the floor beside him, dumping his scrolls in a heap. "I will make you a bargain, Hezekiah. First, you answer a question for me; then I will answer one for you. Is that fair enough?"

Before Hezekiah could answer, Shebna pulled a scroll from the pile and unrolled it. "This scroll tells a story, but you must first learn to read. Then you will know what that story is." He produced a small clay tablet and carved on it with a stylus. "This is the word for 'house.' See? Now, you look at this story and see if you can find 'house' anywhere on the scroll."

Shebna pushed the scroll and the tablet across the floor in front of Hezekiah. For a moment he wasn't sure if he should read it or not, afraid he might betray his grandfather. But the scrolls in the Temple library had fascinated him, and he wanted to unlock their mysteries. In the end his curiosity won, and he studied the scroll. It was a jumble of strange markings, and he nearly pushed it away when suddenly he spotted the word Shebna had drawn on the tablet. Then he saw it again and again, and he felt the power of deciphering a secret. He could read.

"There . . . and there, there . . . and there," he replied, pointing his stubby finger to several places on the scroll.

Shebna smiled broadly. "That was very good. You found all of them. You have learned to read one word already. Soon you will be able to read the story. Now, what about numbers? Do you know your numbers?"

"I can count to 12."

"Good." Shebna scraped the tablet clean and began drawing circles in the soft clay. "Suppose you had six figs and you ate two. How many would—"

"Four." Hezekiah answered before Shebna finished drawing, and the tutor's thick, black eyebrows rose in surprise.

"And suppose I had five figs. How many would we—"

"Nine."

"Have you done this before?"

Hezekiah gave him a puzzled look. "I've eaten figs lots of times."

"That is not what I meant. Anyway," he quickly continued, "if we wanted to divide up all the figs between us—"

"You'd have to cut one in half, or it wouldn't be fair."

Shebna's eyes widened in surprise. "I did not realize my division problem worked out unevenly, but you solved it anyway. You seem quite bright."

"Can I ask you a question now?" Hezekiah asked.

Shebna smiled weakly. "Certainly. That was the bargain."

"Why do you smile all the time if you're not really happy inside?"

Shebna's smile faded, and he looked at Hezekiah in surprise. "And what makes you say I am not happy?"

"Because your eyes aren't happy."

Shebna leaned back on his elbows and studied his pupil. "You seem quite perceptive as well," he mumbled. "Tutoring you could be a tremendous challenge. But you do not like me very much, do you?"

"I don't know . . ." Hezekiah shrugged, gazing sadly at the scroll on the floor in front of him. "Where's my grandpa?" he asked quietly. "He said he'd come back for my lessons, but it's been days and days!"

And for the first time, Hezekiah formed the question in his mind that he had been trying so hard not to ask. If his grandfather had abandoned him, would Yahweh, his Savior and Protector, abandon him too?

"I do not know where your grandfather is," Shebna sighed. "That is the truth. I will try to find out for you. But in the meantime, I must teach you. Is there something you would like to learn about?"

Hezekiah thought of the soldiers who had come for his brothers and him. They had been armed with swords and spears, and he had been helpless against them. "I want to learn to be a soldier, like King David."

"Really? Do you like to read about warriors and battles?" Shebna shuffled quickly through his scrolls. "I have many stories about brave warriors and the battles they fought. We can read one of them."

"Do you have the one about David and Goliath?" For the first time, Hezekiah was almost interested.

"Maybe . . . somewhere . . ." Shebna rifled through the pile and the scrolls rustled noisily. "Let me see. There must be one here."

"My grandpa has lots and lots of stories about David. They're in the Temple library. He'll let us borrow some."

"I am certain he would." Shebna sounded annoyed, and he abruptly pushed his scrolls aside and studied Hezekiah again. "So, you want to be a soldier, yes? Can you shoot a bow and arrow? Fight with a sword? Throw a spear? Can you ride a horse?"

Hezekiah shook his head to each of these questions.

"Would you like to learn how?"

"Yes!" Hezekiah's eyes grew wide, and he managed a quick smile. If he had his own sword and learned to use it, he could save himself from Molech. He wouldn't have to wait for Yahweh or his grandfather, who might never come back again.

"Follow me, then." Shebna grinned and stood up. "First we will go to the stables and find you a horse, then to the armory to get some swords."

The tutor strode briskly from the classroom with Hezekiah trotting close behind.

A tremor of fear went down Abijah's spine when Ahaz's two servants suddenly appeared in her room. Her father had disappeared many days ago, never returning from the morning sacrifice, and now Ahaz's escorts, who followed him everywhere like sinister shadows, stood at her door.

"His Majesty wants you in his chambers." They held her door open, waiting.

Abijah's heart began to race. Ahaz always came to the harem. She had never been summoned to his rooms before. She wanted to ask "Why?" but the servants' menacing presence overwhelmed her. They looked directly into her eyes, something palace servants were forbidden to do.

"Yahweh, help me," she prayed as she followed them, and she felt her father's God, the God who had restored her son, filling her with courage.

When she entered Ahaz's chambers, Abijah knew by his smoldering, angry expression that she had been discovered. A tall, lanky man in Egyptian clothing stood beside him. The servants closed the door behind her and followed her into the room.

"By whose authority did you invite your father into

my palace to brainwash my son with myths and lies?" Ahaz shouted.

For a reason she couldn't explain, Abijah felt no fear and she heard the words that came out of her mouth as if someone else spoke them.

"He is my son too."

Ahaz slapped her face with the back of his hand, and she stumbled backward, blood trickling from a cut where his ring split her cheek. The servants pushed her forward.

"You gave birth to him. That's all. You have no other part to play in my son's life. How dare you try to influence what he is taught?"

Abijah didn't answer, but she felt no fear.

"Your father is dead," Ahaz continued. "I ordered Uriah to execute him for disrupting my sacrifice." He paused and studied her closely, as if waiting to enjoy her reaction, like a cat toying with a mouse.

Abijah never doubted that Zechariah was dead, but she steeled herself to show no emotion. It was the only way she could beat Ahaz at his game. His face grew red as his anger mounted.

"And now you will tell Shebna, my son's tutor, exactly which lies your father taught him."

"My father taught him no lies, only the truth," she said calmly, "that there are no other gods but Yahweh, the God of Abraham—and that kings who lead their nation into idolatry, who sacrifice their sons to false gods, will one day suffer the vengeance of a holy God."

Ahaz lunged at her, beating her with his fists until she fell to the floor, dazed with pain. Then he stood over her, kicking her until she nearly fainted.

"I ought to make you a shrine prostitute of Asherah!"

"I'd rather be one than sleep with you." Abijah formed the words through swollen, bleeding lips.

"You'll never see my sons again—ever!"

It was Ahaz's most vicious blow, more painful than all

the others and one she hadn't bargained for. She longed to cling to his feet and plead with him not to take her children from her, to at least let her hold them one last time, to kiss them good-bye, but she knew it was what Ahaz wanted her to do. And she knew she had already lost her sons. She spit on Ahaz's feet instead.

Ahaz wiped the spittle off with her hair, then hauled her to her feet, forcing her to face him again. "You listen to me! You're my wife, to do with as I please, and—"

"I'd rather die than be your wife."

Abijah had nothing more to lose. Her father was dead because of her, and she would never see her children again. She spit in Ahaz's face, welcoming death. Ahaz's eyes turned as cold and gray as granite.

"Very well. Grant her wish." Ahaz shoved her backward into his servants' waiting arms.

But as her last act of defiance, Abijah wanted the final word. She met her superstitious, idolatrous husband's gaze and repeated the words he loathed and feared:

"Hear, O Israel. Yahweh is God—Yahweh alone."

Zechariah painfully climbed the Temple stairs to the courtyard, each step slow and deliberate, but he knew he had to keep his aching joints moving in spite of the pain, or eventually he would be unable to walk at all. The dry summer sun, glaring off the golden roof of the Temple, blinded him as he slowly circled the deserted courtyard, aware of the gatekeepers watching him from their posts. As his eyes adjusted to the bright light, a sudden movement in the middle court caught his attention. He shaded his eyes from the glare and drew closer for a better look. Someone seemed to be beckoning to him.

"Zechariah—it's me, Hilkiah."

"Hilkiah? My friend? Is it really you?" Zechariah hobbled to the gate that separated the courtyards and embraced his little friend.

"Zechariah! Thanks be to God! You're all right."

"I've missed you, my friend."

"Yes, my son and I don't come here any more, since . . . but . . . I had to see you. How are you?"

"I'm fine, just fine," he assured him. Hilkiah was the first person from the outside that he had seen in six months, and he hungrily studied his jovial face. "A little stiff in my joints maybe, but that's what happens when you live in a crumbling old building."

"They told me you weren't well."

"There's nothing wrong with me. King Ahaz wants to keep me quiet—that's all. We've had a major disagreement, you might say, about his new altar, and I think my living arrangements here will be quite permanent."

"Oy! Then you're a prisoner?"

"It's not so bad. I spend a lot of time reading and studying the Torah. And I can walk around the courtyard when there aren't any sacrifices being held. It's not so bad."

"How can you be so calm about it, my friend? You're being held prisoner for no reason, without even a trial."

"It's all right, Hilkiah. Yes, at first I questioned God: 'Why, Yahweh, why?' I asked in an endless refrain throughout the long, boring days and the many sleepless nights. I waited for God to vindicate me and punish my enemies, and I immersed myself in the Holy Torah, always questioning, demanding answers.

"But then I discovered Job, another victim of injustice who demanded answers from God. And you know what I learned from Job? Yahweh doesn't owe us an explanation for what He does. He is sovereign over all: "Can you fathom the mysteries of God? Can you probe the limits of the Almighty? They are higher than the heavens—what can you do? They are deeper than the depths of the grave—what can you know? Their measure is longer than the earth and wider than the sea. If he comes along and confines you in prison . . . who can oppose him?"

"So you see? I don't need to know why anymore."

"Things have gotten worse in Jerusalem since you've been here," Hilkiah sighed. "King Ahaz worships every new god he hears of, and it seems as if the high priest encourages him to. I've heard Ahaz consults witches and mediums."

"I know. I've seen the changes here too. The quiet orderly rhythm of the Temple is no longer the same. Ahaz even had the doors of the holy sanctuary closed. Can you imagine that? The golden candlesticks in the holy place have gone out. And Uriah has instituted a new order of rituals and sacrifices in Yahweh's Temple. I wouldn't come to them even if they allowed me to."

"It scares me, Zechariah. What's going to happen to our nation?"

"Judah is rushing headlong toward ruin, plunging deeper and deeper into sin. I don't suppose there are too many godly men left besides you, my friend. I questioned Yahweh about that too, but He showed me that He is in control of the nation, the king, and even Uriah: 'If he holds back the waters, there is drought; if he lets them loose, they devastate the land. . . . both deceived and deceiver are his. . . . He silences the lips of trusted advisers and takes away the discernment of elders. . . . He deprives the leaders of the earth of their reason; he sends them wandering through a trackless waste. They grope in darkness with no light; he makes them stagger like drunkards.'"

"I came to comfort you, my friend, and instead you are comforting me," Hilkiah smiled.

"Have you heard any word of my grandson, Hezekiah?" Zechariah asked quietly. "How I miss him!"

Hilkiah's face looked troubled. "I've heard that the king hired a scholar, an Egyptian, to tutor his sons. I wish I could tell you more than that, but I can't. I'm sorry, my friend."

Zechariah closed his eyes, as if it might help him bear the pain in his heart. "There is a reason for everything that happens," he said in a trembling voice. "Hezekiah is in Yahweh's hands now. I have to trust Him. I pray many, many times each day for Yahweh's protecting hand to be on Hezekiah. And Yahweh hears. He will watch over him."

Hilkiah wiped a tear from his eye and looked at his friend. "I'm afraid for you, Zechariah. What's going to happen to you?"

"Don't be afraid. Yahweh has given me peace. That doesn't mean that I never have struggles or questions. Our lives will always be filled with those. But the peace of Yahweh comes from knowing that there is an order in the universe and a reason for whatever happens, even if only Yahweh sees it. We have to trust God's sovereign will: 'To God belong wisdom and power. Counsel and understanding are his. What he tears down cannot be rebuilt; the man he imprisons cannot be released.'"

"Then they'll never let you go free again?"

"It doesn't matter, Hilkiah. It doesn't matter. I have Yahweh's peace—and that makes me free."

2

Ahaz . . . shut the doors of the Lord's temple and set up altars at every street corner in Jerusalem. In every town in Judah he built high places to burn sacrifices to other gods and provoked the Lord, the God of his fathers, to anger.

—2 Chron. 28:24-25

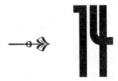

Hezekiah entered his father's opulent private chambers and bowed low, steeling himself for a possible confrontation. He had determined, regardless of what happened, not to allow Ahaz to anger him.

"You wanted to see me, Your Majesty?" The king aroused a broad range of emotions in Hezekiah, from fear and hatred to pity and revulsion, but rarely respect and never—that he could recall—love. His bitterness extended back as far as he could remember, though the exact cause of it was long forgotten. He avoided Ahaz as much as possible and dreaded being summoned to his chambers, never knowing whether to expect censure or praise.

"Yes, I did," Ahaz answered. He reclined on his divan among a clutter of silken cushions with two pretty concubines seated on the thick carpet at his feet. His expression was one of boredom, and Hezekiah wondered if he had been summoned to be Ahaz's entertainment, to be toyed with as a small boy would torment a captured beetle. "I may have some interesting news for you." He didn't offer Hezekiah a seat but left him standing while he took his time coming to the point.

"Pour him some wine," he gestured to his servants.

"No, thank you." Hezekiah knew his refusal would irritate his father.

Ahaz eyed him narrowly, accusingly. "How old are you now?" he said at last.

"I'm 25, sir." He wondered why Ahaz always made him feel like an inadequate child who never quite measured up to his expectations.

"Twenty-five . . . is that so?" he mused. "Well, I'm fairly pleased with your education so far. You've done well in your studies and your military training." He rose ponderously from his seat and made a show of striding grandly around the room, occasionally picking up an ornament or trinket and examining it casually.

"Tell me—has Shebna taught you how to conduct yourself at formal ceremonial proceedings?"

With disgust, Hezekiah thought of his father's frenzied sacrifices at the many altars throughout the city. "If you mean taking part in formal religious rituals, I really don't have much interest in—"

"No, no," Ahaz interrupted impatiently. "I don't mean religious sacrifices. I know you never participate in those." The truth was that Ahaz rarely allowed Hezekiah to join him at public ceremonies or even at the Temple worship services. The physical contrast between Hezekiah and his father was great, and it was almost as if Ahaz didn't want his heir to compete with him in the public eye. So he kept Hezekiah in the background as much as possible.

"No, what I mean is, how much do you know about formal diplomatic protocol?"

"I'm fluent in a few languages, and I've studied international diplomacy, if that's what you mean." Hezekiah was already tired of his father's games and wondered where these questions were leading. He tried to sound patient.

"Yes. That's exactly what I mean. And do you like to travel?"

"I've traveled throughout most of our nation, Your Majesty, and it was quite enjoyable." He deliberately pretended indifference, even though the prospect of leaving the confining walls of the palace excited him.

"Good, good," Ahaz beamed, and for no apparent reason he began to laugh uproariously, triggering a coughing fit that left him wheezing and flushed. His concubines floated around him, gushing in alarm, and helped him back to his divan. He took a few sips of wine and gestured to a servant.

"Tell my cupbearer to bring something stronger than this." He looked up at Hezekiah again through watery eyes. "I may have some good news to announce very soon. My trade minister is negotiating a new agreement, and if he's successful, I've promised that his daughter will be wed to you. I've been thinking that perhaps it's time I arranged a marriage for you. Would you like that?"

The king's patronizing attitude infuriated Hezekiah, and he had difficulty hiding it. The idea of being used as a prize, a reward for doing the king a favor, enraged him. For a moment he couldn't speak, but he knew from experience the danger of contradicting his moody, impulsive father.

"I already have several concubines, sir. A legal wife would make no difference."

"Her name is Hephzibah. She sounds 'delightful,' doesn't she?" Ahaz was obviously pleased with himself and laughed at his own joke, a pun on the girl's name, which means "My delight is in her." "Hephzibah's father is negotiating my trade agreement with the Phoenicians. Are you interested in being an envoy?"

"Yes, of course. But why would—" Hezekiah stopped short, catching himself. His father's proposal made no sense, but he didn't dare question it.

"But *what?*" Ahaz asked impatiently.

He hesitated, then proceeded carefully. "Why would we want a trade agreement with the Phoenicians, since we have no direct access routes to their territory?"

Ahaz looked at him blankly. "What are you talking about?"

"When the Philistines conquered our territory in the foothills, they took control of all the northern passes through the mountains to the central trade route. In order to trade with Phoenicia, we'd have to go through Philistine territory and pay duty or else go farther north—"

Hezekiah stopped abruptly when his father's face slowly reddened. He realized too late the mistake he had made in demonstrating his superior knowledge to Ahaz.

"But you're aware of all this, sir," he mumbled. "I didn't mean to imply—" But Hezekiah knew from his father's expression that Ahaz had been ignorant of the situation.

"You have all the answers, I suppose!" Ahaz sprang from his couch to confront him angrily. "Maybe you think you'd be a better king than I am?"

"I wasn't trying to—"

"Don't interrupt me! I'm still king of this nation, not you! Although you'd jump at the chance to take over, wouldn't you?"

Hezekiah did not answer.

"*Wouldn't* you?" Ahaz demanded.

"No, sir. I don't want to take over. But I do feel that I'm capable of holding a position of responsibility in your government, and I'm willing to serve in any—"

"I'm sure you are—just like Absalom served *his* father, King David." He stood in front of Hezekiah, glaring up at him. "I know the fickleness of the masses. And that's all I need is for you to persuade them that you could rule better than I."

His father's accusations infuriated Hezekiah, and in spite of his resolution, he lost his temper in self-defense.

"I never said I wanted to take over! But since I *am* going to be king someday, why can't you allow me to attend the Advisory Council meetings so I can get acquainted with how the nation—"

"No! How dare you?" Wheezing with anger, Ahaz turned his back and stalked across the room. "No! Next thing I know you'll be poisoning me in my sleep. You're not ready to take responsibility yet."

Ahaz gulped some of his wine, which seemed to cool his temper. "Maybe once you have a wife and settle down I will find something for you to do—if you deserve it, that is. Now get out."

"Yes, Your Majesty," he mumbled, furious not only at Ahaz but also at himself for losing his temper. It would probably cost him the opportunity to travel with the trade mission.

He brushed past the royal cupbearer on his way out and stalked through the palace corridors to his own rooms, where his tutor awaited him. Shebna knew him well. He read the anger on Hezekiah's face and sighed.

"It was not good news, I gather?" Shebna was now in his late 40s, and silver streaked his blue-black hair at the temples and in a swath across his forehead. His lanky body was thinner than ever, and he paced restlessly around the room, as if unable to contain his energy. Hezekiah groaned and sank onto a pile of cushions near the window.

"I don't know—it might have been if I hadn't lost my temper. He was about to make me an envoy on a trade mission to Phoenicia." He laughed shortly, ironically. "But when I pointed out the futility of a trade agreement without trade routes, it infuriated him to discover that I knew more about geography than he did."

"Oh, dear," Shebna winced.

"Then he accused me of plotting to overthrow him."

"Oh, dear."

"That's when I lost my temper." His tutor covered his face and shook his head in dismay. "Then he threw me out," Hezekiah shrugged. "That was the end of the meeting. Oh, yes—I almost forgot. He's also chosen a wife for me."

Shebna regarded him with a humorous twinkle in his dark eyes. "You do not appear very happy about taking a wife. Do you plan to remain unwed all your life, like me?"

"He's using me, Shebna, like—like some kind of trophy. I'm a reward for some trade minister or other. I'd like a more useful function in his kingdom than that."

"Why does he make you so angry, my lord? Why can you not hold your fiery temper when you are with him, be patient, and listen to him without comment?"

"I don't know. I honestly tried this time, but it was all so idiotic—a trade agreement with Phoenicia!"

"Well, idiotic or not, it was an opportunity to prove yourself to him."

"And I messed it up."

"You will have to get back in his favor, my lord. Perhaps if you showed interest in the wife he has chosen—"

"No. I don't want a wife he has chosen."

"It is your stubbornness that always gets you into trouble."

Hezekiah looked at Shebna, then laughed. "You're right, as usual. Do you have any other advice I need to hear?"

"My lord, you have finished your education, as far as I am concerned. You already know more than I do. Perhaps I should suggest to the king that he allow you to gain practical experience in running the nation. He could make you a lower court judge or civic administrator. At the very least, you could sit in on his advisory meetings and find out what is going on in the nation."

"I agree, Shebna, but unfortunately my father doesn't. In fact, I suggested it today, and that's when he accused me of trying to overthrow him." Hezekiah shook his head. "It would never work. I'm afraid of him, Shebna. He's too impulsive. He lets his emotions rule him. And he doesn't have to make me his successor, you know. He has no shortage of heirs, as he's always quick to remind me. My brother, Gedaliah, gets along with him much better than I do."

Shebna looked thoughtful. "But you say he hinted about making you an envoy?"

"He said 'maybe.' But my father has hinted at a government position before, and nothing ever came of it. So I'll just have to wait and see this time too. He's not even 40 years old, Shebna. I could be waiting years to inherit the throne."

"That is true, my lord," Shebna sighed.

"Maybe you'd better start teaching me to be patient."

15

Hephzibah lay on a pile of cushions in her favorite spot, beneath the fig tree in her courtyard. She gazed up at the rich, shiny green leaves and pale brown fruit, dreaming the dreams of every girl who has finally reached the age of marriage. Hephzibah knew she had several suitors, and, one by one as they paraded through her mind, she considered each of them as a husband. Her opinion wouldn't matter, but she loved to dream all the same. When her father negotiated her dowry, she knew she would command a high price, not only because he was a prominent government official, but because she was very beautiful as well.

Petite and fine-boned with thick dark hair that fell in soft curls, Hephzibah had natural grace and elegance and the indefinable aura of wealth and breeding that was part of her social class. She had been told all her life she was beautiful, but only recently had she become aware of the effect and power she had over men, even with her face discreetly veiled.

The afternoon sun warmed her as it dappled through the trees. The tranquil, hazy afternoon and the quiet hum of insects made her drowsy. She closed her eyes, and the next thing she knew she awoke to see her father smiling down at her.

"Is this any way for the future bride of the prince to spend the afternoon?" he said, laughing.

He wore the richly ornamental linen robe of the royal court, too hot for summer, and beads of perspiration dampened his hair and forehead. His face was flushed, not only with heat but also with excitement. Hephzibah quickly sat up, not sure if she was dreaming.

"What did you say, Abba?"

"I suppose I shouldn't tell you about it until the arrangements are final," he laughed. "But I can't keep quiet about a secret this big." His narrow face with its immaculately trimmed beard and arched brows beamed with pride and self-confidence.

"What, Abba? What? Please tell me." She grabbed both his hands and pulled him down beside her onto the cushions.

"I've been working on a special project for King Ahaz for several months, and he's very pleased with what I've accomplished so far. This morning he told me that if my trade agreement is finalized, you will be betrothed to his son Prince Hezekiah."

"Oh, Abba!" The news astonished her, and although Hephzibah knew she should be overjoyed, a cold fist of terror gripped her instead.

"You mean, live in the palace? Me? Married to a prince?"

"Yes, my darling. And your future husband is also heir to the throne. He will be the next king of Judah."

The news overwhelmed Hephzibah. Her shock, combined with the afternoon heat, made the courtyard seem to spin, and she felt as if she might faint. This had to be a dream. It couldn't possibly be true.

"Oh, Abba," she whispered again.

"What's the matter, darling? I thought you'd be thrilled—but you look as if you've seen King Uzziah's ghost."

"I never dreamed . . . I never thought . . . Abba, I don't know what a king's wife is supposed to do."

"She's supposed to bear him sons—many, many sons!" Her father laughed indulgently. "It's what every man expects from his wife, whether he's a king or a slave."

Hephzibah's terror began to subside, replaced by the excitement of her betrothal, and she was filled with questions.

"What does he look like, Abba? Have I ever seen him? How old is he? What's he like?"

He laughed. "Slow down—one question at a time! Besides, does it really matter what he looks like? He's going to be the king someday."

Hephzibah had seen King Ahaz on ceremonial occasions and remembered him as grossly fat and pasty-faced. Not even the aura of royalty or his fine robes and jewels could disguise that fact. The thought of being married to him, being held against his doughy belly, made her shudder. Once again she was afraid.

"Yes, Abba—of course it matters. Is Prince Hezekiah pale and fat like his father?"

"Hephzibah!"

She clapped her hand over her mouth, as shocked as her father by her outspokenness.

"That's the king of Judah you're talking about. How can you be so disrespectful?"

"I'm sorry, Abba." She lowered her eyes and tried to look repentant, but she shuddered at the thought of being married to someone like Ahaz, whether he was the king or not.

"Ah, I forgive you. You're bound to be a little jittery before your betrothal." He brushed her thick, dark hair from her face affectionately. "To tell you the truth, I don't know much about the prince, darling. I've seen several princes, but I don't know which one is Hezekiah. They never come to council meetings. I've heard they study under an Egyptian tutor, a genius of a man, so they say, and spend a lot of time with the captain of the palace guards for their military training. I promise I'll try to find out more once you're betrothed, all right?"

"Yes, Abba," she answered quietly.

For the rest of the evening Hephzibah alternated between joy and terror as she dreamed of being wed to an unknown prince. The pampered life appealed to her, with elegant clothing, dazzling jewels, and hundreds of servants. And she longed for a husband who would love and adore her the way her father cherished her mother. But her dream man was supposed to be handsome and strong, not flabby and pale. What would she do if Prince Hezekiah resembled his father? How could she hide her revulsion every time he held her or pressed his bloated cheek to hers?

Long after the household retired for the night, Hephzibah tossed and turned restlessly, unable to sleep. Weeks might pass before she would be certain if the betrothal would take place, and Hephzibah decided that she could never cope with the terror of the unknown that long. She had to find out whom she was marrying and stop the betrothal, if necessary, before it was too late.

All night Hephzibah watched the stars sweep slowly past her open window and the sliver of moon rise and set. By the time she had formulated her plan, it was dawn. She rose from her disheveled bed and silently crept into her younger sister's room, gently shaking her awake.

"Miriam, wake up."

"Hephzibah?—what?"

"Shh—be quiet and listen to me. You've got to help me. I'm going to go out of my mind if you don't."

"What's wrong?" she asked sleepily.

"Abba's betrothing me to the prince."

"I already know that," she said in a cranky voice. "You woke me up to tell me what I already know?"

"Shh—listen to me. I've got to find out what he looks like before it's too late. What if he's really horrible? What then?"

"You'll marry him anyway, like a dutiful daughter should. Now let me sleep." She rolled over with her back to Hephzibah and closed her eyes.

"Will you listen to me? If I really hate him, maybe I can pray to all the gods to cancel the betrothal or take a vow or something. Please, Miriam. Suppose it was *your* betrothal. Wouldn't you want to know? You've got to help me."

It required no effort on Hephzibah's part to plead desperately. She merely had to think of sitting beside the fat, pompous king, and helpless panic overwhelmed her. Miriam rolled over again to face Hephzibah.

"It depends—what do you want me to do?"

"We'll stuff cushions in our beds so it looks like we're sleeping. Then we can sneak out and try to get a look at Prince Hezekiah."

Miriam sat up straight. "Are you crazy? We can't wander around the city by ourselves. If Abba catches us, he'll have us stoned."

"Shhh. We'll dress up as servant girls and pretend we're on our way to the spring for water. Listen—I have it all figured out. Abba said the prince spends a lot of time drilling with the captain of the palace guards. I know where that is. It's close to the Water Gate."

"You're really crazy! Go back to bed." She shook her head in disbelief.

"Miriam, name your price. I'll do any favor for you if only you'll help me." She gripped her sister's hand.

Miriam studied Hephzibah as if she were a stranger. "You're actually serious about this, aren't you?"

"Yes. Very serious. I'll give you anything you want."

"I sure hope I don't act this crazy when it's *my* turn to get betrothed." She swung her feet out of bed with a sigh and stood up.

"Then you'll help me? Oh, thank you! Thank you!" Hephzibah hugged her sister quickly.

Miriam held up her hand in warning. "For a price, remember? First of all, swear to me that you'll help me find a royal husband too."

"I swear it."

"And you'll give me those golden earrings that Abba bought you in Beersheba."

Hephzibah hesitated a fraction of a second, then agreed.

"And . . ."

"Don't get greedy, Miriam. I think that's more than enough, don't you?"

"And swear to me that if we get into trouble, you'll say I was innocent but you forced me to do it."

"We won't get into trouble."

"Swear?"

"OK. I swear. By Asherah and Baal, I forced you to do it. Now please—let's hurry!"

They padded their beds with cushions and crept down to the kitchen, where Hephzibah bribed two servant girls into lending them their clothes. Then, with their faces discreetly veiled and balancing water jugs on their heads, they headed down through the back lanes to the Water Gate.

The sun had not quite appeared over the top of the Mount of Olives, but it bathed the streets with hazy, golden-pink light. Hephzibah shivered in the thin, cheap gown as she pulled Miriam through the streets behind her. Curiosity and fear propelled her forward at a rapid pace, but Miriam, who didn't share her motivation, lagged as if wishing she had never come.

As they neared the Water Gate, they heard hearty shouts coming from the courtyard near the guard tower and the metallic ring of sword against sword.

"See?" Hephzibah whispered. "I told you they practice here every morning."

They followed the wall of the courtyard until they

came to an open gate and peeked cautiously inside. Dozens of men stood around the perimeter of the yard, cheering two guardsmen engaged in a duel. Some of the observers wore the tunics of the palace guard, some wore ordinary clothes, and a few wore the richly embroidered robes of the nobility.

"Great. So how are we going to know which one is your prince and future husband?" Miriam asked.

"Let's listen for a minute. Maybe we can find out."

"I don't like this," Miriam said nervously.

Hephzibah scanned all the faces of the young noblemen, looking for one that resembled King Ahaz, but it seemed hopeless.

As they watched, the older of the two dueling men seemed to be winning the advantage, and his young opponent finally threw down his sword in defeat.

"You win, Captain Jonadab," he conceded. The watching men cheered.

"Psst—we can't stay here forever," Miriam whispered. "We're going to get caught."

"Please. One more minute."

"Who's going to challenge me next?" the victorious captain cried. "How about you, my prince?"

Hephzibah froze as the captain nodded toward a young man in his early 20s. He took off his embroidered outer robe and casually tossed it aside. Amid a chorus of shouts and cheers, the dark-haired man strode forward.

Hephzibah's heart began to pound, not with excitement but with fear. He had a trim, compact build, very different from King Ahaz's, but there was something in his swagger, a hint of danger or cruelty in his eyes that frightened her.

"Oh, please, Lady Asherah. Don't let it be him," she silently prayed.

The young prince seemed to have more self-confidence than skill, and the captain repeatedly cut short his attempts to show off before his audience. Before long, the prince seemed to realize that he was making a fool of himself and angrily flung down his sword.

"I'm not in the mood for a real fight." His eyes flashed dangerously.

The captain gave a respectful bow. "Another time then, my prince."

"Is he Prince Hezekiah?" Miriam whispered.

"I don't know," Hephzibah shrugged.

"Come on. We've been gone too long already. Let's get the water and go home." Miriam pulled her by the arm, and they headed through the gate and down the steep slope to the spring.

Neither of them spoke as, surrounded by chattering servant girls and slaves, they clumsily filled their jugs. The water was cold, the work harder than Hephzibah bargained for, and even with her jug only half full she could barely lift it.

"They're full enough, Miriam—let's go," she whispered, and they headed back up the ramp to the city. As they neared the courtyard again, Hephzibah pleaded with her sister.

"One more minute. That's all—I promise."

When they peered through the open gate, the captain had a new opponent. He was tall and strongly built, yet amazingly quick and agile for his size, darting out of the captain's reach, then lunging swiftly to take the offensive, his curly brown hair and thick beard flashing with copper in the morning sun. His skill with the sword was breathtaking, and Hephzibah's pulse raced as she watched him sparring.

He was poised, confident, handsome, and she prayed fervently to every god she could think of that this man would turn out to be Prince Hezekiah. It was too much to hope for, but if only she knew who he was, maybe her father could arrange a betrothal to him instead.

Suddenly Miriam cried out, and icy water drenched Hephzibah's legs as her sister's water jug crashed to the ground. A strong hand clamped down on Hephzibah's shoulder and swung her roughly around. Four guardsmen who had moved up unnoticed behind them circled around, leaving no escape. Their leering faces and mocking grins left no doubt about their intentions.

"I've never seen you two before," their leader grinned, pawing clumsily at Hephzibah's veil. "Let's have a look at you."

"Yeah—I want to see what I get for my money," a second one added and snatched Hephzibah's water jug from her hands. As they closed in around them, Miriam collapsed in fear, sobbing uncontrollably.

"No! Leave us alone!" Hephzibah cried. She twisted away from the soldier, and her veil tore partly away from her face.

"Hey now! She is a pretty one," the soldier yelled. "Remember: I saw her first."

"No, please! Let me go!" Hephzibah cried in terror as she tried to break free. The soldier moved behind her and pinned her arms to her side, his huge, strong hands bruising her arms, while another soldier pulled her screaming sister to her feet and clamped his hand over her mouth.

"Let them go." The command was spoken with authority. The knot of soldiers parted, and Hephzibah saw the captain and his opponent standing before her. They were both breathless from the duel, the fronts of their tunics wet with sweat. The tall one stepped forward and spoke again.

"These girls are terrified, can't you see that?"

"They're just common servant girls, my lord," said the soldier who held Hephzibah. "They come around here for only one reason."

"Resisting is part of their game, sir," a second soldier added.

"No, please . . . we weren't!" Hephzibah stammered while Miriam sobbed pitifully.

The stranger studied Hephzibah's unveiled face as if trying to determine if she told the truth. His deep brown eyes were somber, almost melancholy, and they dominated his handsome face. The intensity of his gaze unnerved her.

"Soldiers under my command will never misuse their power on defenseless people," he finally said. "Do you understand?"

"Yes, my lord," the soldier muttered, and Hephzibah felt herself free. The stranger retrieved her water jug and handed it to her.

"Go home. And don't come here again."

Hephzibah gripped her sister's trembling hand and tried to walk, the street unstable beneath her watery legs. She had completely forgotten about her betrothal when a voice from the crowd suddenly shouted, "Prince Hezekiah, I'll challenge you next."

She froze at the name, then glanced over her shoulder. As if in a dream, she saw the tall stranger acknowledge the offer.

"I accept that challenge." A smile flickered across his solemn features.

Hephzibah thought she would faint as she clutched her water jug and stumbled up the hill toward home, with Miriam weeping beside her.

"It's all your fault. I never should have come with you."

"Miriam, I'm sorry. But it's all right now—we're fine."

"We were nearly raped!"

"Shhh—not so loud. And stop whimpering. We're almost home. If Abba finds out what happened, we'll be disgraced. Then we'll both die old maids."

By the time they reached the servants' entrance at the rear of the house, Miriam had composed herself. But when Hephzibah reached the safety of her bedroom, she collapsed onto her bed and began weeping. Miriam shook her angrily.

"What's the matter with you now? You saw your stupid prince, didn't you?"

"Oh, Miriam, I want to marry him more than anyone else in the whole world. If Abba doesn't get him for my husband, I know I will surely die."

—◆—

Hephzibah paused for breath when she reached the sacred grove of Asherah on the hill outside Jerusalem. This day following her daring escapade to the spring was blistering hot. The servants who led the young bullock and carried her grain and wine offerings sweated from the exertion of their climb and the size of their loads. They gazed at her expectantly, hoping for a share in the feast after the sacrifice.

Hephzibah felt a sense of awe as she considered the enormity of her mission and its importance for her future. She must please the goddess, must somehow win Lady Asherah's favor and secure her betrothal to Prince Hezekiah. Her other suitors no longer interested her. Not content to leave her destiny in the hands of others, Hephzibah had decided to appeal to the ultimate source: Asherah, goddess of love and fertility.

The high priest of Asherah, undoubtedly impressed with the extravagant offering her servants bore, hurried over to greet her and bowed slightly. He was a Phoenician from Tyre, imported to Jerusalem by King Ahaz. Foreign priests seemed to be multiplying throughout the land, growing in boldness as well as in numbers.

"How may I help you?"

"I wish to make an offering to the goddess," she told him, "and pour out a drink offering, and burn incense."

The priest's brows arched slightly, and he licked his lips. "The goddess will be pleased at such devotion. Do you have a petition to make?"

"Yes—and also a vow."

He smiled faintly and led the way into the grove. Within the stone enclosure stood an altar and several incense burners. Beyond them were an inner grove of images and an Asherah pole.

As the priest lit Hephzibah's incense and prepared to slay the bullock, she knelt before the golden image of Asherah, her eyes closed in prayer.

"Oh, Queen of Heaven," she prayed silently. "I bring my offering before you with this petition: that you would bring to pass my betrothal and marriage to him whom I love . . ."

Tears sprang to her eyes as she thought of Hezekiah, the glint of sunlight on his sword, the soft sheen of sweat on his tanned arms and legs, the burnish of copper in his dark hair and beard. She imagined being held in his arms, becoming his wife.

"And I vow this day, I pledge to your service, a daughter from this union that you bring to pass."

She never doubted her ability to fulfill her vow. Kings were interested only in sons. A daughter would be hers to do with as she pleased.

Hephzibah kissed the little statue reverently and, suddenly overcome with emotion, hurried from the sanctuary to preside over the sacrificial feast with her family and friends.

16

"Hephzibah, my darling, how beautiful you look!" Hephzibah saw a glow of pride in her father's moist eyes.

"Oh, Abba, do you really think so? Do you think the prince will be pleased to have me for his wife?"

"When he sees you, he will faint for joy. Turn around and let me look at you."

Hephzibah did a small pirouette in the center of the room, and her father sighed, slapping his arms to his side in a gesture of helpless awe. "You are beautiful! Fit for a king!"

Hephzibah wore a magnificent wedding gown of embroidered linen, fashioned by the finest craftsmen in Jerusalem. Her dark, wavy hair had not been pinned up by her maids yet, and it flowed loose down her back. Shining jewelry, her betrothal gifts from the palace, adorned her— golden bracelets on each arm, thick loops of gold in each ear, and a heavy rope of gold around her neck, from which hung a ruby the size of her fingertip.

"You're too beautiful to cover with a veil," her father decided. "The whole kingdom should see Prince Hezekiah's beautiful bride. Let's leave the veil off."

"Abba, you're teasing." Her father cupped her face in his hands affectionately.

"I have a right to be proud of my beautiful daughter."

Hephzibah's mother bustled into the room behind

him in a flurry. "Hephzibah, why are you standing around? Fix your hair. Put your veil on. You should be down in the courtyard with your bridesmaids already. He could come for you any minute."

"Mama, there's lots of time. We'll hear the groom's procession coming. It's still early." She felt surprisingly calm and happier than ever before in her life. She had dreamed about Prince Hezekiah for months, sacrificed and prayed and made vows to reach this day, and now the goddess had answered. Today he would come to take her for his wife.

"Is your sister ready? Have you seen her?" her mother fussed. "What's taking her so long? I'm going to check on Miriam. Papa, go watch for the procession."

"I'd better do what I'm told," her father said with a wry smile, but there was love in his eyes as he watched his wife bustle off. *My husband will look at me that way too,* Hephzibah thought and felt a tingle of excitement spread through her. She hugged her father fiercely.

"Thank you, Abba! Thank you for this wonderful day!"

"May the goddess bless you with many, many sons," he said, and as he turned to leave, Hephzibah saw a tear in his eye.

She knew she should go downstairs and let her maids pin up her hair, then take her seat in the flower-strewn chair beneath the fig tree, but her heart was too full of joy for her to sit quietly and wait. She wanted to dance and leap and sing. She ran to her window, listening for the music of the groom's procession, but in the hot streets below, the still air carried no song. Servants and slaves and merchants went about their affairs as if it were an ordinary day.

Didn't they know? Couldn't they tell that today would mark the beginning of a love so deep and strong that it would outshine the love of Solomon for his Shulammite maiden? Hephzibah smiled as she remembered the beautiful words of Solomon. Then as she gazed longingly toward the palace, she picked up her lyre and sang them softly to herself: "Listen! My lover! Look! Here he comes, leaping across the mountains, bounding over the hills. . . . My lover spoke and said to me, 'Arise, my darling, my beautiful one, and come with me.'"

―――◈―――

Hezekiah stood before a tall bronze mirror as his servants dressed him in his wedding robes and placed the small crown of gold on his head. Shebna stood behind him watching, nodding his head in approval.

"I hope you realize this is all your fault, Shebna. I'm only doing this because you said I should appease my father."

"You look magnificent, my lord—like a king."

"Well, I don't feel like a king. I feel trapped. My life is controlled by a man I despise.

"Try to smile anyway. It is your wedding day."

His wedding day. Hezekiah knew he should enjoy this day, but instead he brooded over the fact that months had passed and King Ahaz had not said another word about a government position. He regretted losing his temper that day and wished he had kept quiet about Ahaz's trade agreement, but maybe Shebna was right. Maybe after his wedding he would regain his father's favor.

As Hezekiah's procession journeyed down the hill from the palace, crowds of people thronged the streets to join in the revelry. Hired musicians and dancers paraded before him, scattering palm branches and flowers at his feet, but Hezekiah felt as if he were on display, like an article in the marketplace under a gaudy striped awning. He wished he could do something to earn cheers besides get married.

Mercifully, Ahaz's trade minister lived close to the

palace, so Hezekiah didn't have to parade through the entire city. The procession waited in the street while he and his brother Gedaliah, who was his groomsman, went inside to claim the bride.

She waited for him in her courtyard, surrounded by bridesmaids. He couldn't see her veiled face, but she seemed tiny in the massive chair under the fig tree, like a child, too young to be given in marriage. Heavy layers of embroidered linen swaddled her, and Hezekiah thought she must be even hotter and more miserable than he.

When he took her hand, it felt icy cold, and she trembled like an old woman with palsy. He felt a rush of pity for the girl. Perhaps she was as unwilling to endure this charade as he was. Hezekiah spoke his wedding vows without comprehending them, as his heavy wedding garb seemed to suffocate him. He wished the day would end, but when the procession returned to the palace, he had to preside over the lavish wedding banquet Ahaz had ordered.

The feasting and drinking lasted all evening and far into the night. Long before the moon rose, the king was drunk, his pale face flushed, his bellowing laughter heard in every corner of the banquet hall. He could scarcely walk without help, and his eyes were glazed and bleary as he made the rounds of his guests, staggering and lurching as if crossing the high seas. His behavior disgusted Hezekiah, and he barely touched his own wine. He avoided his father most of the evening, but later that night Ahaz staggered up to him with a twisted grin on his face.

"I think you'll enjoy my delightful little gift tonight. Picked her out for you myself. Delicate little child, isn't she?"

Suppressed anger and hatred surged through Hezekiah until he was almost physically sick. He didn't want to accept any gift from Ahaz, and if his father had personally chosen Hephzibah, then he didn't want her. As he struggled against the urge to lash out at Ahaz, his father slurred his words again.

"But don't wear yourself out too much, because I've decided to send you to Phoenicia as an envoy with your new father-in-law when your wedding week is over."

At that moment Hezekiah hated Ahaz more than he thought possible. Even more, he hated his own helplessness and the power his father held over his life, causing him to grovel and beg for each miserable favor Ahaz granted. He was about to tell Ahaz to keep his gift and his worthless appointment when Shebna gripped his arm, squeezing it until he winced in pain.

"Your son is speechless with gratitude, Your Majesty," Shebna said with a grin. "I thank you on his behalf."

Hezekiah silently willed Ahaz to leave before he lost control, but instead his father inched closer, nudging him like a conspirator. Ahaz's hot breath, reeking of wine, fanned his face.

"But maybe you won't want to go away and leave her when the week's over. Such a pretty little child. Find out if she has a sister I can use for a concubine."

A hot rush of uncontrollable anger swept through Hezekiah. But once again his tutor gripped his arm painfully and spoke before Hezekiah could respond.

"We will look into it, Your Majesty. Thank you for your generosity, but will you excuse your son now? There is something he needs to attend to."

Hezekiah pushed his way through the crowd and out to the palace courtyard, beckoning the chilly evening air to cool his fury.

For Hephzibah, the long day of wedding festivities seemed endless as she waited for Hezekiah to take her away to their bridal chamber. Music. Dancers. Unending courses of food. An almost incoherent, rambling speech by the king that seemed to honor her father. Then more music, more dancing, more food. The opulence of the palace dazzled her. The attention lavished on her by everyone except her husband overwhelmed her. She had been in such a state of heightened excitement all day that she neared exhaustion.

But suddenly Hezekiah appeared beside her and reached for her hand, drawing her to her feet. The room fell still for the space of a heartbeat, then rang out with a frenzy of deafening clapping and cheering. Her face grew hot, and she was grateful for the veil.

Hezekiah stared straight ahead as he led her out of the din, up the stairs, through the maze of hallways. She felt the pressure of his hand on her arm but had no sensation of her feet touching the floor. At last he came to their wedding chamber, led her inside, and closed the door. The sound of her own heart pounding in her ears drowned out the noise of the wedding feast below.

Neither of them spoke as Hezekiah unfastened her veil to see her for the first time. As his dark gaze searched her face, studying her, she hoped her father was right, that he would find her beautiful. Instead, an unspoken question filled his eyes. He scowled slightly as if deep in thought; then his thick brows arched in surprise.

"Is your father paid so poorly that he has to send you to fetch the water every day?"

Hephzibah's heart stood still. In her joy she had never considered that he might remember her or recognize her from that day. Cold terror overwhelmed her, and she began to tremble until she could barely stand. The marriage would not be official until it was consummated. He could still change his mind. He stared at her curiously, waiting for her answer.

"No, he isn't, my lord," she whispered.

"Hmm. I didn't think so. Then maybe you can explain why you were standing by the guard tower a few months ago with a jug of water in your hands. Or am I mistaken?"

"No, my lord. You're not mistaken."

Hephzibah's heart pounded so loudly she was certain he could hear it, and she searched his dark eyes for anger. Would he annul their marriage and expose her shame before the entire wedding party? She felt a cry of despair rising from deep inside her, but it stilled before it reached her lips. She looked down, afraid to face him to see rejection on his face, but he put his hand under her chin and gently lifted her head until she had to look into his dark eyes again.

"You must have had a very good reason to venture out unescorted like that."

Hephzibah saw no anger in his eyes, only curiosity as he waited for her explanation. It tumbled out of her in a spurt of fear.

"When my father told me I would be married to a prince, I was terrified. I didn't know what you looked like, and so I had to find out before it was too late, because I was so afraid that you'd look like your—"

She stopped abruptly, horrified at what she had almost said.

"Like my father?" he finished for her.

Hephzibah felt the rising flush of heat on her face and knew it betrayed her guilt. She had committed a grave mistake. How many times had Abba scolded her for being outspoken? How many times had he said it was unladylike? What would happen to her for insulting the king?

The silence between them seemed endless. Then she saw his broad shoulders begin to quiver, the hard lines of his mouth split into a grin, and suddenly Hezekiah dissolved into helpless laughter. It was the most welcome sound Hephzibah ever heard. Still, she knew she must apologize.

"I . . . I'm sorry, my lord. I didn't mean to say it. I didn't mean to insult the king."

His laughter gradually died away, and he dismissed her protests with a shake of his head. "I like your honesty,

Hephzibah. It's very refreshing. But tell me, now that you've seen me—do you think I resemble my father?"

He stood before her with his hands on his hips, his chin held high, smiling broadly as he waited for her appraisal. He was so disarmingly handsome when he smiled that Hephzibah's chest tightened until each breath hurt.

"No, my lord. You don't resemble the king."

"I see. And what if you had gone to the guard tower that day and discovered a resemblance? Would it have made a difference to you?"

Hephzibah panicked. She could see no way to answer his question without insulting either Hezekiah or his father. She groped for words, aware that she had to say something.

"I did a very foolish thing, my lord. I never should have left my father's house. Thank you for saving my sister and me."

His magnificent smile faded, and his eyes grew serious once again. "I'm sorry, Hephzibah. It wasn't fair of me to put you on the spot like that. It's just that I was curious to know what would motivate a beautiful young woman like you to take such a risk. I suppose I was vain enough to believe that any woman in the nation would be honored to marry a prince, no matter what he looked like."

"Oh, yes, my lord! It's true! Most women would!"

"But not you?" His smile returned, and she managed to smile back weakly.

"I would marry whoever Abba arranged for me, my lord." And as difficult as it was to take her gaze off him, Hephzibah looked down again, submissively.

"Your honesty is refreshing, Hephzibah, and so is your daring, although I suspect your father would be outraged if he found out about it."

"Yes, my lord."

"And I trust you'll be more cautious in your exploits now that you're a married woman?"

She felt a glimmer of hope and met his gaze solemnly. "I promise, my lord."

He reached for her, drawing her into his embrace, and the top of her head barely reached his chin. She felt the hard strength in his arms and broad chest, and she clung to him, trembling, unable to believe it was real. Then, still holding her close, he gave a heavy sigh.

"I guess noblemen's daughters have a lot in common with kings' sons. Neither one of us has anything to say about who we will marry."

Hephzibah's panic returned as she puzzled over his words. Was he unhappy about his father's choice? Was there someone else he had wished to marry instead? She longed for the day when she would understand him completely, be able to read his heart in his eyes, to know what each sigh and gesture meant, to understand his half-spoken thoughts, and communicate without words as her parents often did. More than anything else, Hephzibah longed to be truly his wife, his lover, his friend.

His wooly beard brushed her cheek as he bent to kiss her for the first time, and with his lips on hers, Hephzibah vowed that somehow, someday, she would win his devotion, his trust, his undivided love.

But when Hezekiah left the bridal chamber after their week together, he didn't return to Hephzibah again.

17

King Ahaz slouched on his throne, browsing absently through a pile of documents. The heavy, official language in which Uriah had written confused him, and the stiff, tightly rolled scrolls jumped and curled in his hands, making them difficult to read, trying his limited patience. They required only his seal to levy more taxes to meet the Assyrian tribute demands.

The tedious morning routine of signing documents and listening to petitions bored Ahaz. He stared vacantly at the scrolls, sipping his wine, and allowed his mind to wander to the more pleasurable activities he had arranged later in the day.

A small commotion near the door to his throne room distracted him from his reverie, and he looked up to see Uriah embroiled in a heated discussion with one of the chamberlains. Thinking that a good quarrel might be an interesting diversion, Ahaz beckoned to his servant.

"Tell Uriah and the chamberlain to come here." He tossed the documents onto the table beside his throne as the arguing men approached and bowed before him.

"What's the problem, Uriah?" he asked pleasantly, fingering the stem of his wine goblet.

"There is no problem, Your Majesty. I have given the chamberlain my decision, and he has defied me." The chamberlain huffed angrily in protest, but Uriah ignored him. "I was about to summon another chamberlain—that's all. I'm sorry if we disturbed you. We'll continue our discussion outside."

Uriah seemed anxious to leave. He bowed and slowly backed away as if he had something to hide, which aroused Ahaz's curiosity.

"Just a minute. Why did you defy my palace administrator?" Ahaz asked the chamberlain. The man glanced uncertainly at Uriah, then back at the king.

"I was trying to deliver a message to you, Your Majesty, but Uriah wouldn't let me."

Uriah pounced with the swiftness of a striking adder. "The chamberlain knows that all messages and petitions must be cleared through me first."

"That's just the point, Uriah," the chamberlain whined. "They won't give the message to you. They asked to speak directly to the king, and unless you let them we'll never find out what they want."

Uriah glowered at the chamberlain, further heightening the king's curiosity. Uriah was hiding something—he was certain of that. Ahaz sat up, no longer bored.

"Who wants to see me? Tell me what's going on," he demanded.

"Your Majesty, envoys have arrived in Jerusalem from the northern kingdom of Israel," the chamberlain explained. "They've requested an audience with you to present a petition from King Hoshea."

"There can be no audience with the king unless they explain their petition to me first," Uriah responded angrily. "That's standard diplomatic courtesy."

Ahaz's excitement grew. He had not received a foreign emissary in many years, except from Assyria, and they came each year only to collect the annual tribute payments. He shifted in his seat excitedly, then leaned forward to pronounce his decision.

"Bring them to me. Tell them I'll hear their petition."

"No! Your Majesty, wait," Uriah pleaded, his words rushing out swiftly. "We need to take our time and think through all the implications of this. I advise you to postpone a hearing of their petition until tomorrow. Take time to consider—"

"No. I want to know why they've come."

"But receiving an envoy from another nation is a very serious decision, Your Majesty. If word reaches Assyria that we received envoys, they might interpret it as an act of rebellion. They might think we're plotting to form an alliance with Israel." The urgency in Uriah's voice was lost on Ahaz.

"That's ridiculous. I want to know what they're here for, and I want to know now." He waved Uriah away impatiently and nodded to the chamberlain. "Bring them here."

"Wait!" Uriah grabbed the chamberlain's arm to prevent him from leaving. "Your Majesty, I must advise you that the Assyrians—"

"I know what you've advised. You just told me. And your advice is nonsense." Ahaz suddenly smiled. "Besides, Emperor Tiglath-Pileser is no longer a threat to us, because he's dead."

The news of the Assyrian emperor's death had reached Ahaz only recently, but he felt uncharacteristically brave now that the monarch who haunted his dreams was dead.

"Yes, he's dead, Your Majesty, but that's precisely why we need to be even more cautious. Tiglath-Pileser merely represented the huge Assyrian Empire. His death won't mean the end of their domination over us. In fact, his successor will probably act swiftly and ruthlessly to quench any fires of rebellion that flare up in order to confirm his authority to the entire empire."

Ahaz refused to listen. "My mind is made up," he replied. "I will receive the envoy right now."

"Yes, Your Majesty." Uriah's shoulders sagged in defeat. He released the chamberlain and took his seat beside Ahaz, mumbling, "I hope this doesn't lead to disaster."

The chamberlain returned a short time later, followed by King Hoshea's emissaries and a retinue of slaves bearing gifts for Ahaz. They paraded down the long, carpeted throne room and bowed low before him in deference, giving Ahaz a feeling of power and authority he hadn't experienced for a long time, reminding him of the humiliation he had suffered when bowing before the Assyrian monarch.

"Your Majesty, King Ahaz ben Jotham, Great and Mighty King of Judah, we are your humble servants." They touched their foreheads to the stone floor. Ahaz allowed them to remain in that posture for several moments before stretching out his scepter to acknowledge their obeisance.

"Your Majesty, we bear gifts and a message from our lord, King Hoshea of Israel."

"The last emissaries from Israel were soldiers who besieged my city," Ahaz snorted angrily. "I'm pleased to see that your new king has decided to treat me with respect. State your petition."

"Your Majesty, our lord King Hoshea would like to meet with your representatives at a conference in Samaria. He wishes to discuss a united approach in our relations with the new Assyrian monarch, Shalmaneser."

Uriah leaped from his chair. "Do you know what you're proposing? Has your king gone mad?" He turned to Ahaz, pleading urgently. "Your Majesty, you must send them away at once to let it be known that Judah would never consider such a conspiracy. The Assyrians have spies everywhere!"

"Oh, sit down," Ahaz said, waving him aside like a pesky insect. "When I want your advice I'll ask for it. You may continue," he told the envoy. The Israeli glanced triumphantly at Uriah.

"As you know, the Assyrians annexed our northern-most territories as provinces 14 years ago. But lately they have begun using them as staging areas on some of our bordering towns and villages, raping and plundering our land unmercifully. Now that Tiglath-Pileser is dead, King Hoshea feels that it's time to reconsider submitting to Assyria. An envoy has also been sent to the Egyptian Pharaoh, asking him to join with us as well. United, perhaps we can put an end to Assyrian domination."

Uriah again sprang from his seat to confront the Israeli representative. "Has your king forgotten what happened the last time your nation tried to form an alliance against Assyria?" He turned to Ahaz. "Your Majesty, please. You saw what happened to Damascus. Do you want to risk the same punishment for Jerusalem?"

Instantly, Ahaz recalled the tortured, flayed body of King Rezin, the cold, merciless eyes of Tiglath-Pileser, and he shuddered involuntarily. But his euphoria quickly returned when he remembered that his adversary was dead. He had no reason to fear.

"Your petition is very interesting," he told the emissary. "But I will need some time to consider it."

Uriah paled. "There's nothing to consider! They're proposing treason and suicide! Please, stop this discussion before it goes too far—"

Ahaz silenced him with a shout. "No! I'll do whatever I please." Acting a role, playing the part of the dead tyrant he had feared for so many years, Ahaz wouldn't be stopped. The prospect of consorting with the kings of other nations excited him, and he no longer cared about the consequences.

"As I was saying," Ahaz told the envoy in a calm voice, "you will accept my hospitality as royal guests and dine with me tomorrow night. I will have an answer for King Hoshea by then. You are dismissed."

Ahaz laid down his scepter. "Uriah, I want you to assemble the men who took part in my trade delegation to Phoenicia six months ago and have them join me for dinner tonight. We'll send them to Samaria with this delegation. Make sure you include my son, Hezekiah. He'll be my personal representative. I shall return to my chambers now."

Uriah's features, usually unreadable, were creased with frustration, even despair, as he followed Ahaz and his servants across the palace courtyard to the king's private quarters. Uriah's obvious desperation gave Ahaz a feeling of power over the intimidating high priest that he didn't normally experience. He found the sensation gratifying, and he hoped Uriah would plead with him further so he could enjoy the pleasure of refusing him. When they reached Ahaz's chambers, Uriah granted his wish.

"Your Majesty, please listen to me—I beg you. You're endangering the safety of our whole nation. I urge you to have the emissaries stripped and beaten immediately and sent back to King Hoshea in disgrace. The Assyrians would surely interpret that in a favorable light."

Ahaz shook his head. "I don't care about the Assyrians. I've decided to join with Israel and Egypt and gain our independence from Assyria."

"But we couldn't possibly break free from them, even with Egypt's help. Don't you understand? Jerusalem will end up just like Damascus."

The more desperately Uriah pleaded the more it amused Ahaz, but he soon grew tired of the game. He needed a rest.

"Uriah, I'm sick of listening to you. If you can't support my policies, then maybe I'd better look for a new palace administrator." With a smile of satisfaction, he closed his chamber door in Uriah's face.

—◈—

Uriah returned to his own chambers with a sense of dread that bordered on nausea and spent the rest of the morning carefully pondering the unsettling turn of events. Within a matter of moments, Ahaz had pronounced a death sentence on his nation. The royal dinner tomorrow night would be the final knot in the noose that Ahaz had slipped around Judah's neck.

He wondered why a king who had been a docile puppet for so many years would suddenly abandon all reason and commit this act of political suicide. And he wondered how he could regain the control over Ahaz that had fallen so swiftly from his grasp. Ahaz had allowed Uriah to run the nation for years without interfering, and life under Assyrian domination had been safe and predictable, even if it was financially crippling. Why had the king picked this moment to suddenly decide to take control again?

Ahaz refused to listen to reason, and Uriah knew that if he continued to plead with him he was certain to lose his position in the court. He paced frantically around his chambers like a huge lion trapped in a pit too deep for escape, cursing Ahaz and his impetuous decisions. But in the end, Uriah knew he must save the nation from annihilation.

He pondered every possible solution to his dilemma and examined all the implications, knowing with quiet certainty that only one solution remained: he must place a new king onto Judah's throne, one who would refuse to join Israel's conspiracy, one who would appease Assyria before it was too late. Ahaz had to be eliminated—permanently.

His successor, Prince Hezekiah, was not much older than Ahaz had been when he first became king and was completely inexperienced. Uriah felt confident that if the prince were to inherit the throne suddenly, he would ask him to continue as palace administrator. Then he could influence Hezekiah to reject the Israeli alliance. But first he had to get rid of Ahaz.

Uriah's decision made sense to his rational mind, yet

another part of him cried out in horror. For over an hour he paced the length of his room, clenching and unclenching his huge fists, raking his fingertips through his thick mane of hair, gnashing his teeth in anger and frustration as the battle raged between the voice of reason and the vestiges of his conscience—between that of the powerful palace administrator and of the almost-forgotten high priest of Yahweh.

He was contemplating murder. His conscience recoiled at the thought. How could he have degenerated into a murderer? he asked himself. When did the process start? Was it when he turned his back on Ahaz's idolatry? Or when he helped sacrifice those children to Molech? Had planning the first murder made this one a little easier?

But there had been no choice back then, he rationalized. Ahaz chose to murder his own sons, and Uriah had only participated to gain his confidence. It had been a worthwhile decision, enabling him to do a lot of good for the nation since then. And there was no choice now either. The alliance would never work. Assyria would certainly retaliate. Uriah didn't want to be tortured or see his nation destroyed. Ahaz was playing with fire, and Uriah had to act before the alliance went any further. He was the only one who could save his nation.

But what about Yahweh? Wasn't the nation in Yahweh's hands? Or didn't he believe that anymore?

He didn't know what he believed. His beliefs didn't matter anyway. King Ahaz wasn't going to suddenly start trusting Yahweh after all these years. He was placing his trust in the alliance with Israel and Egypt, just as he had once trusted Assyria.

So maybe Zechariah had been right years ago. He had said Uriah would change if he compromised his beliefs. And in his heart Uriah knew that he had. He had wanted to change the king, but instead, Ahaz had changed him.

No. He dismissed that thought with an angry shake of

his head. Zechariah was an embittered, defeated old man who didn't know what he was talking about. And the king was an irresponsible fool. Without Uriah, Ahaz would have destroyed this nation long ago. It was up to him to stop Ahaz now.

But was murder the only way to stop him? It was written in the Torah, "You shall not murder."

True, but didn't the Torah also say somewhere that it was permissible to take a life in order to save a life? In this case, Uriah was saving millions of lives, the entire population of Judah. Certainly the Torah would sanction that.

Gradually, Uriah's frantic pacing slowed, his steps became more firm and assured, his worried expression relaxed into quiet resolve. In the end, the feeble remnants of his conscience couldn't win the intellectual duel. The voice of reason was victorious. King Ahaz had to die.

Uriah now began to direct his energies toward devising a plan. Ahaz had to be killed in a way that would throw no suspicion on himself, for his remaining in power was of the utmost importance. And it had to happen immediately. The dinner with the Israeli envoys tomorrow night must never take place.

With meticulous deliberation, Uriah reviewed every moment of Ahaz's daily routine, searching for the precise time, the exact place of Ahaz's vulnerability. One thread ran through the daily fabric of the king's life with unwavering consistency—his dependence on wine and the Assyrian drugs. He was rarely without a glass of wine close at hand. As his priest, Uriah had access to those drugs. He also understood what too much could do.

Convinced that he was about to perform the courageous act of a hero, Uriah sent for the king's royal cupbearer.

18

Hezekiah impatiently drummed his fingers on the banquet table. His father often arrived late for his meals, sometimes staggering in drunkenly. "But he has outdone himself tonight," Hezekiah mumbled to himself.

He had been waiting with the other banquet guests for over an hour and had watched in disgust as the steaming platters of meat had grown cold and the bloody fat congealed into hard puddles on the plates. The waiters who had carried the huge meal into the banquet room stood evenly spaced like mute statues around the perimeter of the table.

For Hezekiah, the last several months had been nothing but perpetual waiting for Ahaz. After making the trip to Tyre six months ago, he had been given no other duties in Ahaz's government, and the trade agreement had proved worthless, just as he had predicted. Ahaz had not summoned him at all until tonight's mysterious dinner.

Gradually, the polite conversation around the banquet table had dwindled into anxious silence as everyone waited. The guests eyed each other uneasily, but no one dared begin the meal without the king.

Finally Hezekiah's drumming fingers stopped, and he slapped the tabletop with his open hand.

"Why are we all left waiting here?—what is keeping the king?" he asked the nearest servant.

"I don't know, my lord."

"Well, has anyone bothered to find out where he is?"

"He's in his bedchamber. We have knocked repeatedly on His Majesty's door, but he doesn't answer. We were afraid to disturb him."

"He's probably passed out cold," Hezekiah muttered bitterly to Shebna. He hoped his assumption was true so he could return to his room and forget about the dinner. It was ruined anyway, and so was his appetite.

"He has never been this late before," Shebna agreed, shifting his position and flexing his long legs, which were cramped beneath him. "Do you know what could be keeping him, my lord?" he asked Uriah.

The high priest sat across the table from Hezekiah in his habitual stony silence, saying very little to anyone in the long hour they had been waiting. He showed no trace of impatience or boredom but had sat passively, occasionally stroking his gray-flecked beard.

"I haven't seen the king since this morning," he shrugged. "He returned to his chambers after holding court, and I believe he ate lunch there as well."

Jonadab, captain of the palace guards, flushed with embarrassment as his stomach rumbled and gurgled in the silent hall. "Pardon me," he mumbled. Shebna passed him a platter of date cakes, but he refused. "No, thank you. I'll wait for the king."

"This is ridiculous," Hezekiah cried, motioning again to the servant. "Send the king's personal valet into his chamber. Tell him to see what's keeping King Ahaz. I'll take responsibility for disturbing him."

The servant slipped from the room, and several minutes passed, the silence broken only by Hezekiah's drumming fingers and the incessant rumblings of Jonadab's stomach. Suddenly the king's valet burst into the room, pale and trembling.

"Oh, no—somebody come! It's the king!"

Uriah leaped to his feet with surprising swiftness and strode from the room with Captain Jonadab close behind. The other dinner guests sat frozen in their places, but Hezekiah hurried around the table and grabbed the frightened valet by the shoulders.

"What's wrong with the king?" he demanded. The valet shook his head, unable to answer, and covered his mouth with his hand as if he might vomit. "Show me, then." Hezekiah said and grabbed the trembling man by the arm and pulled him along behind him.

Hezekiah had no idea what to expect as he hurried down the covered walkway to his father's chambers. "Oh, no—oh, no . . . ," the valet murmured, and Hezekiah's body tingled with dread. Uriah had reached the king's bedchambers first and tried to stop Hezekiah at the door.

"Don't go in there," he advised, but Hezekiah pushed past him. He wasn't prepared for what he saw. King Ahaz lay sprawled on the floor in a pool of his own vomit and spilled wine, his back arched in agony, his limbs twisted in grotesque angles from his immense body. His fixed eyes stared, and his mouth gaped wide, permanently fixed in a scream of anguish. Fat, iridescent flies swarmed all over his body and inside his mouth, oblivious to Ahaz's status as king. Hezekiah swallowed back his rising gorge, wanting to look away but somehow unable to move.

"The king is dead," he heard Uriah saying behind him. He sounded very far away.

Hezekiah refused to believe it. He squatted down and touched his father's hand, where it curled clawlike against the carpet, and his stomach rolled over at the feel of his cold, dead flesh. It was true. Ahaz was dead. The room seemed to grow smaller and begin to spin. He shook himself, as if he could wake up from a bad dream, and swatted vainly at the buzzing flies that clung to his father's face.

He heard Uriah's voice again saying, "Long live King Hezekiah!"

He glanced around and saw Uriah on his knees, bowing to him. Then the others followed Uriah's example, slowly dropping to their knees and touching their foreheads to the floor, murmuring, "Long live King Hezekiah!" He stared at the prostrate forms, struggling to comprehend their words. His father was dead. He was the king.

Hezekiah felt no grief for Ahaz—only shock and surprise. Until today his life had been neatly ordered and scheduled with few changes and very few surprises. He hadn't dared to hope he would reign for many years. But Ahaz was dead, and now he was the king.

The news spread quickly through the palace, creating a bustle of noise and confusion in the passageways outside the room, but Hezekiah remained immobile. He turned to stare again at the grisly sight as if trying to comprehend the utter finality of death. At last, Uriah stood up and gripped Hezekiah's arm, squeezing it until the pain broke the spell of his shock. The tall priest pulled him toward the door.

"Your Majesty, there's nothing more you can do. You should leave now." He propelled him into the hall and closed Ahaz's door behind them. "I know that this has come as a great shock to you, but there are several urgent matters of state, Your Majesty. In order to insure an unbroken command of power, I ask for your permission to take care of them right away."

"My permission," Hezekiah muttered ironically. He wondered how it was possible that an hour ago he had nothing important to worry about, and now he was in command of the nation. He felt Uriah studying him, his eyes bold, almost challenging, and Hezekiah had to resist the urge to look away. Uriah knew much more about running the kingdom than he did, but Hezekiah had always had an instinctual dislike for him. He didn't really know why. He attributed it to the fact that, as far back as he could recall, the imposing priest had always hovered close to his father.

In spite of his instincts, Hezekiah decided to let Uriah remain in control for the good of the nation. He knew he would need time to learn his new role as king.

"You may continue with your duties as you did under my father," Hezekiah said at last.

"Thank you, Your Majesty." Uriah's steely features never changed. Hezekiah sensed Uriah's strong will and knew who had been running the nation.

"First, there is the matter of the emissaries," Uriah said. "It is imperative that they be sent back to their own country immediately."

What emissaries? Hezekiah wondered. It seemed to require a great effort to comprehend Uriah's words, as if he spoke a foreign language that needed translation. The hallway tilted as he nodded his assent.

"I will have to trust your judgment, Uriah, until I can be briefed."

"Good. I'm sure you will want to meet with your father's advisers as soon as possible. Would tomorrow morning be too soon?"

"No, that's fine," Hezekiah answered, knowing he needed time to recover.

"Also, there are the details of King Ahaz's burial for me to attend to." At the mention of his father's name, the grisly image returned to Hezekiah's mind.

"How did he die, Uriah?"

"He was alone, my lord. We may never know."

"Find out. Interview all his servants, all his concubines." That he had died in agony was obvious. The fact that no one had heard him or come to his aid seemed inconceivable.

Uriah's features hardened. "It can only tarnish the king's memory to dig too deeply," he said sharply. "I already know what I will discover." He paused, and his voice softened slightly. "You're well aware that your father drank too much. What you may not know is that he misused the ritual drugs from Assyria. I tried to discourage him, but he demanded more and more. He was the king. I couldn't refuse him."

"Are you saying he took a lethal dose by mistake?"

"I'm certain that's what I'll discover, but I will look into his death if you wish." Again Uriah stared at him almost defiantly, and Hezekiah's deep distrust for the priest resurfaced.

"I guess there would be no point," he said at last.

"Then if I may be dismissed, I will take care of these other matters and begin the preparation for your coronation immediately."

"You may go," he mumbled, and Uriah seemed to vanish.

Hezekiah walked slowly down the hall, oblivious to the surrounding flurry of excitement. Ahaz's life was over. And Hezekiah realized that the sheltered life he had always lived was also over. From now on, he was responsible for the entire nation. He knew that Ahaz had often tried to evade that awesome responsibility, and for a brief moment Hezekiah thought he understood why. He only wished there had been more warning, more time to prepare for his new role. But the time had come for Hezekiah to be king, whether or not he was ready.

—◆—

At first Hephzibah thought the king's death was only a rumor. Gossip was plentiful in the palace. But when she heard the high-pitched mourning cries coming from the king's harem and saw Ahaz's wives and concubines draped in black, she knew it was true. King Ahaz was dead, and she was married to the new king of Judah.

Within hours the palace servants prepared to move her and all of Hezekiah's concubines out of their crowded quarters and into the lavish apartments of the king's harem.

"Oh, my lady Hephzibah," her handmaiden Merab gushed. "Wait until you see your new suite. The rooms in the harem are the best in the palace. They have tall windows that overlook the courtyard on one side, and there's a view of the whole city from the balcony on the other side."

For as long as Hephzibah could remember, Merab had taken care of her. She had nestled as a baby on Merab's lap, been carried around on her broad hips. Merab's work-worn hands had soothed Hephzibah's tears, and her crinkly smile had greeted her each morning of her life. Now Merab had come to the palace with her as a wedding gift from her father. Merab loved her like her own daughter, but she was Hephzibah's only friend and companion in her new home.

Rich and spoiled all her life, Hephzibah did not get along well with Hezekiah's concubines, who resented her superior position over them. Then, as months passed and Hezekiah chose to be with them instead of Hephzibah, they began to taunt her, making certain she learned of it whenever he sent for one of them. Merab also knew what was happening, but she did her best to shield Hephzibah from their mockery and buoy her spirits.

"My lady, the concubines will go to the harem, but you'll have one of the beautiful apartments, reserved only for the king's wives."

Hephzibah smiled to hide the pain in her heart that grew greater each day. "Merab, I don't want those clumsy servants to carry these. Will you take them to our new apartment for me?" Hephzibah handed her the carved ivory box that contained her wedding jewels, her gift from Hezekiah.

The little servant's eyes glowed. "With pleasure, my lady," and she waddled out of the room, carrying the box like a treasure.

A few minutes later, when the palace servants returned for another load of Hephzibah's things, she suddenly decided to follow them and see her new quarters for herself. But as she entered the new suite she heard Merab's voice in the next room, arguing, scolding.

"My lady will *not* live with the concubines! She's the king's wife! She'll live here, in the wives' chambers!"

"I'm in charge, and I've already decided." The whiny nasal voice of the harem chamberlain was unmistakable. "The wives' quarters are only for King Hezekiah's favored wives, the ones he's pleased with. Your lady goes in the harem with the rest."

Hephzibah felt as if she had been slapped. She stifled a cry from the pain of his words and leaned against the wall to keep from falling over.

"How dare you insult my lady?" Merab cried.

"The prince spent his wedding week with your lady and hasn't sent for her since. It's been more than six months. Does it sound to you like she's a 'favored' wife?" His voice was biting and sarcastic.

Hephzibah covered her face as if to hide from the ugly truth. But the chamberlain continued to argue with Merab in the next room, and his painful words rained down on Hephzibah like the lashes of a whip.

"He never asks for her. That speaks plainly enough to me. Besides, she's failed to conceive his child. She'll go into the harem until he sends for her again. I'm not going to clutter up the wives' chambers with a wife he doesn't want. Now that he's the king, he can choose any woman in the nation for his wife. And the one he chooses will live here."

Hephzibah crumpled on the floor in a heap, sobbing, as the chamberlain stormed out of the room without seeing her. But in the next minute she felt Merab's arms around her, rocking her, and by the warm tears in her hair she knew that Merab was crying too.

"He doesn't want me, Merab. He doesn't love me."

"Shh . . . don't listen to that hateful man," she sniffed. "Don't listen to him, baby. It's not true."

But in her heart Hephzibah knew the truth. She was unloved, abandoned, rejected. What would her life be like now, she wondered, doomed to a long, lonely existence locked away in the king's harem? She had no husband, no children, no purpose for her life, no role to play except that of a decoration at banquets and feasts. She was not quite 18, and her life seemed to be over.

"What am I going to do?" Hephzibah sobbed. "I don't want to be imprisoned here for the rest of my life. Oh, why doesn't he love me, Merab? Why?" The servant clung to her protectively, her round little body trembling with emotion.

"I don't know, baby . . . one week . . . it's so unfair."

"Why couldn't I have married an ordinary man and been a *real* wife? I could run a household for my husband, like mama does. I could encourage him when he wakes up each morning and comfort him at night—be with him, take care of him, entertain important guests for him, raise his children. I want to love him and have him love me. Why couldn't it be that way? Why?"

"Let's go home, baby, back to your papa's house. This was a terrible mistake—"

"No," Hephzibah cried. "We can't go back home!"

"But, why not? Your papa loves you. He'd rather die than see you this unhappy."

"I can't go back. I don't want them to know I'm a failure."

"But you're not."

"Merab, I heard what the eunuch said. My husband wasn't pleased with me. That's why he didn't come back for me again."

"But he's hardly given you a chance."

"Besides, if I come home in disgrace, Papa will never be able to find a husband for Miriam. Oh, what am I going to do? I can't live like this the rest of my life!"

Merab drew her into her arms, and Hephzibah buried her head on the servant's chest. She stayed there for a long time, pouring out her sorrow, until all her tears were finally spent.

She loved the old servant like her own mother, but there was one thing she would never be able to confide in her, one thing she had not shared with anyone because it was the most painful irony of all—she loved Hezekiah. She loved him more than she loved her own life. She would stay in the harem until the day she died as long as a faint hope existed that one day he would remember her and come for her again. She could never love another man as much as she loved Hezekiah.

She remembered every word he had spoken to her in their one short week together and the way he stretched when he rose from their bed in the morning and gazed out the window at the hills surrounding Jerusalem as if they were his nourishment. She remembered the way he held her face in his hands when he kissed her and how he buried his fingers in her long hair. She could trace by memory every line and plane of his face, for she had studied him by moonlight each night as he slept beside her. She remembered his every movement, every gesture, because she had to—her memories of him were all she had left.

19

The sun had already set when Micah squeezed inside the rabbi's tiny, crowded home with the other disciples, anxious to learn why Isaiah had called this meeting. He was a trim, dark-bearded man with the tanned skin and muscular build of a farmer and the calloused hands and brawny arms of one who wielded a plow behind a team of oxen. Micah greeted those he hadn't seen since he'd gone back to tend his crops in Moresheth and embraced them warmly.

The single-room home that served the rabbi as a kitchen, bedroom, and study, as well as classroom, had few furnishings, and Micah found a place to sit on the stone floor. The fragrant air smelled of fresh bread and onions sizzling in olive oil.

Isaiah stood before the open hearth while his wife continued cooking behind him. Micah and the other men, called by Yahweh to be His prophets, listened with rapt attention.

"Most of you have probably heard the news from Jerusalem," Isaiah began. "King Ahaz is dead. His son Hezekiah will succeed him as king."

The news stunned Micah. It hadn't reached his tiny village of Moresheth. He leaned forward, listening intently.

"How did he die?" someone behind him asked.

"It was very sudden," Isaiah shrugged. "No one will say what happened."

It was Yahweh's judgment on a wicked, idolatrous king, Micah thought.

"The next few weeks will be critical for our nation," Isaiah continued. "We don't know anything about the new king, Hezekiah, whether he'll continue walking in Ahaz's ways or not. That's why I'm leaving to return to Jerusalem tomorrow. Yahweh's voice needs to be heard again."

"But Rabbi," someone protested, "suppose he's as evil as his father? Maybe you should wait until we know for certain. You're risking arrest." The others murmured in agreement.

"I understand your concerns," Isaiah answered, "but I'm not afraid. We have all been praying for a spiritual revival in our nation, and I must take advantage of this opportunity. I'm going to prophesy to King Hezekiah in Yahweh's name." The room fell silent except for the crackling of the fire and the slow stirring of a wooden spoon in the earthenware pot.

Excitement tremored through Micah. Isaiah was right —they had all prayed for an end to the moral decline of the nation, and a new king could reverse that decline. If only someone could convince him to listen to the Word of the Lord.

"I still say it's too dangerous for the rabbi to go," one of the prophets said. "Ahaz had orders to arrest him. He's too valuable to us here."

"I prophesied to King Jotham and to King Ahaz, and now I must prophesy to King Hezekiah. I'm not afraid."

"We're not questioning your courage, Rabbi, but what about Uriah? He's still the high priest, and for all we know, he may still be palace administrator too. He knows who you are, and he will never allow you to speak to the king."

"It's a chance I'll have to take," Isaiah insisted. "Yahweh's Word must be spoken now, while there's a transition of power."

"Then I'll go for you," Micah said, rising to his feet.

"No one knows me in Jerusalem. I'll prophesy before the king."

Isaiah looked at him thoughtfully. "I have no doubt that you could do it, Micah. I recognized the Lord's calling on your life the first time we met, in Moresheth."

Micah was younger than Isaiah, and his simple peasant manners contrasted sharply with Isaiah's poetic sophistication, but they had become as close as brothers in the few years of their acquaintance. And now Micah felt compelled to go to Jerusalem in Isaiah's place.

"But I have access to the palace and to the king," Isaiah continued, "I am of the house of David and—"

"And that's exactly why you shouldn't go," Micah said. "You're too well known. They'll find out you're back before you walk through the gates of the palace. Let me go. I'm a simple farmer from Moresheth, coming for the king's coronation."

"Are you sure you understand the great risks involved?" Isaiah asked his friend. "We have no way of knowing how King Hezekiah will react to a prophecy from Yahweh."

"Yes, I understand. I could be arrested or even killed. But I want to go. Yahweh commands it."

"I don't know," Isaiah wavered. "We'd need to help you formulate a plan to get an audience with the king. If Uriah is still the palace administrator, you'll have to get past him somehow. No one can stroll up to the palace and see the king. Public street prophecy may not be feasible either. And the king will be very heavily guarded."

"Rabbi, would any of your relatives in the palace help us?" someone asked.

Isaiah thought for a moment, then shook his head. "No, I've been out of contact with them for too long. A great deal of political intrigue takes place with a change of administration, and most of the nobility turn whichever way the wind blows until they see who's really in power.

I'm afraid I can't trust too many of my blood relatives to be sympathetic to our cause."

"What about the palace guards?" ventured one of the young prophets. "Could one of them help Micah get close enough to speak to the king?"

"I have an uncle in the palace guard," someone offered. "But he's assigned to a sentry post at the Water Gate, not the palace."

Isaiah stroked his trim beard thoughtfully. "Hmm . . . it's a possibility . . ."

"Rabbi, what about the servants at the palace? Could Micah trade places with one for a day and get close to the king that way? Maybe while he dines?"

"Does anyone have a contact among the palace servants?"

No one answered.

"How about if Micah sold some of his produce to the palace kitchens and made his own contact? A pretty serving girl, perhaps?"

"It's a good idea," Isaiah said, "but I'm afraid that it would take too long for Micah to establish a friendly relationship, in spite of his good looks. No, we will have to act quickly, within the next few days if possible. It will have to be while the new king is still gathering his advisers and deciding how he will begin his reign. It's our only hope. Once Uriah and his followers manage to gain the king's confidence, it will be too late."

Again the room fell silent except for the crackling of the fire. A range of emotions, from hope to despair, flooded Micah. Prophesying before the king could turn the nation back to Yahweh. But how would he get close enough to do it? Then suddenly he knew.

"I know what I must do," he said quietly. Everyone turned to him. "Isaiah said it at the beginning. I will simply walk into the palace and speak to the king." Stunned silence fell.

"Listen," he continued. "The king will probably announce a feast day to celebrate his coronation, right? I will wait until evening, when spirits are high with eating and drinking and everyone has relaxed his guard. Then I will walk boldly into the palace and speak to the king. Isaiah can draw a map so I will know my way around. After that, I am in Yahweh's hands."

Everyone stared at Micah. His plan was simple but outrageously daring. At last, one of the other prophets spoke up.

"Micah, you can't possibly attempt such a plan. It's foolhardy."

Micah turned on him with surprising anger. "I suppose you would have called David foolhardy when he went before Goliath, armed with only a sling? Or maybe Joshua was foolish to think he could conquer Jericho by marching around blowing trumpets? I can't question the way Yahweh chooses to work. I have to obey Him. And if I'm wrong, if I am acting foolishly, then I guess I was never called to be His prophet in the first place."

Isaiah gazed at Micah, and his eyes shone with respect. "May Yahweh bless you, my friend, for your courage."

"Amen," the others breathed. "Amen."

—◈—

Micah left before sunrise, following the winding mountain road through the Judean hills to Jerusalem. By the time he reached the Valley Gate on the city's southern wall, he was hot and tired, and his legs ached from the strain of his steep climb.

He stopped to rest at the Shiloah pool, feeling lost and strange in this bustling city that seemed to move at a breathless rate. He cupped his hands to sip the cool spring water and studied the unsmiling people hurrying past. He longed for a familiar face, but no one acknowledged his greetings. Rich and poor, priest and slave, they went about their business, either regarding Micah and his simple peasant clothing with contempt or else ignoring him altogether. It occurred to him suddenly that this was their attitude toward Yahweh too. They either ignored Him and His commandments or else contemptuously flaunted their sin before Him.

As Micah looked down the valley to the west, he saw the jagged cliffs that marked the entrance to the Valley of Hinnom. Isaiah had described the hideous rites performed at that shrine as parents sacrificed their own children to the terrible idol, but it seemed almost unbelievable to Micah. A clump of spreading oaks nearby marked a sacred grove used for worshiping Asherah, and all along his journey he had seen numerous altars to Baal springing up like weeds in every clearing and hilltop in Judah.

Micah had journeyed to the northern kingdom of Israel and prophesied against their apostasy and idolatry, still believing that his own nation of Judah was different, was true to Yahweh. But her wound is incurable too, he thought now. This scourge has come to Judah. It has reached the very gate of my people, even to Jerusalem itself.

Weariness and depression settled over his soul. It was too late for his nation. The futility of his mission overwhelmed him. His was only one voice against thousands of others. What could he possibly hope to accomplish? They would never listen to a poor peasant farmer. He would be ignored and scorned by the sophisticated city dwellers. Isaiah was of noble blood, from the royal house of King David, well educated and highly cultured, yet they hadn't listened to him.

"What am I doing here anyway?" Micah wondered aloud. "What's the use?"

He considered turning around and going home to his land in Moresheth without even entering the city. But then he remembered how Isaiah and his disciples had prayed for him throughout the night, and he knew that they would pray for him continually until he returned. They relied on him to be their spokesman, to remind King Hezekiah of Yahweh's covenant with the nation. If the new king would forsake idolatry and return to Yahweh, maybe the whole nation would repent as well.

It might be too late, but he had to try. He pushed his weariness and depression aside and walked through the crowded gate into the city.

The sun stood directly overhead, and Micah's shadow formed a small pool beneath his feet. In a few more hours he would watch the coronation at the Temple, and then the feasting would officially begin. After that, he would wait until everyone at the king's banquet had his fill of wine and meat. Then he would go. He would speak Yahweh's words to King Hezekiah.

The golden roof of Yahweh's Temple shone on the hill above the city, and Micah started walking in that direction. He had not made a pilgrimage to Jerusalem since before Ahaz closed the sanctuary and set up the Assyrian altar, and he could scarcely remember a time when the holy festivals were celebrated. The city had seemed beautiful back then, but now as he made his way through the steep, narrow streets, it seemed dirty and decayed, cloaked in rags of poverty. Micah knew how greatly the Judean farmers had suffered under the heavy burden of taxes that went to Assyria, but all around him he saw proof of how much the city dwellers had suffered as well. The splendor of Jerusalem, the once-great city perched at the hub of busy international trade routes, had faded. The city walls and houses seemed to be tumbling down, and many merchants had boarded up their shops. Beggars of all ages sat in the dust, pleading for alms from everyone who passed by. Hungry children ran naked in the streets. At least in the country the people have food to eat, Micah thought.

When he reached the royal palace below the Temple mount, Micah saw thousands of people jamming the outer courtyard, where the coronation procession would begin in three hours. He wondered what drew them. Did they hope for a better life under a new king, with renewed prosperity and peace? Only Yahweh could give them what they longed for.

He saw no joy in the thousands of faces he passed in the crowd, in spite of their merriment. Their frenzied drinking and laughter seemed like pathetic attempts to forget the overwhelming misery of their lives. A deep burden for these wretched, misguided people descended on Micah, and he knew that Isaiah had been right: the time had come for Yahweh's prophets to speak His message once again.

Micah leaned against the wall of the courtyard, away from the crush of people, and took out the sketch of the palace Isaiah had drawn for him, now limp and rumpled from being folded and unfolded countless times. He had studied it every spare moment along the way to Jerusalem until he had memorized it, and now he compared the drawing to the actual palace in front of him, trying to decide which route he would take to the banquet hall later that night. He didn't know exactly what he would say to King Hezekiah. Yahweh would provide the words when the time came.

As Micah watched, a squadron of palace guards, armed with swords and spears, roughly pushed back the crowd, then moved down the central staircase and assembled in a protective circle around the perimeter of the palace stairs. He wondered how he could get past them and what would happen to him after he prophesied—if he could quietly walk away and return to his home in Moresheth or if he would be imprisoned or even killed. To his surprise, he felt no fear. He would listen to the voice of Yahweh and speak the words He gave him, and what happened after that didn't matter.

The restless crowds milled about the courtyard, pressing in on him. Micah wanted to be alone with God, to prepare himself for his task. He folded the worn map once again and pushed his way out of the palace gates, feeling in the folds of his cloak for the silver pieces Isaiah had given him. He wanted to use them to purchase a dove for a burnt offering of purification. He climbed the steep steps to the Temple mount with growing anticipation, aware that he approached Yahweh's holy dwelling place on earth. Years had passed since Micah had seen it, and he recalled its shining splendor as through the eyes of a child.

But as soon as Micah entered the Temple gates, the sight of the huge Assyrian altar dominating the courtyard stopped him. Isaiah had warned him that a heathen altar had been erected in Yahweh's Temple, but that had not prepared him for the overwhelming sense of violation that hit him. The altar loomed above him, blatant evidence of the rape of Yahweh's holy place. The forbidden idols carved around the altar's base seemed to mock the Living God in what had once been His holy habitation. Yahweh's altar of burnt offering had been pushed aside, just as God had been pushed aside in men's hearts, to make room for the works of their own hands, the blasphemous creations of their own evil imaginations.

Micah groaned aloud, and his entire body trembled in outrage. He could never offer his sacrifice to Yahweh in the presence of idolatry. Never. God no longer dwelled here. No wonder his nation suffered and bled.

He turned and fled from the Temple, plowing through the winding streets, not caring where they led him. The teaming crowds jostled and buffeted him, but he didn't feel it. His anger and grief numbed him, and he wanted to lash out in vengeance for the sake of his God.

Micah strode blindly down the hill and found himself in the marketplace, where the tumultuous noise and activity brought him back to the present. Voices assaulted him from all sides as merchants hawked their wares, competing with each other for customers. Micah was still dazed when a short, swarthy man with a thick accent abruptly blocked his path.

"Come over here and look at these," the man invited, pointing to his booth. "I sell the finest household gods in the city. See? I have olive wood, gold, ivory . . . what'll it be, friend? Baal, for good crops? Only 30 shekels—"

"Leave me alone." Micah shook his head in disgust and tried to push past, but the merchant grabbed his arm. The man's breath reeked of garlic, and his touch repulsed Micah.

"You won't find any gods better than these. For you, 25 shekels."

"I don't want your filthy idols," Micah cried and wrenched free of the man's grip, shoving him backward a little harder than he intended to. The man lost his balance and stumbled, knocking over some of the images on his table.

"Hey! You can't push me around, you filthy peasant! Come back here!"

Shaken, Micah elbowed through the crowd and disappeared before the man could follow. He wanted to get away from the marketplace and find a quiet spot somewhere outside the city to be alone. He looked around for the street leading to the Valley Gate, but he couldn't see past the swarm of jostling people.

Suddenly, from behind, someone gripped his arm. He spun around to face a gnarled old man who grinned at him toothlessly. "Say, mister, you're not from around here. I can tell. Came to the big city for the celebrations, huh? Listen, I can give you a good deal on Arabian incense for the gods. It's imported stuff—10 shekels."

"No!" Micah cried, and as he turned away a woman smoothly stepped into his path. Micah stopped in shock. She wore no veil or headcovering but approached him immodestly, face-to-face, her eyes heavily painted with kohl like an Egyptian.

"Is that old toad bothering you?" she asked Micah, pointing to the incense merchant. "Want me to cast a spell on him?" Micah was too shocked to answer. To speak to such a shameful woman was improper.

"Maybe you have a departed loved one you wish to speak to?" she smiled. "Why don't you come home with me, honey, and I might even conjure up King Ahaz for you." She tossed her long black hair over her shoulder and laughed seductively.

Micah turned away and plowed through the crowd, brusquely shoving people out of his path. He felt contaminated and unclean, tainted with the filth of idolatry. But in his haste to leave the marketplace, he unwittingly stumbled into a gathering of Asherah worshipers. Cult prostitutes stood on a small raised platform while an eager group of men bartered vigorously with the priests for their services. As Micah burst through the crowd into the open space in front of the platform, the bartering suddenly stopped. Everyone looked at him in amazement, waiting for an explanation for his rude interruption.

Micah's entire body began to tremble. As the power of Yahweh flowed through him, he suddenly saw the masses of people through God's eyes. Strained to the limit, Yahweh's grace was about to run out. Wrath and judgment loomed ominously above the whole nation, yet the people were blind to their peril. He had to warn them. They needed to know.

He leaped onto the platform, shoving the prostitutes into the street. "Hear, O peoples," he shouted, "all of you." His dark eyes blazed, and his body shook with anger. "Listen, O earth and all who are in it, that the Sovereign Lord may witness against you, the Lord from his holy temple."

Micah's powerful voice carried across the marketplace, and the chattering and bartering stopped as a curious silence swept through the crowd.

"Look!" he cried. "The Lord is coming from his dwelling place; he comes down and treads the high places of the earth. The mountains melt beneath him and the valleys split apart, like wax before the fire, like water rushing down a slope. All this is because of Jacob's transgression, because of the sins of the house of Israel. . . . In that day, declares the Lord, . . . I will destroy your witchcraft and you will no longer cast spells. I will destroy your carved images and your sacred stones from among you; you will no longer bow down to the work of your hands. I will uproot from among you your Asherah poles and demolish your cities. I will take vengeance in anger and wrath upon the nations that have not obeyed me. . . . Zion will be plowed like a field, Jerusalem will become a heap of rubble, the temple hill a mound overgrown with thickets."

Micah leaped off the platform and, before the startled merchants could react, he overturned a table of carved images, dumping its contents into the street. Carried away by the wrath of a jealous God, Micah smashed all the images and idols that lay in his path.

"I will pour her stones into the valley and lay bare her foundations. All her idols will be broken to pieces."

The crowd stared at him in astonishment, and, as he paused for breath, Micah wondered if they would listen to him and repent. But in the next horrible moment he realized his mistake as a gang of drunken youths, following Micah's example, joined in the destruction of other booths, overturning tables of fruit and vegetables, smashing bottles and jars and furniture. Then the crowd went wild, scrambling to loot the smashed booths, and the marketplace erupted into a riot. Too late, Micah realized that his prophecy had exploded out of control.

"What have I done?" he cried. "No, wait! Stop! You don't understand!" He had never intended for this to happen, and he felt as if he were in a nightmare as the violence raged around him.

Suddenly the idol merchant stood in front of him, brandishing a club. Micah tried to step back and realized that angry merchants, armed with bats and sticks, were all around him, closing in from all sides. His heart pounded with fear.

This couldn't be happening to him. He had to get away. He had to prophesy to the king. He tried to run, but there was nowhere to go.

The idol merchant swung at him, and Micah dodged, only to catch a blow from behind him. He tried to fight back, to defend himself, but the force of their attack overwhelmed him. Clubs rained down on him in a torrent of pain. He raised his arms to shield his head and felt a sickening crack as a bone in his left arm fractured, leaving it limp and useless. They meant to kill him.

"Help me—Yahweh, help me!" he cried, as he struggled with all his strength to get away, to keep from collapsing. A violent blow smashed into his forehead, and pain ripped through his body like a knife. He staggered forward as his vision shrank into a throbbing blur and blood poured down his face, into his eyes, blinding him. Another blow knocked him to the ground, and the angry merchants closed in on him, kicking and beating his motionless body long after he had lost consciousness.

From his stall in the marketplace, Hilkiah watched in horror as the angry merchants swarmed over Micah's battered body. It had happened so fast. One minute Hilkiah had listened, spellbound, to the prophet's warning vision, and the next thing he knew they were killing him.

"Stop, stop—you'll kill him!" he cried as he raced from his booth into the street. He had to save him. But before he could reach Micah, his son Eliakim grabbed him from behind.

"Abba, no. Don't go out there."

"Let me go, Eliakim! Let me help him! They're killing him! They're killing God's prophet!"

Hilkiah struggled to break free, but his son, taller and stronger than he, would not let him go.

"They'll kill you too, Abba. Stay out of it. It's none of your business."

"Let me go," Hilkiah panted. He felt each blow that the angry men rained down on Micah, but he couldn't break free from Eliakim.

"God of Abraham—somebody! Help him," Hilkiah cried as Eliakim dragged him back to his booth. Then came the sound of horses as soldiers from the palace guard thundered into the marketplace. "Oh, thank God—thank God," he whispered.

"That's enough!" Captain Jonadab shouted above the chaos. "Stop where you are! All of you!"

The mob quickly backed away from Micah, and all over the marketplace the destruction and looting suddenly stopped as people scrambled to disappear and avoid arrest.

"Spread out," Jonadab ordered. "Arrest anyone who moves." He stood with his sword drawn, gazing in amazement at the destruction before asking, "What's going on here? Who's responsible for this?"

"Let me go!" Hilkiah begged. "Let me explain to him—" But Eliakim wouldn't loosen his grip.

"No, Abba. Stay out of it."

One of the angry merchants pointed to Micah's crumpled body. "He's the one who started it all. He destroyed my booth, and he has to pay for it!"

"Is this true?" Jonadab asked.

"Yes—I'm also a witness," another merchant added. "He claimed to be Yahweh's prophet."

Jonadab studied Micah's bloody body and rough peasant clothing as if he were an item for sale. "A prophet of Yahweh?" he muttered.

"Yes . . . yes," Hilkiah tried to shout. His arms ached from Eliakim's grip.

"Shh . . . Abba, please. Don't get involved."

The crowd stood hushed as Jonadab paced the length of the street, surveying the damaged booths carefully. Then he walked back to where Micah lay.

"Whoever wants to press charges should bring witnesses before the judges at the city gate. If the prophet lives, he will have to pay for the damages. In the meantime, take him to the guard tower. And the rest of you, go about your business or I'll arrest you as well."

Two soldiers lifted Micah by the arms and dragged him away. Hilkiah's shoulders sagged wearily as he watched the soldiers leave with the prophet. Only then did

Eliakim loosen his grip, and Hilkiah, angry and frustrated, turned to face his son.

"What is the matter with you? That man is God's prophet. Why didn't you help me instead of stopping me?"

"Abba, I helped you the best way I knew how. I kept you out of it. They were out of control. The mob would have killed anyone who helped that man, even you."

Wearily, Hilkiah sank onto his stool, shaking his head. He felt impotent against the evil that surrounded him and disappointed that his son didn't share his outrage. Instead, Eliakim seemed accustomed to it. He had been so young when the evil started creeping in and probably had no memory of a city that wasn't violently opposed to God. He wondered if there was any good left in the world or if he and this prophet were the only faithful followers Yahweh had left. He sighed in frustration.

"It's been so long since I've heard the Eternal One's prophets speak. You probably can't even remember them."

Eliakim rested his hand on his father's shoulder. "Yes, I do, Abba," he said quietly. "I once met Rabbi Isaiah—remember? I went to warn him for your friend, Zechariah."

"They are the only hope for this nation," Hilkiah said sadly. "The prophets. They're our only hope."

"We have a new king now, Abba. Maybe things will be different."

Hilkiah sadly shook his head and stared out into the street, watching the merchants sweep up the remains of their damaged booths. "No, I don't think so. Each new king has been worse than the one before him: Uzziah, Jotham, Ahaz—oh, God of Abraham, what can we do?"

"Come on, Abba. I'll help you close up. At least they didn't damage your booth."

"Yes, I suppose we may as well."

As Hilkiah rolled and stacked the colorful bolts of cloth, he had a sudden thought that steadily grew into a pressing conviction of what he must do. Carefully concealing his sense of urgency, he walked over to where his son was stacking cloth and took a bolt from his hand.

"The coronation will start soon. Why don't you go on ahead, Son, and pick a good spot for us to watch? I'll close up here and meet you in a little while."

"You'll finish faster if I help."

"No, no, no. You go, Son. I'll be along."

"Are you sure?"

"Yes, yes! Are you sure, he asks? Of course I'm sure. Go, already!" He motioned for him to go, then turned his back and, with deliberate patience, continued rolling up bolts of cloth and straightening the piles.

Eliakim shrugged. "OK, then. I guess I'll see you later," he said and then set off up the street toward the palace.

Hilkiah busied himself with his goods until he was certain Eliakim was out of sight. Then he hurried over to the idol merchant's booth.

"Shalom, my friend," he said cheerfully and bent down to help him pick up the remnants of his booth. "What a mess—what a mess!"

"Lousy religious fanatics," the merchant grumbled. "I hate them. They're bad for business."

"Yes . . . yes . . . ," Hilkiah cooed sympathetically, as he silently prayed for God's forgiveness for handling the idols. His hands felt contaminated.

Together they cleaned up most of the debris and tried to repair some of the damage. Then Hilkiah stood back to survey their work, idly jangling the silver pouch that hung at his waist.

"So—how much do you figure it'll cost you to make things right again?"

The merchant eyed him suspiciously. "What do you mean?"

Hilkiah hung his thumbs in his waistbelt and patted the money pouch conspicuously. "It's a holiday, and my business has been good. I was lucky. I'm willing to help you out a little so we can both forget this whole nasty mess as quickly as possible and get back to business." He chuckled merrily, but the merchant still peered at him suspiciously.

"What's in it for you?"

Hilkiah laughed. "What's in it for me, he asks? Look at this mess! It's an eyesore. It's bad for business. And a lawsuit at the elders' gate will be even worse."

"But why would you want to help that filthy peasant?"

"I'm not helping him—I'm helping *you*. Besides, the poor beggar has suffered enough, don't you think?"

"Yeah, we did get him pretty good." His lips curled into a mirthless smile that revealed crooked, yellowed teeth.

"Precisely. You already got more justice than the elders at the gate will ever give you. And I'll wager that poor beggar hasn't a shekel to his name."

"That's probably true—"

"Of course it's true." Hilkiah clapped a friendly arm around the man's shoulder and steered him toward the inn down the street. "So. Round up these other merchants, and let's all forget about the fellow. We'll drink a toast to the rebuilding of your booths. It'll be my treat!"

———◆———

Uriah watched as his servants prepared his bath, and for the first time in days he started to relax. He had taken a great risk when he assassinated King Ahaz, but the risk had paid off. The emissaries had been sent back to Israel, avoiding a disaster that might have destroyed his nation. And so far, Hezekiah had not pursued the cause of Ahaz's death.

The new king had not only allowed him to continue as palace administrator but in a few hours he would preside as high priest over the coronation as well. He fingered the mitre and ephod that he would wear for the ceremony. He had remained in power as he had hoped.

"Your bath is ready, sir," a servant announced. But before Uriah had a chance to undress, someone knocked at the door.

"Come in!" he boomed cheerfully. Captain Jonadab entered, and his worried expression made Uriah uneasy.

"Forgive me for disturbing you, sir, but you wanted to stay informed on all aspects of security for the coronation."

"Yes—what is it?" A stab of fear punctured his elation.

"Well, a short time ago my soldiers and I broke up a riot in the marketplace. Now, that's not too unusual, considering that this is a festive occasion and the people are starting to celebrate, if you understand what I mean. In fact, people are coming into the city from all over the countryside, and the feasting and drinking are well underway and—"

Uriah quickly grew impatient with the long-winded captain's rambling story. "What about the disturbance in the marketplace?" he demanded angrily.

"Well, sir, I know how much trouble his kind has caused you in the past and . . . ," Jonadab stammered nervously for the right words, obviously aware of Uriah's reputation for blaming the messenger for bearing bad news. ". . . the fellow who started the disturbance claimed to be a prophet of Yahweh."

Uriah shouted a curse, and his bustling servants froze in their places.

Jonadab took an unconscious step toward the door.

"Was it Isaiah?" Uriah thundered.

"No, sir," Jonadab answered. "He was younger than Isaiah, a coarse and common fellow—a peasant from the countryside, judging by his clothing."

"Where is he now?" Uriah demanded. He knew with certainty that if a prophet of Yahweh came to Jerusalem, he would try to reach King Hezekiah, perhaps by disrupting the coronation ceremony. Uriah could not allow that to happen.

"I've arrested him, sir. The soldiers took him to the tower. The mob beat him pretty badly during the riot, and he's all but dead."

Uriah felt only slightly relieved. He knew better than to forget the incident, though. "I want him brought to me at once so I can question him. And I want you to double the security measures at the coronation ceremony. There may be more than one prophet, and they are a great threat to the king."

"Yes, sir. I'll take care of it right away." Jonadab bowed and swiftly left the room.

The news greatly disturbed Uriah. Yahweh's prophets had been silent for so many years that he had hoped the last of them was finally gone. If they reappeared now, competing with him for King Hezekiah's confidence, they could topple the delicate balance of power that Uriah had worked so hard to build.

He was proud of the reforms he had made in the strict Jewish religious system, reforms that Isaiah and his followers would call too liberal. He had centralized the state religion at the Temple of Yahweh, with himself as high priest. The prophets, with their narrow, conservative, outdated views, opposed all that Uriah had worked for. He would not risk the possibility that they might influence the king. He had to make sure they never reached Hezekiah.

21

Zechariah shaded his eyes, squinting in the glare of the afternoon sun as he stood with the Levites on the Temple porch. He rose to his toes, craning his neck from side to side, but he couldn't get a clear view of the king's platform.

A rumble of applause thundered from the huge crowd assembled in the courtyard, and he pushed forward frantically. A guard rested his hand on the old man's shoulder and drew him back.

"Please, Zechariah—I have orders to make sure you keep quiet. That's the only way Uriah would agree to let you watch the coronation."

"But I can't see. Let me move a little closer. I'm not going to disturb the ceremony."

Shimei, who stood nearer to the front, turned around. "Here, let him trade places with me. You haven't missed anything yet, Zechariah. The nobles and king's advisers are making their entrance."

"Very well—go ahead," the guard conceded. "I can't imagine how you could cause any trouble," he mumbled.

Zechariah quickly traded places with Shimei. Now he had an unobstructed view of the raised platform in the center of the Temple courtyard, the site of the coronation. The nobles and advisers leading the procession had taken their places near the Assyrian altar. In a moment, Hezekiah would make his appearance and come forward to be anointed king of Judah. Zechariah had never dreamed he would live to see it.

The trumpeters, assembled on the broad wall surrounding the Temple, sounded their fanfare. The gates to the courtyard slowly swung open. Zechariah held his breath.

The deafening cheers of the crowd drowned out the sound of the trumpets as the people caught their first glimpse of their new king. Carrying himself with the posture and bearing of a soldier, he strode to the platform and took his place, wearing a sword strapped to the belt of his royal tunic. He was tall, broad-shouldered, trim, a startling contrast to King Ahaz. His curly brown hair and beard had an auburn luster in the sunlight.

Zechariah's vision blurred as tears filled his eyes. He still looks the same, he thought to himself. He is older and taller, but he still looks the same. And he remembered the curly-haired little boy who had run through the rain-washed streets to the Temple, splashing his feet in all the puddles. He longed to hold him in his arms as he had so long ago.

With a faint smile, Hezekiah acknowledged the wildly cheering crowd, but his dark eyes remained serious. At last he held up his hand to call for silence, his other hand resting casually on the hilt of his sword. The noise slowly subsided.

"Men of Jerusalem and Judah," he shouted. "I, Hezekiah ben Ahaz, lay claim to the throne of my father, Ahaz ben Jotham, as rightful heir of the royal house of King David." He spoke slowly and clearly, and his deep voice carried an aura of authority. "My reign will be equitable and just—and absolute. When I sit in judgment over this kingdom, you may expect my decisions to be impartial. And in return, I will expect the honor and tribute that is due me by virtue of my position as king and heir to the throne of Judah."

A roar of approval went up from the crowd, and,

amid the shouts and cheers, the trumpets sounded their fanfare once more. When the din died away, Uriah stepped forward, wearing the mitre and ephod of the high priest, carrying a horn of oil in his hand. As Hezekiah sank down on one knee, Zechariah watched, biting his lip.

"May all the gods of Judah bless your reign with peace and prosperity," Uriah prayed as he anointed the king's head with oil.

"No!" Zechariah gasped. The guard shot him a threatening glance. "But Hezekiah knows there is only one God! Why would he allow Uriah to pray that way?" The priest's words had struck him like a fist in his stomach, and his pain was greater than any he had ever known. All his years of waiting, all his prayers had been in vain. Hezekiah no longer believed in Yahweh. He fought back tears as his faith and hope withered like green shoots in the desert sun.

He wondered where Isaiah was, where all the prophets of Yahweh were. If only one would prophesy to Hezekiah. Maybe he would listen—maybe he would remember. Zechariah scanned the huge crowd, hoping to see Isaiah pushing his way to the front to prophesy as he used to do in the days of Jotham and Ahaz. But no one attempted to challenge the double ring of guards that stood at the base of the king's platform.

When Uriah finished his prayer, a scribe stepped forward from among the Levites and presented the manuscript scroll that contained the divine law for kings.

Maybe Hezekiah would read it. Maybe it would help him remember all that he had been taught. But Zechariah realized bitterly that Uriah had probably altered the divine law as well to conform with all his other deviations from the Torah.

Another priest walked forward, carrying the royal crown of Judah and the emblem of David, the heavy gold and velvety gems glinting in the sunlight. Zechariah watched in pride and pain as Uriah solemnly placed the crown on Hezekiah's head and draped the emblem around his neck. The new king rose to his feet, his chin held high, while the jubilant crowd roared, "Long life to King Hezekiah!" over and over again.

Zechariah gazed at Hezekiah, his beloved grandson, standing with strength and dignity, the crown of the kingdom on his head. He remembered all the other kings he had known: Uzziah, Jotham, Ahaz. They had once stood here too, full of promise like Hezekiah. Now they were dead. And Zechariah's hopes and dreams for Hezekiah died as well. Hezekiah no longer believed in Yahweh. Zechariah felt as if his heart would break.

As the sound of the cheering throbbed in the old man's ears, he took his gaze off Hezekiah to search the crowd one last time for Isaiah. For a moment he considered going forward himself, but the guard at his side watched him carefully.

"Ah, Yahweh! He doesn't believe in You," Zechariah groaned as he looked longingly at Hezekiah. "He doesn't believe in You." He could no longer stop the flow of tears that streamed down his face. He felt old and withered suddenly, and he longed to crumple into the dust of the courtyard in disappointment.

As the Temple priests prepared to offer sacrifices for the new king on the Assyrian altar, Zechariah covered his face. "Hezekiah doesn't believe," he moaned again.

"Come on, old friend," Shimei said, taking his arm. "Let's get out of this hot sun. It's all over for now. Let's go inside."

Zechariah took a final look at the new king of Judah. "Yes, it's over," he said. Then, leaning heavily on Shimei's arm, he walked slowly back to his rooms.

—◈—

Uriah sent all his servants away and sank onto his couch, exhausted and greatly relieved. The coronation had gone smoothly, without any disturbances. Perhaps the prophet in the marketplace today was the only one left, he thought as he began to relax.

He could enjoy the ceremony now, in retrospect. Hezekiah had made a striking impression, and the crowds seemed pleased with their new king. Uriah smiled to himself and felt his good mood begin to return.

A servant entered quietly and bowed before him. "Captain Jonadab wishes to see you, sir."

"Good. He has brought me the prophet. Send them in." He wanted to question the prophet himself and see how many other prophets remained in Judah.

But Jonadab entered alone. He appeared more worried than the last time. Uriah sprang to his feet. "What's the matter? Where's the prophet? Is he dead?"

Jonadab cleared his throat. "No, sir. He didn't die, yet. But I don't have him."

Uriah exploded in a storm of furious cursing. "Why not? Didn't I tell you to bring him to me?"

"When I got back to the guard tower, he was gone. The guards released him while I was overseeing the extra security measures you ordered for the coronation." There was an inference of guilt on Uriah's part, but Uriah ignored it.

"They did *what?*"

"No one showed up with witnesses to press charges. Someone paid his fines and paid for the damages in the marketplace, so we had to release him. He was gone when I got back to the guard tower."

"You *fools!*"

"How could we hold him if no one pressed charges?" he said defensively. His dislike for Uriah was ill-concealed.

"Who paid the prophet's fines?"

"I don't know. My men didn't ask his name."

"Fools!" Uriah repeated in disgust.

"I can order my men to search for him again. It

shouldn't be hard to find him. The prophet was beaten half to death during the riot and still hadn't regained consciousness when the soldiers released him from the guard tower. My men said it would be a miracle if he lived." He was silent for a moment and then added, "I will resign my position, sir, if you wish."

But the news upset Uriah too much to worry about Jonadab's resignation. If someone had redeemed the prophet from prison, then he was not acting alone. There were more of them, and they would probably try to reach the king unless he stopped them. He turned to the waiting captain.

"I don't want your resignation—I want you to find the prophet and the men who are helping him. They are a threat to King Hezekiah. Do you understand? I want to be notified the minute you have them in custody, and this time guard them well. Is that clear? Do it right this time!"

"Yes, sir. I understand."

———❖———

Hezekiah sat in his old classroom, on the bench he had occupied for so many years, still wearing the royal robes from his coronation that had ended a few hours earlier. Scrolls littered the table in front of him, and he pored over them in desperation, his stomach a knotted lump of nameless apprehension and dread.

If only he'd had more time to prepare, to learn to handle the reins of government gradually instead of having them thrust into his hands without warning. He felt as if he were a passenger in a driverless cart, careening down a mountain slope out of control.

He picked up a scroll from the top of a pile and read the title: "Annual Assyrian Tribute Payment." He skimmed over the long list of items that followed and tossed it aside. The next scroll contained the following year's payments, and its list of tribute was even longer, the financial demands much greater. He crushed it between his hands and hurled it to the floor. Suddenly the door flew open, and he looked up.

"Your Majesty!" Shebna cried in surprise. "I did not think I would find you here. I am sorry for disturbing you. I will come back later."

"What do you want, Shebna?" For a reason he couldn't explain, he felt angry with his tutor for the first time that he could recall.

"I have come back for some of my things. I did not expect to find you here. I assumed my duties were over now that you are the king." He grinned proudly, displaying his even row of white teeth.

Hezekiah's stockpile of frustrations exploded into rage. "You haven't finished your job, Shebna! In fact, I'd say my real education has just begun!"

"I do not understand what you mean. I have tutored you since you were a child. You have exhausted all of my knowledge."

Hezekiah sprang from his bench, knocking it over backward, and swiftly crossed the room to stand before Shebna, confronting him angrily. "Everything you taught me is worthless knowledge. It has nothing to do with real life."

"What do you mean? I do not understand." He groped for the nearest bench and sat down as Hezekiah towered over him in rage.

"I'm king of a nation that lies in ruins! My kingdom is in shambles. My reign is a joke. That's the reality. And you never taught me any of this." He knew he was using Shebna as a convenient outlet for his frustration, but he couldn't stop his fury once it had been unleashed.

"Your Majesty, you have been the king for only a short time. You will learn what you need to learn quickly. You have a sharp, clear mind, and you learn so fast . . ."

"Oh yes—I learn very fast," Hezekiah answered bitterly. "Do you want to know what I've learned in the few days that I've reigned? I've had my first briefing with Uriah and my advisers. Do you want to know what I've learned? First of all, that my father's advisers are all worthless! Uriah's the only intelligent one of the bunch, and I don't trust him. I've also learned that our nation is bankrupt!"

"That cannot be true." Shebna's eyes widened in shock.

"Yes, it's true," Hezekiah assured him. "While you and I sat in this classroom and studied all these dusty scrolls, my father and his advisers sold Judah into slavery to Assyria. Sure, you taught me that Judah has a treaty with Assyria, but never the fact that his treaty makes us virtual slaves! Look at these tribute demands! And the list gets longer every year." He shoved one of the scrolls into Shebna's hands.

"I am sorry," Shebna stammered. His face turned pale as he scanned the list. "I am sorry. I did not know—"

Hezekiah raged on. "Our nation's territory has shrunk to half the size it was 50 years ago. The Philistines, Edomites, Israel, Aram—everyone has carved out his share. We have no strategic seaport, no fortified cities except Jerusalem, and even these walls are crumbling down around us. The national treasuries are empty. There is no surplus in the storehouses. Everything our people labor to produce goes to Assyria."

He paced in front of Shebna, tugging helplessly on his beard. "I have no real power. Judah is one of dozens of puppet states in the Assyrian Empire. I have no army, no defensive weapons, and I can't afford to raise an army, because we're bankrupt." He stopped pacing and shook his head in disbelief. "I never dreamed I'd be king so soon—or that I'd inherit such a mess."

He sank onto a bench opposite Shebna and covered his face. "I'm supposed to preside over a banquet in a few minutes, and I've never been so depressed in my life."

"I am truly sorry, my lord," Shebna said softly.

"You know what infuriates me the most? I sound just like my father did with his lousy temper. No wonder he never wanted me to learn about running the government. He's made such a mess of it."

"Well, it certainly explains why he drank so heavily," Shebna ventured.

"I don't want to escape from responsibility like he did. I want to find solutions. The question is, how? The more our country produces, the more Assyria takes. And the chronicles tell what happens to nations that try to rebel. None of them have succeeded. How did Judah get into this predicament? And how am I going to get out of it? I've been poring over all the records, trying to figure it out, but I haven't found any answers."

"At least you have tremendous popular support. At your coronation today the crowd loved you. I never saw them that supportive of King Ahaz."

"Is that supposed to make me feel better?" Hezekiah turned on him angrily again. "They expect something of me. They are counting on me to solve all the problems my father created. And I don't have any answers. I don't even know where to begin. How popular will I be a year from now if things aren't any better?—or if things get worse?"

He remembered all the hopeful, expectant faces gazing up at him from the crowd, and he felt sick. He longed to do something to help them, to repay their loyalty and hard work with renewed prosperity. But he didn't know how. Several minutes passed as the two men stared at each other.

Finally, Shebna said quietly, "I have failed you, my lord. I am sorry."

"Sorry?" Hezekiah shouted. "Sorry? I don't need your apologies, Shebna. I need your advice!" He sprang from his seat, grabbing a pile of scrolls from the table and flinging them onto the floor. "Where are the rules that tell me how to govern? Where are the instructions for kings to follow? Where is the order in all this chaos?" Hezekiah turned to the shelves and hurled those scrolls onto the floor too. At last the shelves were empty and his anger was exhausted. He sagged onto a bench, staring at the littered floor.

"I care about my country, Shebna," he said at last, "every rock-strewn, sunbaked acre of it. Its future is entrusted to me." Hezekiah gazed out the window at the green-and-brown Judean hills surrounding the city and realized how very much he did love his tiny country. He bent down and began slowly picking up the scrolls.

"You do not need to do that, Your Majesty," Shebna said hesitantly. "I will call a servant."

Hezekiah didn't reply but continued gathering up the scrolls. When he finally looked up, his face was strained.

"I don't know what I'm going to do, Shebna," he said quietly. "But I am the king of this beautiful, pitiful little nation. And I will find a solution."

22

Micah slowly opened his eyes, and an explosion of pain ripped through his head. He moaned and fought the urge to sink back into unconsciousness to escape the agony. He tried to move, but he felt as if a huge stone rested on his chest, making it difficult to breathe.

Help—he needed help. He tried to cry out, but all that emerged from his swollen lips was a hoarse rattle. Through painful spears of light he saw a dark-skinned face peering at him with soft hazel eyes. Then the face disappeared, and he heard her calling, "Master, Master—come quickly! He's awake!" When the woman reappeared, Micah noticed a slave ring in her ear.

He tried to talk, to move, but the woman gently placed her hands on his face and shook her head. "Stay very still," she commanded.

Micah felt too weak to struggle. He heard footsteps, and then a second face appeared, round and jovial with a broad smile and twinkling brown eyes. A small skullcap covered his balding head.

"Well, now, my dear fellow," his pleasant voice boomed. "We've been quite concerned about you. We weren't sure if you'd live through the night or not. But Botheina knows all about the medical arts of Egypt, and she's taking good care of you." He patted Botheina's arm to show his appreciation and chuckled to himself.

Through the night? thought Micah. Could it be night already? Was he too late for the banquet? How long had he lain unconscious? He moaned and struggled to sit up.

"Steady, my friend," the little man soothed when he saw Micah struggling. "It's all right—you're among friends. Take it easy, now. You've had a terrible beating. In fact, I'd say you're lucky to be alive at all. But you'll have to lie here a while longer and rest. I'll have Botheina mix you one of her concoctions to ease the pain and help you sleep." He nodded to Botheina, and she slipped from the room.

Micah felt desperate. He had to get to the palace. He couldn't let them drug him into unconsciousness. "No . . . ," he moaned. "No . . . ."

"What's that?" the man asked, then his sparkling brown eyes lit up. "Oh, I know," he chuckled. "You're probably wondering where you are and what happened. Just lie still, and I'll tell you the whole story. My name is Hilkiah, and I'm also a follower of the Holy One of Israel—blessed be His name. But unlike you, I don't go around causing riots in the marketplace." He laughed merrily.

"Anyway, I'm a merchant, an importer of fine linen and dyed cloth, and I heard you prophesy today. I watched the whole ugly riot from my booth. Such a beating you had! Terrible, terrible!" He shook his head.

"After the soldiers carried you away and things calmed down a bit, I had a chat with the merchants whose stalls were destroyed. Now, I don't blame you a bit for what you did. I agree that their idolatry is an abomination to the God of Abraham—blessed be He. And I wanted to help, because I could see that you are a true prophet of Yahweh. So I bargained with them a little. They drove a hard bargain," he laughed, "but in the end I paid for their losses, and they agreed not to press charges. Then I went to the guard tower, paid your fines, and here you are." He chuckled again. "As I said, we weren't sure if you'd live through the night or not."

Night? Please, God, don't let it be too late! Micah summoned all his strength in an effort to speak. "Night . . . ?"

"Eh?" Hilkiah asked, leaning closer.

"What . . . hour . . . ?"

"You want to know what hour it is?" Micah nodded. "I don't know—it must be close to midnight."

"Oh no," Micah groaned and closed his eyes, praying silently for strength. Why hadn't he kept silent in the marketplace? How had everything gone awry? Maybe he could still make it to the palace if he left right away, if the palace wasn't too far. He had to try.

"I've got . . . to . . . go . . . ," he whispered and struggled to get up against tremendous pain and the dead weight of his body. It was no use. His head pounded violently, and something sharp stabbed his chest with every breath he took. The throbbing pain in his lifeless left arm was agonizing. He began to cough from his efforts to move and tasted blood.

"Now listen, my friend," Hilkiah said with concern. "You've got to take it easy. What is it that's so important? Are you supposed to be someplace else?"

"Yes," Micah breathed. "The king . . ."

"Yes, yes," Hilkiah soothed. "Just lie still a minute." He looked up at the slave girl who had returned to the room. "Botheina, our friend the prophet seems anxious to go somewhere, and he's quite determined, in spite of all his injuries. Can you bring him a little broth to sip for strength?"

"Yes, Master," she replied and hurried from the room again.

"What's going on, Abba?" a new voice asked. A young man in his late 20s entered the room, tall and thin, scholarly looking, with a high forehead and tousled black hair and beard. His deep brown eyes had the same jovial sparkle as Hilkiah's. "Has the prophet recovered?"

"Yes, he's conscious now. This is my son, Eliakim," he told Micah.

"Here, Abba—let's help him sit up," Eliakim suggested.

The two men stood on either side of the narrow bed and gently lifted Micah to a sitting position, propping him up with pillows. He coughed up more blood, but his breathing seemed to ease, and he found talking easier.

"I still don't know your name," Hilkiah said.

"I'm Micah of Moresheth."

"OK, Micah. Botheina has some broth for you, and it should give you a little strength. Then maybe you can tell us what it is that's so important."

The slave girl returned with a small bowl of liquid, and she carefully fed him several spoonfuls. He felt like a helpless child as some of it trickled past his swollen lips and ran down his chin. Again, he blamed himself for his failure. However, he hadn't eaten since he left Isaiah's house early that morning, and the warm, delicious broth renewed his strength. He drank all he could, stopping several times to cough. Each time the piercing stab in his chest dug deeper.

"I think his ribs are broken, Master," Botheina said, feeling Micah's chest gently. "Can you move your arm?"

Micah tried in vain to raise his limp left arm, and the throbbing pain increased.

"Yes," she soothed as he groaned. "It is broken as well."

"Oh dear, oh dear," Hilkiah clucked. He turned to his son. "Can you fix it for him, Eliakim?"

"I'm an engineer, Abba, not a physician. Buildings and roads I can fix. But people?" He shrugged helplessly. "He needs a physician."

"Oh dear," Hilkiah repeated. "We'll have to wait until morning to send for one. Will he be all right until then?"

"No! I have to leave right now," Micah panted.

"What must you do that's so important, my friend?"

"I'm in Jerusalem on a mission for the prophet Isaiah."

"Isaiah!" Hilkiah shouted. "Isaiah is still alive?"

Micah nodded.

"Oh, hallelujah! We thought he was dead. God of Abraham, thank You!"

"Abba, let Micah finish," Eliakim said.

"Oh, I'm sorry. It's just that after the way they've locked my friend, Zechariah, up in the Temple all these years I was worried that—well, please go on, Micah."

"I must go to the palace tonight. I have a prophecy from Yahweh for King Hezekiah."

Hilkiah looked at Micah with awe. "A prophecy?" he muttered incredulously. "For the new king? No wonder you're so anxious." He turned to his son. "Eliakim, we have to help our friend get to the palace."

Eliakim spread his arms wide in amazement. "What? You can't be serious, Abba. He can't even sit up by himself. How can he possibly go to the palace? Listen, Micah— you'll have to wait until you're stronger. You're in no condition to prophesy to anyone."

Micah shook his head. "No. It must be tonight. Please help me get there. I won't get a second chance."

Eliakim stared at him as if unable to fathom his tremendous determination. "OK, then," he finally sighed. "Let's get him ready to go."

Eliakim took charge with levelheaded efficiency, for which Micah was grateful. "You can't wear these bloody clothes. Bring one of my father's robes. And we'll have to bind your ribs to ease the pain. Maybe Botheina and I can bind your arm too."

"Just hurry, please," Micah begged. "There's not much time."

Botheina worked swiftly and gently, binding Micah's throbbing ribs with long strips of cloth soaked in a fragrant mixture of aloe and balm. With Eliakim's help she tried to realign the bones in his arm, and he cried out, nearly fainting in pain. But once they had finished, wrapping the arm tightly in strips of cloth, the throbbing eased. As they helped him into one of Hilkiah's robes there was a furious pounding on the front door.

Eliakim looked at his father. "Who can that be at this late hour?"

A knot of dread tightened in Micah's stomach. "It's someone searching for me," he said with quiet certainty.

"Who?" Hilkiah asked.

"I'm not sure, but they probably found out about my prophecy in the marketplace. I can't stay here. I've got to get to the palace." Again, Micah cursed his own stupidity for botching the task Isaiah had entrusted to him.

The pounding thundered once again, and an angry voice cried out, "Open the door, or we'll break it down!"

———⬥———

Outside the door, Captain Jonadab's patience diminished with every second. If someone didn't open the door soon, he would tear it from its hinges. He was tired and hungry and had grown more anxious and irritable as the day had progressed. The prophet still hadn't been found. And if he posed a threat to King Hezekiah, then he must be found.

Jonadab had retraced every step Micah had taken since he had arrived in Jerusalem that morning, had interviewed everyone who'd witnessed the riot in the marketplace, had questioned the soldiers exhaustively about the man who'd paid for Micah's release.

With every hour that passed, the witnesses had become more incoherent as the coronation festivities and the drinking had escalated. And Jonadab had grown more apprehensive at the thought of facing Uriah again without the prophet. He could never hope to make him understand the difficulty of finding an ordinary peasant in a city teeming with them.

Then, just when Jonadab had been at the point of despair, one of the merchants remembered the name of the man who had paid for his damaged booth. And he remembered that Hilkiah also had a booth in the marketplace. Jonadab and his men had painstakingly searched for Hilkiah's house, and now, close to midnight, they had finally found it. Jonadab scarcely dared to hope the prophet would be inside.

He couldn't wait any longer. "Prepare to break it down," he commanded.

───◆───

Inside, Eliakim took charge. "Abba, get a couple of servants to help you with Micah. Go out through the back. I'll stay here and stall as long as I can. Hurry!"

"How will I ever thank you?" Micah asked.

Eliakim looked at Micah's bruised, puffy face, his oddly twisted left arm, and it seemed as if the prophet would crumple to the ground if the servants weren't supporting him. He'll need a miracle to be able to walk up the hill to the palace, he thought.

"You need to thank Abba, not me," he said. "Now hurry. And God go with you."

The pounding on the door intensified. "I'm coming!" Eliakim shouted, then waited as long as he dared, holding his breath. But they were no longer pounding—they were trying to break it down.

"Who is it?" he shouted again. "What do you want?"

"Jonadab, captain of the palace guards. Open the door, or we'll break it down!"

Eliakim fumbled with the heavy oak bar and opened the door a crack, hoping to stall for a few more minutes. But as soon as Jonadab saw an opening, he kicked in the door, and it slammed into Eliakim's head, nearly knocking him off his feet.

"Are you Hilkiah, the merchant?" he demanded.

"No, I'm his son, Eliakim." The blow had stunned him, and he fingered the rising welt on his forehead.

"Where is Hilkiah? And where is the prophet?"

"My father isn't here," he said, trying to stay calm. "And I don't know anything about a prophet."

"Liar!" Jonadab shouted and delivered a blow to Eliakim's jaw that knocked him to the floor. "Your father and anyone else who is helping this man are enemies of the king."

Eliakim tested his jaw tenderly, hoping it wasn't broken. Blood poured from his split lip. He was furious with his father for getting him into this mess, for always sticking his nose into other people's affairs and trying to help. He saw the look of angry determination on Jonadab's face and was tempted to tell the truth. But he loved his father, and the situation was serious. He didn't care about Micah, but he had to get Hilkiah out of it somehow.

"Search the house—he must be here," Jonadab commanded. Then he grabbed Eliakim by the arm and yanked him to his feet. "Where is your father? Tell me, or I swear I'll beat it out of you."

Eliakim never doubted that he meant it. He wiped the blood from his lip, but before he could answer a soldier emerged from the room where Micah had been, carrying his bloody tunic. Eliakim's heart sank.

"Captain, look—the prophet's clothing. He was here."

Before Eliakim could react, Jonadab unsheathed his sword, and in one smooth, swift movement pinned Eliakim's arms to his sides and held the blade to his throat.

"Where is he?" he demanded through clenched teeth.

Eliakim's forehead beaded with sweat. "You mean the peasant who owned those clothes? He's dead. My father tried to save him, but he was too badly hurt. He died several hours ago."

"Are you telling the truth?" Jonadab pressed the sword tightly to Eliakim's neck, then drew it slowly across his throat until a ribbon of blood trickled down the blade. Eliakim cried out. He was going to die.

"Yes! I swear it!" he gasped.

Jonadab lowered his sword and cursed in frustration. "If the prophet's dead, then he's no longer a threat to the king," he told one of his men. "But Uriah won't be content until he sees his body—and Hilkiah's."

One by one the soldiers returned to Jonadab with no other sign of Hilkiah or the prophet, leaving the house in shambles from their search. Eliakim sank down on a bench by the door, pale and shaken, and fingered the wound on his burning neck. It was only skin-deep, performed with the skill of a surgeon, but the front of his tunic was soaked with his sticky blood, and it hurt to swallow.

"Where did you bury him, and where is your father?" Jonadab demanded wearily. He placed the tip of his sword below Eliakim's breastbone and applied just enough pressure to make him wince.

"My father has property outside Jerusalem. He left hours ago to bury the man there—in the tomb of his ancestors."

"Then you'll show us where this property is," he informed Eliakim, hauling him to his feet. Eliakim wished he was a better liar.

"Listen—it's a long, difficult journey over the mountains, especially at night. I'll gladly take you there at dawn."

"Then we'll have to wait until dawn. Let's go."

"Where are you taking me?"

Jonadab didn't answer. He ordered two of his men to stand guard at Hilkiah's house, then shoved Eliakim ahead of him into the street.

23

He looks so sad, Hephzibah thought, so strained, so somber. She sat across the banquet hall from Hezekiah at the women's table, staring at him all evening, waiting for his gentle smile to light up his face. But he hadn't smiled once throughout the entire coronation banquet, and she wondered why.

Hephzibah felt lost and alone. Surrounded by hundreds of people, at a banquet that celebrated a momentous occasion in her husband's life, she felt waves of desolation washing over her. Spoiled and indulged, Hephzibah had obtained everything she wished for all her life—until now. For the first time she was powerless to change her situation.

Beside her, Hezekiah's concubines drank cup after cup of wine and giggled foolishly, but Hephzibah had barely touched her food. She simply stared across the room at her husband, wondering why he looked so melancholy, what thoughts went through his mind.

Hephzibah wished she could go to him, say something to him to make him smile, to make him laugh out loud again—to make him love her. But he still hadn't sent for her since the week of their marriage, and tonight, at his coronation banquet, she saw him for the first time since then.

The other concubines knew he preferred them, and

they lorded it over Hephzibah, making her life nearly unbearable. But Hezekiah hadn't married another wife yet, and the feisty Merab had won Hephzibah the right to live in the wives' quarters until he did. In her heart she knew a new wife of Hezekiah's own choosing would soon occupy her rooms. Like kings everywhere, he would marry many wives besides her, even the daughters of foreign kings.

She had to accept that he would never belong to her alone or that she could be the love of his heart. Hezekiah didn't belong to her and he never would. Kings didn't love their wives as other husbands did. She was only one of many women whose sole job was to provide heirs for the kingdom.

She had known this truth ever since the day she had overheard the chamberlain and wept with Merab. But she had never accepted the truth in her heart until tonight, until she had watched him, distant and remote, a stranger who had never once looked her way.

Soon the banquet would end, and the eunuch would escort her back to her lonely prison cell in the harem. Months or even years could pass before she saw him again. Now that he was king, all hope that he would ever love her had died.

She wanted to cry out, to wail the high-pitched scream of mourning, to pour out her grief and despair. Instead, she stared at her husband across the crowded room and wondered what he was thinking and why he looked so sad.

Hezekiah stifled a yawn and refused the servant's offer of more wine. He was emotionally drained, sick in heart and soul, and wished he could go back to his rooms, but duty obligated him to preside at his coronation banquet. His guests showed no signs of leaving, even though it was well after midnight.

He had not enjoyed this banquet. Talking with Shebna about the state of his kingdom had left him depressed and discouraged. All around him, the tables in the banquet hall were heaped with empty plates and platters of discarded bones, but Hezekiah had barely tasted the sumptuous feast, knowing that every bite he ate further impoverished his people.

He leaned toward Uriah, seated at his right, to ask him when he could discreetly leave. It barely occurred to him that as king he could do whatever he pleased. Uriah seemed to know a great deal about running the kingdom, and he relied heavily on him for advice, although it frustrated him to do so. As soon as Hezekiah got the high priest's attention, however, the musicians began to play.

"Never mind, Uriah," he said. "I was going to leave, but maybe I'll stay a bit longer to hear the music."

"In that case, have more wine, Your Majesty." Uriah signaled to the servant.

———◈———

Micah paused halfway up the flight of stairs and leaned against the wall to keep from fainting. "Please, dear God. Only a little further," he prayed. He knew from Isaiah's map that this was the last flight of stairs he had to climb. He was almost to the banquet hall. He had left Hilkiah and the servants outside, and so far he hadn't seen any palace guards. The few people he'd passed had barely noticed him.

He thought briefly about Hilkiah's son and wondered what had happened after he and Hilkiah had left. He whispered a prayer for him, then summoned all his strength to climb to the top of the stairs.

Micah turned down the hallway to the left and suddenly stopped. Two palace guards stood in front of the banquet room doors. They looked directly at him. Micah momentarily lost his composure and stood frozen, swaying slightly, trying to decide what to do. One of the guards took a few steps toward him.

"Help me, Yahweh," he silently prayed. "Help me."

Suddenly the guard smiled. "You look as though you could use some assistance, my lord," he said to Micah. "You've been celebrating a bit heavily, I see. They must be serving good wine." He smirked at the other guard. "Would you like help getting back to your table?"

"Yes . . . thank you," Micah breathed. The soldier took Micah's left arm to steady him, and Micah moaned in pain.

"And you'll probably feel even worse tomorrow," the soldier said with a laugh. The second guard opened the door for them, and Micah gazed dizzily at the hundreds of people who packed the enormous room.

"Do you remember which table is yours, my lord?"

Micah easily spotted the king, seated on a raised platform at the front of the room.

"You can leave me now," he told the guard. "I know where to go." The guard bowed slightly, and the door closed behind him.

As he limped up the long center aisle toward the king's table, Micah began praising Yahweh in his heart. He put all his mistakes, all the disasters of this day, behind him. His goal was within reach. As he felt the power of God surging and swelling within, he forgot his own physical condition and concentrated on the words that Yahweh spoke to him.

—◈—

When the musicians finished their song, Hezekiah decided to leave the banquet. He rose from his seat, then suddenly stopped. Below the platform stood a man, staring at him with an intensity that made his heart beat faster.

"What's wrong?" Hezekiah asked.

"Listen, all you leaders of Judah," the man shouted. Hezekiah was certain he had never met the man before; yet something about his piercing eyes seemed familiar. The hall gradually grew silent.

"You are supposed to know right from wrong, yet you are the very ones who hate good and love evil; you skin my people and strip them to the bone. You devour them, flog them, break their bones, and chop them up like meat for the cooking pot—and then you plead with the Lord for his help in times of trouble! Do you really expect him to listen? He will look the other way!"

"Guards!" Uriah shouted, leaping to his feet. "Take this man out of here!"

"Wait." Hezekiah held up his hand. "Let him finish." He knew some of the accusations were true, and he felt the sting of guilt as he saw the remains of the sumptuous banquet feast all around him. He wondered if this stranger had answers. And something about the man seemed familiar to Hezekiah. He struggled to define it but couldn't.

"Yahweh has filled me with the power of his Spirit, and with justice and might. I've come to announce Yahweh's punishment on this nation for her sins."

"Yahweh?" Hezekiah mumbled. One of Israel's gods? This all seemed like a dream he once had, and he had the peculiar feeling that this had happened once before. His mind groped for the key, but it eluded his grasp.

"Listen to me, you leaders . . . who hate justice and love unfairness, and fill Jerusalem with murder and sin of every kind—you leaders who take bribes; you priests and prophets who won't preach and prophesy until you're paid . . ."

"Your Majesty, let the guards take him out of here," Uriah pleaded. "This man is either drunk or insane."

All the color had drained from Uriah's face, and he glared at the intruder with mingled hatred and fear. Hezekiah had the eerie feeling that his elusive dream involved Uriah too. He turned back to Micah.

"You have made some serious accusations," Hezekiah began.

"My judgments are not my own. I'm here to plead Yahweh's case."

"All right," Hezekiah replied. "Let's make this a formal hearing. You may present Yahweh's case." The strange interruption and the misty memories it evoked intrigued him. He sat down to listen, and Uriah sat grudgingly beside him, his face chalky.

"Hear, O mountains, Yahweh's accusation; listen, you everlasting foundations of the earth. For Yahweh has a case against his people. . . .

"O my people, what have I done that makes you turn away from me? Tell me why your patience is exhausted! Answer me! For I brought you out of Egypt, and cut your chains of slavery. I gave you Moses, Aaron, and Miriam to help you.

"Don't you remember, O my people, how Balak, king of Moab, tried to destroy you through the curse of Balaam, son of Beor, but I made him bless you instead? That is the kindness I showed you again and again. Have you no memory at all of what happened at Acacia and Gilgal, and how I blessed you there?"

"I have studied the history of Israel," Hezekiah interrupted. He hoped to learn something from this strange intruder, but the growing uneasiness he felt increased his impatience. He wanted him to make his point. "What is it that Yahweh wants from His people?"

Micah's tone changed suddenly as he switched roles, pleading the case for the people. He dropped to his knees.

"With what shall I come before the Lord and bow down before the exalted God? Shall I come before him with burnt offerings, with calves a year old? Will the Lord be pleased with thousands of rams, with ten thousand rivers of oil? *Shall I offer my firstborn* for my transgression, the fruit of my body for the sin of my soul?"

"*Offer my firstborn*"—the floodgate burst open, and suddenly the memories poured into Hezekiah's mind with the force of a tidal wave.

The rumble of voices and trampling feet. *"Which one is the firstborn?"* The hand had rested on his head. *"This one."*

The column of smoke and pounding drums. The terror.

Molech.

Hezekiah began to tremble. "Yahweh," he whispered unconsciously. Now he remembered. He remembered everything. And above all, he remembered the terror as the nightmare returned. But it wasn't simply a childhood dream. He knew with certainty that the horrible sacrifices had really taken place—that his brothers Eliab and Amariah had burned to death; that if it hadn't been for Yahweh, he would have burned to death too. He sat frozen in his chair, shaken, unable to speak.

Micah rose from his knees and approached him, his voice soothing and quiet. "He has showed you, O man, what is good. And what does the Lord require of you? To act justly and to love mercy and to walk humbly with your God."

A hushed silence filled the room. Hezekiah's heart pounded in his ears as he remembered another piece of the puzzle.

"Tell me . . . ," he said hoarsely. "My grandfather, Zechariah . . . ?"

"He is alive," Micah said with a nod.

"Take me to him."

24

"It's no use," Zechariah thought. "I can't sleep." He threw back the tangled bedcovers and groped in the dark for the oil lamp, coaxed it into a sputtering flame, then put on his outer robe and sandals. There were many nights like this, when sleep refused to come, when questions filled his heart and soul, questions only God could answer. Tonight his mind replayed Hezekiah's coronation, reviving the pain of Uriah's prayer to "all the gods" of Israel.

Hezekiah would never have allowed such a blessing if he still believed in the one true God. The long years of waiting, all of Zechariah's prayers and hopes, had been in vain. Hezekiah would not be the king to restore Judah's covenant with Yahweh.

Bearing his burden of grief, Zechariah limped down the dark, deserted corridors to the Temple library, hoping to find comfort, to find answers in God's Word. He loved this room and the scrolls that lined its shelves. He loved to pray here, feeling somehow closer to Yahweh when surrounded by His Word. He lit the oil lamps mounted on the walls and scanned the shelves, trying to decide what to read. Finally he chose the fifth Book of Moses and sat down wearily at one of the tables. But tears blurred his vision. He was too heartbroken to open it.

He hadn't been given enough time with Hezekiah. He hadn't taught him enough. He remembered the first time he had brought him here, how he had read to him from this scroll.

"O Yahweh! Hezekiah knows there are no gods except You. I taught him, Lord. He knows."

He remembered the day they had walked to the spring and he had recited the Shema for the first time. *"Louder, Grandpa! Make the goats bellow!"*

Zechariah cleared the lump from his throat and began to recite the words, slowly, solemnly. They soothed the pain in his heart like balm in an open wound.

"Hear, O Israel . . . Yahweh is God—Yahweh alone . . ." A sob choked off the rest, but from the darkness behind him a voice continued to recite.

". . . Love Yahweh your God with all your heart and with all your soul and with all your strength."

Zechariah leaped from his seat. Hezekiah stood in the doorway.

At first Zechariah thought he was dreaming, but in the next moment he felt Hezekiah's arms surrounding him, crushing him close to his heart, and he knew it was real. They held each other, without saying a word, for a long time.

—◈—

Hezekiah had remembered his grandfather as tall and strong, but the man he held in his arms now seemed very small and frail. He finally released his grasp and stepped back to gaze at the man he had loved so much as a child, the man who had delivered comfort and the assurance of God's protection and strength. He saw the familiar kindness and love in his grandfather's eyes and was ashamed that he could have forgotten someone who had once been so precious to him.

"I'm so sorry, Grandpa—"

"No, Son. It's not your fault." Zechariah put his hand over Hezekiah's lips and silenced him with a shake of his head. "Everything happens according to the will of Yahweh."

"I haven't thought about Yahweh for many, many years," he said softly. He felt the need to apologize, to explain himself to his grandfather. He groped for words. "My father insisted that I have the very finest education, the very best tutor. And I loved learning. I couldn't get enough of it." He smiled slightly. "Languages, history, literature. But my tutor didn't believe in any gods, and my father worshiped hundreds of them."

Hezekiah hadn't realized until now why he hated his father. Ahaz had killed his two brothers—and he had intended to kill Hezekiah as well.

"I hated him. I hated his idolatry, and I wanted no part of it. And when he polluted Yahweh's Temple with his sacrifices, I guess I discarded Yahweh as well. I gradually forgot about the things you taught me.

"After a while, even the sacrifices to Molech seemed like only a fairy tale or a bad dream I once had as a child. I didn't think about Yahweh until His prophet spoke at the banquet tonight—"

"Forgive me, Yahweh!" Zechariah moaned, leaning against the table. "Forgive my unbelief."

Hezekiah reached out to support him. "Are you all right? What's wrong?" He helped Zechariah sit down, then pulled up another bench facing him.

"I'm fine," Zechariah said shakily. "Please, tell me about the prophet. Was it Isaiah?"

"His name is Micah, from Moresheth."

"What did he say?"

"He told me that Yahweh had a case to plead against Judah, and he reminded me of our history and everything Yahweh has done for the nation. When I asked what Yahweh required in return, he answered, '. . . shall I offer my firstborn?' And suddenly I realized why he looked so familiar to me. He was so much like the prophet I met in the

Valley of Hinnom. And that's when I realized that it wasn't a dream."

Hezekiah's hands trembled slightly as the memories returned after all these years. "I remember being so afraid. The sacrifice of the firstborn—and I was the firstborn after Eliab died. I knew I was going to die, just like Eliab. And then when it seemed there was no way out, the prophet spoke. '. . . you will not be burned,' he said. 'Yahweh is your Savior.' And they sacrificed Amariah instead of me . . ."

It was a few minutes before he could continue. "I remember being so afraid it would happen again. Another sacrifice. Then you came and you promised that Yahweh would protect me from Molech."

He stared at Zechariah for a moment. "But one thing you never told me, one thing I guess I never asked you: Why? Why did Yahweh save me?"

"Because He loves you, Hezekiah." Zechariah could barely speak.

Hezekiah shook his head incredulously. "But why?" he asked again.

"'When I consider your heavens, the work of your fingers, the moon and the stars, which you have set in place, what is man that you are mindful of him?' King David wondered the same thing. I don't know the answer, but I do know that He loves us."

"But I've done nothing to deserve His love. Why would He save me?"

"Whether or not we deserve His love is irrelevant. Of all men, I am proof of that. I have sinned so greatly against Him . . ." For a moment he was unable to speak. "But He forgave me. And I know that He loves me."

His grandfather's conviction deeply moved Hezekiah, but he still couldn't comprehend all that Zechariah said. He shook his head. "But why me? Why not Eliab or Amariah?"

"Because Yahweh has chosen you," Micah interrupted

from where he had been waiting in the hallway outside the library. "Forgive me, Your Majesty, but Yahweh urges me to speak, and I can't keep silent any longer. Yahweh has chosen you to lead this nation back to Him."

Another memory stirred in Hezekiah's mind. The other prophet had told him the same thing long ago, in the Valley of Hinnom: *Yahweh has ransomed you. He has called you by name. You belong to Yahweh.*

"Yahweh still loves His people," Micah continued. "And He remembers the covenant He made with them. But we have broken our covenant. We have disobeyed all His commandments and have walked in idolatry. So, like a loving father, Yahweh chastises us, giving us over to our enemies, pleading with us to walk in obedience to Him again. Everything has happened just as the Torah said: 'But if your heart turns away and you are not obedient, and if you are drawn away to bow down to other gods and worship them, . . . you will certainly be destroyed.'"

Hezekiah stared at Micah. "Are you saying that our nation is in such a disastrous state because we have broken our covenant with Yahweh?"

"Yes," Micah answered.

Hezekiah expected a lengthy debate from the prophet, but he stated his answer with simple, quiet confidence. Hezekiah exhaled slowly.

"Wait a minute, Micah. Your answer is too simplistic and naive to take seriously. Judah is entangled in the web of world politics. We're not an isolated nation living quietly with our God."

"Nevertheless, it is true, Your Majesty. Yahweh's wisdom often seems foolish in man's eyes."

Hezekiah looked at his grandfather in surprise. "I remember. You taught me that once—David and Goliath?"

"Yes," Zechariah smiled.

"Your Majesty, Yahweh is actively involved in the affairs of men," Micah continued. "In the affairs of *all* nations, not only ours. He is the God of Assyria too, and He's not a passive observer from His heavenly throne. Yahweh has made Assyria an instrument of His wrath, and when He is through judging our nation, Assyria will also be judged. Yahweh is sovereign over all."

"If you believe that Yahweh saved you as a child," Zechariah said earnestly, "why is it so difficult to believe that Yahweh could save our nation as well?"

"I don't know . . ." Hezekiah sighed and rubbed his tired eyes. "I've been reviewing our nation's history trying to see how Judah got into this mess, looking for answers, for a way out. But I haven't found one. Now you say that Yahweh is the missing key?"

"Yes," Micah replied excitedly. "Didn't our nation achieve great power and prosperity under King David? And David loved Yahweh with all his heart."

"Judah hasn't seen peace or prosperity since King Uzziah's days," Zechariah said quietly. "And Uzziah also worshiped Yahweh—until his pride destroyed him. When Uzziah died, the people slowly turned away from Yahweh, and Judah has declined as well."

"My father was the worst idolater of them all," Hezekiah said bitterly, remembering Molech's blazing image. "And Judah has been reduced to poverty and slavery under his rule."

Micah and Zechariah offered him the solution he had struggled to find. Yet he hesitated, his rational mind refusing to believe in a supernatural answer.

"Can you prove any of this? Perhaps some kings were better equipped to rule than others. Or maybe it was the era in which they lived. I can't rest the fate of my nation on a superstition. I have to believe in things that can be proved in a tangible way. Can you show me that it's not just a coincidence?"

Micah shrugged. "I don't have the kind of proof you're asking for. I believe it by faith."

"I wish it could be true. I wish I could renew this covenant with Yahweh and see my kingdom miraculously restored, but—" Hezekiah shook his head. His mind refused to believe it. He felt torn between his seeds of faith in Yahweh and his sense of reason. He turned to his grandfather, pleading wordlessly for help.

"Belief in Yahweh doesn't come with your mind, Hezekiah," he said softly. "It comes with your heart. When you choose to believe only in the things you can see with your eyes and touch with your hands, it is idolatry."

Zechariah's words stunned him. "Then I'm an idolater too?"

"To have faith in Yahweh is to know that there is a realm of the spirit beyond the comprehension of our minds," Zechariah said. "Trusting in Molech, as Ahaz did, or trusting in your own wisdom and intellect—there is no difference in God's eyes. It is all idolatry."

Hezekiah looked at him in horror. "Then in God's eyes I'm as guilty as my father?"

Zechariah nodded.

Idolatry repulsed Hezekiah, the orgies in the sacred groves, the innocent children burned to death. To discover his own guilt, that he was a sinner in the sight of God, shook him.

"What does Yahweh want me to do?" he asked his grandfather quietly.

"The Torah says, 'But if . . . you seek the Lord your God, you will find him if you look for him with all your heart and with all your soul. When you are in distress and all these things have happened to you, then in later days you will return to the Lord your God and obey him. For the Lord your God is a merciful God; he will not abandon or destroy you or forget the covenant with your forefathers which he confirmed to them by oath.'"

The room fell silent as Hezekiah struggled. His grandfather told him to accept it by faith, but nothing Shebna had taught him prepared him to do that. The one certainty in his life was that Yahweh had saved him as a child. Nothing could change that conviction. His belief seemed small compared to Micah's unshakable confidence, but perhaps it was a place to start.

At last he spoke. "Then I want to do that. I want to get rid of all idolatry and renew our covenant with Yahweh. I want to ask Him to heal this land."

"Who is a God like you," Micah cried, "who pardons sin and forgives the transgression of the remnant of his inheritance? You do not stay angry forever but delight to show mercy. You will again have compassion on us; you will tread our sins underfoot and hurl all our iniquities into the depths of the sea."

The banquet guests sat in stunned silence for a long time. The king had left so abruptly with the prophet that most of them had no idea what had happened. But Uriah knew it was all over for him. He had seen Hezekiah's face when the prophet spoke of the sacrifice of the firstborn. It was only a matter of time before he remembered that Uriah had presided over that sacrifice.

He had expected to be arrested then and there, but instead Hezekiah had asked to see Zechariah. Uriah regretted not having killed the old man years ago. Now the king would learn about Zechariah's long imprisonment. Uriah knew his days of power were over.

At first Uriah seemed resigned to his fate. But as the banquet guests shook off their shock and one by one began to leave, Uriah also began to shrug off his resignation. Anger replaced it. He had run the nation of Judah many years for King Ahaz. Why should he give it over to Hezekiah simply because Hezekiah was born to the house of David? What did that matter? A descendant of King David hadn't ruled the northern tribes of Israel for centuries. The throne belonged to anyone who had the power and strength to grab it.

Uriah leaped from his seat, planning furiously, determined to fight to the end. Many of the government officials hated Ahaz as much as he had. They owed more loyalty to

Uriah than to Ahaz's son. With his persuasive power, he could easily convince them to revolt. And Hezekiah had no sons. Once Uriah got rid of him, there would be no heir to replace him. But he would have to act quickly.

He strode across the banquet room, fighting the urge to run. Two palace guards stood outside the main doors, puzzling over the evening's strange events.

"Guards!" Uriah thundered. "Follow me." They hurried to keep pace as he strode down the hall.

Uriah knew that he couldn't stay in the palace, but he needed to get a few things from his private chambers. He hadn't decided where he would go or exactly how he would start the rebellion against King Hezekiah, but he had fought too long and hard to give up now.

When he reached his rooms, Uriah ordered the guards to remain outside. In spite of his nation's poverty, he had carefully saved a small sum of gold for himself, stolen over the years from the tribute he had gathered for Assyria. He would use it to buy the support of his nation's top officials and of Jonadab, captain of the palace guard. The guards were the only army Judah had, and with Jonadab on Uriah's side, Hezekiah would be defenseless.

Uriah quickly gathered the stolen gold and tied it in a bundle. He didn't bother to pack any personal things, assuming he would return to the palace again as king, if everything went according to his plan.

With his bundle tied securely, Uriah scanned the room to see if he had forgotten anything and spotted the short, sharp dagger he had used to slay the sacrifices when he was a priest. He tucked it securely into the belt of his tunic, hidden beneath his outer robe—just in case.

Spotting the knife helped him decide where he should go first. He was the high priest, and he knew his fellow priests and Levites would back him. He would go to the Temple and gather as many of his supporters as he could find. He tucked his bundle inside his robes and strode from the room.

"Find Captain Jonadab," he commanded the two guards. "Tell him to meet me in the Temple council chamber at once."

—◆—

For the first time since Ahaz had died, Hezekiah was eager to begin his reign. Zechariah and Micah had offered him hope that his nation's staggering problems could be solved.

"I'll need your help," he told Zechariah. "Tell me where to begin."

"We'll begin here," he motioned to the shelves of scrolls. "With the Torah, Yahweh's divine Law."

Hezekiah liked the prospect of Zechariah once again teaching him. But at the same time he was puzzled. "Why did you stop coming to the palace to teach me?" he asked.

"I wanted to come, but I was held prisoner here."

"By my father?" Hezekiah's revulsion and hatred returned.

"No, Son—it was Uriah's decision. I opposed the blasphemous changes taking place in the Temple, and so I had to be silenced. King Ahaz wanted me killed, but instead Uriah kept me here."

"All these years?" Hezekiah thought of how much time had passed since he had last seen his grandfather, and he shuddered. Then, as his anger against Uriah mounted, he suddenly recalled something else. It was the huge high priest, dressed in the ceremonial robes of Yahweh's Temple, who had placed his hand on Hezekiah's head, marking him as the firstborn.

"Uriah led that sacrifice to Molech!" Hezekiah said incredulously. "He was the one who came for me!"

"Uriah's sins against Yahweh are very great. He was in a position of leadership, but he led many, many people into idolatry."

Zechariah slowly walked to the shelves of scrolls and

pulled one down from its place, scattering dust. "This is what the Torah says," he read quietly.

"'If a man or woman living among you . . . has worshiped other gods . . . take the man or woman who has done this evil deed to your city gate and stone that person to death . . .'"

He paused and looked up somberly at Hezekiah.

"Is there more?" Hezekiah asked. "I need to hear it all."

"'Any Israelite . . . who gives any of his children to Molech must be put to death. The people of the community are to stone him . . .'"

Zechariah looked up again, and his eyes were filled with compassion. "You can't stone every man in Judah who is guilty of idolatry. We'd all be guilty . . . even me."

"I know. But Uriah was the high priest of Yahweh. When he led the sacrifice to Molech, the people blindly followed him. And he also silenced the truth. It's more than a matter of revenge. Before I can start any reforms, I have to get rid of the evil. Uriah must die."

Hezekiah didn't know how much time had passed since he left the banquet with Micah, but he suddenly realized that he had given Uriah more than enough time to appreciate the danger he was in and make his escape.

"I have to find him," he told Zechariah, and he strode abruptly from the room, leaving Zechariah standing alone with the dusty scroll still in his hand.

Hezekiah raced through the dimly lit maze of Temple hallways, driven by his sense of urgency. Many of the flickering oil lamps had burned out, making it difficult to see where he was going as he sprinted down the confusing tangle of passageways. He had traveled a considerable distance before realizing that in his blind rage to find Uriah he had lost his way. Anxious and frustrated, he decided to turn around and retrace his steps, hoping to find someone who could lead him out.

He came instead to an intersection of two hallways. At the end of one he heard the faint mutter of voices and saw a shaft of light glowing in the darkness under a closed door. Hezekiah followed the sound of the voices and the light, but when he reached the end of the hall he stopped. Uriah's booming voice filtered through the closed door. The high priest was shouting, arguing, and someone seemed to be answering him in a low mumble, but Hezekiah couldn't make out what they said.

The king condemned his own stupidity when he realized the frustrating dilemma he faced. He had found Uriah, but he had no one, not even a Temple guard, to help him make an arrest. He knew there were men in the room with Uriah, but he had no idea how many or where their loyalty lay. Nor could he go for help. He was lost in the maze of Temple passageways. Beads of sweat formed on his brow. He wished he hadn't removed his sword for the banquet.

But Hezekiah didn't have long to ponder the situation. All at once the door burst open, and he stood face-to-face with his enemy. Uriah seemed as startled as he was, and the men stood motionless, staring at each other.

"You're under arrest, Uriah. You sacrificed my brother to Molech. The Torah condemns you to die."

Uriah stood still as stone, staring coldly. "And the Torah also says that this Temple is a place of refuge. No one can touch me here."

Hezekiah had no idea if Uriah had told the truth or not. He hesitated, reluctant to violate the Torah, and in that split second of hesitation Uriah made his move. He quickly thrust his hand inside his robe and drew out a dagger.

The glint of metal activated Hezekiah's reflexes, honed to swiftness by years of military training with Captain Jonadab. He grabbed Uriah's right arm with both hands to stop the plunging dagger and threw all his weight at the high priest, knocking him off balance. But Uriah quickly regained his stance and locked his other arm in an iron grip around Hezekiah's throat, slowly squeezing off his air supply.

Hezekiah twisted his body, trying to break Uriah's hold, then used his powerful legs to kick Uriah, but his efforts seemed useless. Like a mighty oak, Uriah was rooted to the ground. His grip tightened with each of Hezekiah's movements.

Minutes passed as Hezekiah struggled to break free, prying with one hand at Uriah's arm, which choked him, and holding the knife at bay with the other. A black curtain circled around the edge of his vision and slowly closed in. The floor tilted precariously. He needed air. He had never imagined that Uriah was so strong.

Hezekiah's arms quivered from exertion. The dagger, only inches away, was slowly moving closer to his chest and pointing directly at his heart. If Uriah found a reserve of strength, it would be over. He only needed to close the circle of his arm and plunge his dagger.

Stars of light exploded painfully as Hezekiah's vision shrank. With a hideous rasping, he strained desperately to pull air into his lungs. He wondered why the powerful priest showed no sign of fatigue. Instead, Uriah slowly tightened his death hold and brought the dagger closer. Hezekiah's lungs felt as if they were about to explode. Why would no one help him?

In a few more seconds his air supply and his strength would give out. Uriah was going to kill him. Hezekiah didn't want to die. He wanted a chance to reign—a chance to renew the covenant with Yahweh as he had just vowed. He wanted desperately to live. In his last moment before darkness closed in, Hezekiah prayed.

"O God! Help me!"

Suddenly Uriah released his grip and cried out in pain. The dagger fell from his hand and clattered to the floor. Then he staggered forward and fell on Hezekiah, pinning him to the floor.

For a few seconds Hezekiah lay beneath him, stunned, gulping deep breaths of air, amazed to be alive as he felt a warm dampness slowly soaking his chest. Then he pushed Uriah off and sat up. A sacrificial knife protruded from Uriah's back, and the high priest's blood stained his own tunic.

Hezekiah looked up to see who had saved his life and saw his grandfather standing over him.

26

As the morning dawned cold and gray, Hezekiah saw the door at the end of the passageway that led outside. He was weary of the damp, stuffy Temple and wanted some fresh air. He slowly rose to his feet and found that his legs would hold him. His quivering, overworked muscles had relaxed again, and, except for a dull pain behind his eyes, he felt all right.

Uriah's body was covered with a robe, and it lay in the hallway where he had fallen. The atmosphere was still charged with tension after the night's startling events, and the priests and Levites moved about in tight little groups as if afraid of being alone. Everyone seemed dazed, benumbed, and they talked in low, furtive whispers. Zechariah was the only one who seemed unshaken, as if what he had done had been inevitable.

"Would you do something for me, Grandpa?" Hezekiah asked. "Gather all the priests and Levites who are left and meet me in the courtyard in a few minutes." Then Hezekiah went outside, into the fresh air of the new day.

He shivered in the cool morning breeze. He was still dressed in the clothes he had worn to the banquet, sticky and damp, indelibly stained with Uriah's blood.

The eastern sky was lightening, but clouds that hung damp and leaden over the city obscured the sun. He wandered across the courtyard to the east side of the Temple, out of the cold chill of the shadows. The only sounds were the chirping of swallows and the crunching of gravel beneath his feet as he walked.

When Hezekiah reached the middle of the courtyard, he stopped and looked around, seeing it as if for the first time—the Assyrian altar that Ahaz had erected dominated the courtyard, covered with images of idolatry. Nearby, the giant brazen laver sat crookedly on its improvised stone base. In another corner stood a tall brass pole, a brazen serpent draped in a twisted coil around it.

He slowly walked to the sanctuary porch and looked through the grating. The doors were boarded with rough planks of wood that appeared to have been in place for many years. The once-beautiful building looked decayed, neglected.

No wonder, he thought. No wonder Yahweh has turned His back on us.

He stood between the crumbling pillars that flanked the Temple door. Long ago, Zechariah had taught him their names, and for several minutes his tired mind struggled to recall what they were. It seemed important that he remember. One was Boaz: "In Him is strength," and the other was
. . .

He finally shook his head and turned away. He tried to picture how the Temple had looked the day he had watched the sacrifice with Zechariah. But nothing seemed the same.

After several minutes he heard the sound of approaching footsteps. The priests and Levites had come out of a side door and were silently crossing the courtyard to meet him. Hezekiah was surprised to see that only about 30 men had come, most of them quite elderly.

"Aren't there more men than this in the tribe of Levi?" he asked.

Zechariah shook his head. "Uriah's supporters fled when he died. The rest left Temple service years ago, either because they disagreed with Uriah's changes or else to make a decent living for themselves and their families. The handful of·us who are here remained out of loyalty to Yahweh and a desire to preserve the Temple buildings and the sacred books."

Hezekiah looked again at the Assyrian altar, surveying the confusing mass of foreign images and forbidden idols, then gazed at the handful of faithful men standing before him. He felt as if he were beginning a long journey up a steep mountain. He knew the time for the first difficult step had come.

"Listen to me, you Levites." His voice echoed off the Temple walls. "I want you to consecrate yourselves and make the Temple of Yahweh, the God of your ancestors, holy. Clean all the trash and idolatry from the holy places. For our forefathers have sinned before Yahweh and His Temple and have turned their backs on it and defiled it. The doors to the holy place have been boarded up. The flame that was always supposed to burn has been put out. The incense has not been burnt, and the burnt offerings have not been given. Therefore, Yahweh's wrath has been upon Judah and Jerusalem. He has made us the object of horror, amazement, and contempt in the eyes of other nations."

The Levites seemed to come alive at his words. Their faces reflected their wonder, their incredulity, their joy. A slow, triumphant smile spread across Hezekiah's tired face as well.

"But now I want to make a covenant with Yahweh, the God of Israel, so that His fierce anger will turn away from us. Levites, don't neglect your duties any longer, for Yahweh has chosen you to minister to Him and burn incense."

A shout went up from the men and they rushed forward to bow at his feet, stating their names and pledging their support.

"Mahath, son of Amasai."

"Joah, son of Zimmah, and this is my son, Eden."

"I'm Shimri, from the descendants of Elizaphan."

"Mattaniah, from Asaph, the musicians of Yahweh."

"Shimri of Heman, and my brother Jeiel."

"I am Uzziel."

One after another they came. The last one, Zechariah, embraced him.

"Take the gold that Uriah carried," Hezekiah told him, "and use it to make repairs to the Temple."

"I will send word to all the priests and Levites who have scattered to come back to Jerusalem. Today we will begin reconsecrating ourselves to the service of Yahweh."

"Let me know as soon as everything is purified," Hezekiah said. "Then our nation will renew our covenant with Yahweh, beginning with a sacrifice."

Zechariah and the other Levites slowly filed back into the building, talking, dreaming, making plans, leaving Hezekiah alone in the courtyard. He walked over to the huge Assyrian altar that stood where Yahweh's altar should have been and studied the forbidden idols that decorated it, running his fingers over the intricate carvings. These were gods you could see and touch. But they were as cold and lifeless as the brass they were carved from. Yahweh, whom he could never see or touch, was a *living* God.

"Hear, O Israel! Yahweh is our God—Yahweh alone!" he recited softly. "And thou shalt love Yahweh your God with all your heart and with all your soul and with all your strength." Yahweh required nothing less than a total commitment. And that was what he had promised.

A misty rain began to fall, chilling Hezekiah to his bones, but it seemed to him that it washed the city clean, cleansing away the dirt and defilement. He left the Temple courtyard through the main gate and walked slowly down the hill alone, back to the palace.

Hezekiah was twenty-five years old
when he became king,
and he reigned in Jerusalem
twenty-nine years.
His mother's name was Abijah
daughter of Zechariah.
He did what was right
in the eyes of the Lord,
just as his father David had done.
In the first month of the first year
of his reign, he opened the doors
of the temple of the Lord
and repaired them.

—2 Chron. 29:1-3

Scripture Credits

Scripture quotations from *The Living Bible* (TLB) are found on the following pages (see page 4 for copyright information): 75 (fifth full paragraph), 276, 277 (first and sixth full paragraphs), 278 (fourth and fifth full paragraphs), 282.

Scripture paraphrases by the author are found on the following pages: 62 (sixth full paragraph), 63, 76 (sixth full paragraph), 77, 78, 88-89 (carryover paragraph), 93, 94, 114, 117, 156 (second full paragraph), 180, 277 (fourth full paragraph), 283 (first full paragraph), 284 (first full paragraph), 297.

All other Scripture quotations are from the *New International Version*® (NIV®). See page 4 for copyright information.

Previews of Forthcoming Books

The Lord Is My Song
Book 2

The Lord Is My Song begins with Judah's nationwide spiritual revival led by King Hezekiah. As he grows in faith and seeks to obey God in every aspect of his life, Hezekiah discovers that the Law forbids him to marry multiple wives. He must then decide whether or not Hephzibah—whom he has ignored for so long—will remain part of his harem.

Hezekiah's reforms promise to bring God's blessings and renewed prosperity to the nation, but his brother and many other officials oppose these changes and conspire against him. The situation reaches critical proportions when the Assyrians threaten the northern nation of Israel. This nation's plight is dramatized through the story of Jerusha and her family, who must find a way to escape the ensuing Assyrian holocaust.

As Hezekiah is challenged by enemies on every side—even in his own household—his newfound faith in God is put to the ultimate test.

The Lord Is My Salvation
Book 3

The Lord Is My Salvation tells of King Hezekiah's later reign and the climax of events surrounding the Assyrian invasion. God has brought him great wealth and power; but after many years, Hezekiah still has no heir. His wife, in desperation, makes a vow to Asherah, the fertility goddess, betraying all that Hezekiah believes in and works for.

As his international stature increases, Hezekiah is tempted by Egypt and Babylon to join a military alliance against Assyria—an alliance that the prophet Isaiah warns him not to join. As the Assyrians march westward with a lust for vengeance and conquest, Hezekiah will discover whether or not his faith in God will sustain him against an overwhelming enemy.